BARK AND BOLT

SANDY ST. JOHN

SOUTHPAW PRESS

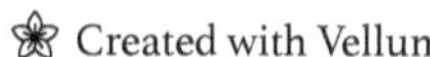 Created with Vellum

~

For Anne—
My traveling companion on this crazy cosmic journey—I can't
imagine the ride with anyone else.
To happiness, tenacity, and sliding in sideways

~

They say staying connected to family and friends helps you live longer. I'm not so sure.

This whole episode started out innocently enough. My friend Evan invited me to go to a book signing. Frankly, I didn't even know Evan read beyond the back of his cereal box, so I was surprised when he called me up and asked if I wanted to go with him. My name is Jessie Gallagher, and I'd been working really hard to get my little gourmet dog biscuit company, Barker Street Bones, up and running for the better part of a year. I hadn't taken a break in weeks, so I was game for anything that didn't involve puréeing liver in a food processor, which is how I found myself on a hard metal folding chair next to Evan at four thirty on Thursday afternoon.

"I thought you said this guy's sold ten million books. How come we're the only ones here?" I glanced over my shoulder at the only other person in the store, a long-haired lanky guy who'd just finished setting out the last row of chairs. "And what time does this thing start anyway?"

"I wanted to get here early," Evan said, running his fingers over his new book. The way he was caressing it made me a little uncomfortable.

"Let me see," I said, reaching a hand out.

He tightened his grip and tucked it under his arm. "You should go buy one." He tried to scoot his chair away. We were in the front row, as close to the podium as we could get. We'd tried out every chair before Evan had decided that these were the best seats.

I'd never even heard of Lander Jones; then again, I hadn't had much time for pleasure reading lately. Instead, I'd been reading articles about how easy it is to start your own business, no doubt written by people who had never actually done so.

"What time does it start again?" I repeated.

He mumbled something, pulled his phone from his pocket and began scrolling with his free thumb.

"I'm sorry, what?" I asked.

"Six thirty," he said.

"*Six thirty?* That's two hours from now."

"I wanted to get a good seat," he said, glancing over his shoulder. "See? They're coming in already. Any later and we'd be standing along the back wall."

Well, okay. A couple more people had wandered in and taken up positions in the rows behind us. But he wasn't far from wrong. By five thirty all the chairs were taken and the heat in the room had ratcheted up to an uncomfortable level. I fanned my shirt against my chest and pulled up the weather app on my phone.

The bookstore's old air-conditioning unit strained against Houston's late-May humidity. Every time it cycled on, a loud thud sounded, as if someone was dropping a dumbbell in the attic. I hoped it would make it through the next couple of hours. The screen on my phone showed a line of red on the radar developing out to the west. I hit the animate button and watched as the line moved closer to the city.

"Uh-oh." I poked the phone in front of Evan. "More thunderstorms. I hope they hold off until I get home." My Border collie, Addie, lives in fear of storms. Houston is perhaps not the best place for her to live. "Those storms last night nearly did Addie in."

"I'm sure it'll be fine," he said, not even glancing at the screen. He stared straight ahead at a brown panel door that presumably led to a storeroom or offices. He hadn't looked away in at least twenty minutes. It reminded me of how Addie watches me when it's getting close to dinnertime.

"How long do you think this will go?" I asked, trying to estimate when I thought the storm would hit. Judging by the radar, I would guess we had about an hour or two before the worst of it got here.

"He'll probably read some from his new book before he gets to the signing." He pulled an orange slip from the front of his book. "I'm first for the signing!"

Maybe getting here so early did have its perks. By six fifteen, the hum in the room had intensified, along with the heat. A bead of sweat ran down my back and joined the others pooled at the back of my underpants.

Evan jiggled in his seat, shifting side to side. I glanced behind us at the crowd jammed in along the back wall and spilling along the edges of the room.

"Wow, it's packed." Several people eyed me as if judging whether I was going to relinquish my seat. Vultures.

"I have to go to the bathroom," Evan said, suddenly shooting to his feet. "Save my seat." He took off, pushing up the aisle, and before I even had a chance to throw my purse on his chair, a woman flew in sideways, landing like a receiver in the end zone.

Her oversized tote clipped my shoulder and she shoved her thigh up against me as she settled onto the chair.

"Excuse me," I said. "Someone's already sitting there. He'll be right back." The woman shifted slightly, easing away from me and began rummaging in the bottom of her tote. "I'm not sure you heard me," I said louder as heads around us turned to watch. "But someone is already sitting there. You're going to have to move when he gets back."

She pressed her lips together and turned away, pretending not to hear me. She was probably close to my age, maybe late twenties or early thirties, but she was dressed matronly in an oversized prairie dress that would have looked better on a frontier schoolmarm. From her bag, she drew out a rolled-up poster board and began to carefully unfurl it. I leaned forward to see what was on the front. "Welcome Lander Jones!" The lettering was hand-drawn and the *o* in Jones was a red heart shape. An owl swooped across the middle of the sign and underneath its wings it said, "From the Houston Chapter of the Lander Jones Fan Club." It looked like it had been carefully designed by a junior high pep squad.

"I need to sit in the front row," she said. "I'm the president of the Houston chapter of his fan club. I need to be in the front row."

I didn't even know fan clubs still existed.

"Okay—well, then, you should have gotten here earlier like we did."

Between the heads in the crowd, I could see Evan approaching. The look on his face changed from excitement to incredulity when he saw someone occupying his chair. He pushed forward and raced up the aisle.

"Hey! You're in my seat," he said, reaching for the back of the chair. He turned to me. "I told you to save my seat."

"I tried," I said. "She just grabbed it. You need to move," I said to the fan club nut.

She sat motionless, staring straight ahead just as Evan had been doing for the last hour. What was with these people? You might expect this kind of devotion at a cult meeting or a rock concert, but at a book signing?

Evan grabbed the back of the metal chair and began trying to tip it forward to dislodge the woman. She pushed her behind more firmly into the seat and braced her legs. A murmur went up in the audience and several people in the back rows stood to get a better look.

"You. Are. In. My. Seat," Evan grunted as he bent his legs, intent on getting more traction to tip the chair over.

"What are you doing?" I asked. He looked committed to dumping her on the floor.

"She's in my seat," Evan repeated through clenched teeth. The long-haired bookstore guy came trotting over from behind the counter.

"Is there a problem here?" he asked pushing through the crowd.

"Yes. She's in my seat," Evan said, relinquishing his hold on the chair. The fan club lady stared straight ahead, refusing to acknowledge the activity going on around her.

"Okay, kids. Surely we can work this out." He looked at Evan and then at the fan club lady. "Ma'am, he was here first. Actually he's been here quite a while."

Evan leaned forward over the woman. "See?" he said.

She didn't budge. I glanced at my watch. It was nearly time to start this show. I stood up. "Here, Evan. Take my seat. It's fine. I know how much this means to you. I'll just go listen from over there. We'll meet up after, okay?"

The bookstore guy looked relieved. "Okay, then. That works out perfect."

Evan didn't take my chair. He stood rooted. "I want my seat back."

The door opened and an electric excitement shot through the room. A young guy wearing a blue blazer, khaki pants and sneakers made his way to the table in front of us. He was younger than I expected, his face unmarred by lines, his skin as smooth as a child's. He struck me as the kind of guy who'd be more at home at a skateboard park than a bookstore. His pale brown hair flopped over his forehead and he brushed it back, taking in the overflow crowd. He looked nervous.

"Oh, for crying out loud," said an older man in the second row. "Lady, just move over. I can't see past you yahoos."

I headed up the aisle as she finally hoisted herself over into my vacated seat and Evan harrumphed into his original chair.

The bookstore guy made his way to the author's side and held up his arms to quiet the crowd. "Thank you all for coming. This is a big night for us. It's not often that we can welcome such a renowned talent into our little store."

All the chairs were taken and I made my way towards the rear. Even the standing room was limited.

"Mr. Jones is going to read from his new release. Then he'll take a few questions, and following that, he'll sign books. Please hold on to the number you were given when you arrived here tonight—that's the order we'll have you line up for the signing. And without further ado, ladies and gentlemen, Lander Jones!"

The room exploded with applause. I'd still not found a place to settle myself, so I inched farther along towards the sales counter, slipping past sweating bodies and garnering dirty looks.

"Sorry, sorry, excuse me," I murmured as I made my way along. I finally found an opening behind a bookcase. I couldn't see much, but at least it was about a degree cooler over here.

"I can't believe I'm here with the release of my sixth book," said Lander Jones. At least I presumed it was Lander Jones, being that I couldn't see anything past the shelves of books and a few random heads.

"Been waiting a year for this!" shouted someone in the crowd.

"You sound like my publisher." The crowd laughed. "Anyway, I thought I'd read a little from Chapter 1, then take some questions. That okay with you guys?"

A wave of assent rolled through the room. The audience settled in like a kindergarten class at story time. His voice was pleasant, like listening to an audiobook, and I sank down on the carpet and leaned against the bookcase behind me. He seemed to relax as he read, and I found myself getting caught up in the story. He read for about twenty minutes, stopping every now and then to throw in a personal story.

By the time he finished reading, I was hooked. I couldn't wait to buy a copy. Hauling myself up, I peered out past the bookcase. The crowd was subdued, sluggish from the heat and lulled by the story.

The author hugged his book against his chest and looked out at the crowd. "Does anyone have any questions?" he asked. His thumb flicked along the spine of the book. He looked very much like he hoped no one did.

A woman in a pale blue pantsuit cleared her throat and raised a spindly hand into the air.

"Yes, in the second row."

"I can't help but notice you use a number of bad words in your books. I know that a lot of people find that acceptable these days, but I think you should try to minimize those types of words." She folded her hands and looked around the room for approval. Someone snorted. Everyone else looked away.

"I'll certainly keep that in mind," Lander said, his lips pulling back in a pained smile. "Anyone else?"

"Yes, I have a question," said an older gentleman in the last row. He pulled a pair of readers down on his nose and opened his book to a place he'd been holding with his finger. "On page 174 you say 'the dog's snout.' Why would you call a dog's nose a snout? Usually people refer to a pig's snout, not a dog's snout." He closed his book and sat back, as if he'd been waiting a long time to win a point like this.

Lander Jones set his own book on the table and took a slow breath. "I just use whatever word choice seems right to me at the time."

"Well, I just think it sounds wrong to refer to a dog's nose as a snout."

"Okay, thank you for the feedback." He clearly wasn't thankful for the feedback. I wasn't sure how he showed so much restraint with these dumb questions. "So, if that's all the questions, maybe we could go ahead and move on to the book signing."

A chorus of voices protested. I pulled out my phone and hit the weather app, pulling up the local radar. The storms were closer and the red blobs had grown into bigger red blobs with purple centers. That couldn't be good. I edged my way to the counter, where a stack of Lander Jones hardbacks sat near the register. The woman behind the counter smiled at me.

"He's very good, isn't he?" she said in a hushed voice. From the room behind us I could hear the author trying to explain the difference between fiction and reality to someone who was quibbling about something that had happened in a prior book.

"Right, so there is an element of the paranormal in most of my books," he was saying, obviously trying to sound patient. "Not a lot, but there are a few things that happen that are a little off-center."

"So, you expect people to believe that an owl could come swooping down from out of nowhere right when this guy is cornered in an alley by a drug-crazed mugger? Owls don't even live in the city."

"The owl was in the first book too," said a lady from the far side of the room.

"I love the owl!"

The question-and-answer session was morphing into a sideline brawl.

"I hope the owl is in this book."

"The owl can't be real," said the owner of the original question. "It doesn't make sense."

"It doesn't have to make sense," shouted the guy sitting right next to him. "That's why it's called fiction!"

The first guy stood up. "But it can't happen that way!" His face flushed with mottled patches of red.

"That's why it's called fiction!" said his neighbor, lumbering to his feet.

And I'd been afraid this would be boring. The bookstore guy started waving his arms.

"Okay, folks! Why don't we move along to the book signing portion of tonight's event? If you could line up according to your number. Who's number one? Anyone? If you could please check your numbers that we gave you when you purchased your books and start to line up over this way."

I turned back towards the counter. "Actually, I haven't read any of his books yet," I said to the clerk. "Truth be told, I'd never even heard of him until my friend invited me to this tonight."

A huff of breath rasped behind my head. I turned and found the fan club lady nearly pressed up against me.

"You've never read a Lander Jones book?" She asked it in the same tone you'd expect if you'd just admitted you'd never bathed.

"No," I said, inching away. She was standing so close I could feel her breath on my face.

The lady behind the counter picked up a different book. "Perhaps you should start with the first one," she said. "You can read them out of order, but it's better if you don't. He does have a lot of character development, so it just works better from the beginning."

I paid for the book and sidled away. The fan club president was still staring at me.

"We'll see if I like it before I get the next one," I said to her as I turned away to look for Evan. She gasped aloud.

The crowd had surged towards the table where the signing was happening, and the author had disappeared behind the mass. I searched for Evan's head in the throng but didn't see him. A clap of thunder overhead momentarily caused the lights to flicker, and I looked towards the front windows, where it looked like full night outside. Rain lashed at the panes, and in the dimness I could see a tree across the parking lot bending and swaying in the wind. It appeared that the red storm blobs had made it to the city.

I stretched up on my toes and caught a glimpse of Evan's dark head near the front of the crowd. He was supposed to be first, so why wasn't he done yet? I'd give him a few more minutes and then I was going to go. We'd come in separate cars since he'd had to sneak out of work early, so there was no reason to wait. Then again, I hated to just ditch him without saying goodbye. This had certainly been more fun than I'd thought it would be.

I watched people file out, clutching their newly autographed books, looking like kids who'd just met their favorite player at a ball game. The crowd around the table had dwindled to a few die-hards, including Evan and the fan club lady. She was holding her sign directly in front of the table, as if perhaps the author hadn't noticed it yet. I waved my hand, trying to get Evan's attention, but he was standing transfixed, head cocked as if trying to make sure he caught every word spoken. A crack of thunder finally broke through, and he looked up. A few of the others also turned, and like a startled herd of sheep, they moved in unison towards the door.

"I need to get home to Addie," I called to Evan. "She's going to be frantic."

"Yeah, I'm going too. I'll see you."

I moved with the crowd towards the door, where we jammed up as everyone balked at going out into the storm. One by one, people dashed into the deluge, some trying optimistically to open umbrellas, only to have them flip inside out. Others just ran, shoving their treasured books inside their shirts. I'm not sure how he got past me, but I saw Evan racing towards his car.

Another crash of thunder shook the building. I was at the door now, edging outside. Everyone else had already made a break for it. I huddled against the building and groped in my purse for my car keys. The rain pelleted down, exploding off the parking lot surface with its intensity and forming small but raging streams along the curb.

My car was in a spot near the side of the building, and I inched along under the awning as far as I could before running a high-stepping canter the rest of the way. Throwing myself into the driver's seat, I slammed my door shut and pushed my wet hair back off my face. Rain hammered on the top of my car like a fire hose against a tin roof.

The cars behind me were blocking me in, and I had to wait several minutes before they began to clear the lot. I pulled my phone from my purse and pulled up the weather app. Oh boy. So much for hoping this would blow over. If anything, it appeared the clouds were converging and growing like a bad algae bloom. My phone dinged. It was a text from Evan. *Thanks so much for coming with me tonight! That was awesome! Be careful going home.*

I smiled at his enthusiasm. It had been a long time since I'd seen Evan this excited.

Thanks for inviting me. I had fun. You be careful out there too.

Just as I hit send, the passenger-side door of my car flew open, letting in a burst of rain as a hunched figure dove into the seat and pulled the door closed with a bang.

CHAPTER TWO

My initial thought was Evan, but that made no sense, and almost immediately I knew it wasn't. A leather bag knocked me in the shoulder and a whiff of unfamiliar male scent rushed in on the wind. I leaned into the door, grasping for the handle, pretty sure I was being carjacked. My phone slipped out of my hand and thudded to the floor. Another figure ran towards the car and the person beside me hit the door locks, obviously something I should have done myself. Outside, someone started beating on the passenger's window.

"Hey, wait!" a female voice was shouting, and I struggled to make sense of what was happening. Should I race out of the car and back to the bookstore? But the person outside was starting to move around the front of the car towards my side. Through the dim light and driving rain, I could make out a sodden cream-colored dress. She stood in front of the hood, waving her arms, a bag weighing one down.

"Wait!"

It was the fan club president.

"Hey, sorry," the guy in my passenger seat said, turning toward me. "It's me." I stared wordlessly. "Lander Jones. I was just in there…" He gestured towards the bookstore and trailed off. "Sorry," he repeated, taking in my obvious panic. "Hey, I didn't mean to scare you. Do you think you could go?" I stared at him while registering how ineffective my reactions were had this been an actual carjacking. He peered out the windshield, then turned and looked out the rear window. "My car's blocked in back there by the employee cars, and clearly I need to get out of here." He said this as if it explained everything. He buckled his seat belt, obviously not going anywhere.

The fan club president was moving towards his side of the car again. I could see her reaching into her bag. I still wasn't sure what was going on, but I turned the key and started the ignition. The cars behind me had cleared, and I shifted roughly into reverse, looking over my shoulder since the backup camera was water-spotted and worthless. Shifting into drive, I steered as quickly as I could through the emptying parking lot.

"Is she following us?" I asked.

"I don't see her," he said, twisting over the seat staring out the back window. I took a breath and turned right.

"So that was weird," I said. "This is kind of weird too. Where do you want me to take you?"

"It doesn't matter. I just need a minute."

"Do you want me to maybe go around the block and then take you back to your car?" We were just outside downtown and I was headed west, instinctively heading home. He slouched down into his seat, eyes trained on the side mirror as I stared straight ahead, trying to see through the downpour.

"Could you turn right at the next street?" he asked. I complied, and we ended up in a neighborhood lined by small apartment buildings and large midcentury homes. I continued on, slowly making my way north, still wondering where we were going.

He sat silent for a few minutes, clutching a dripping

messenger bag in his lap before glancing over at me as if noticing me for the first time. "I'm sorry, I didn't ask your name," he said, sounding embarrassed.

"Jessie Gallagher." I glanced over for a split-second acknowledgment before turning back to peer out the windshield. "What was that about?"

"It's a long story," he said.

"Wasn't that lady the president of your fan club?" I asked. "I would think as a writer it would be good business to have a fan club, maybe not so great to run away from the president of it."

"Yeah, I've never even heard of this fan club, and her story was a little sketchy."

"You mean that poster wasn't official?" I laughed, but he was silent. I tried again. "Was she like a crazed fan or something?" After seeing Evan's performance tonight, I was starting to wonder about his following.

He turned towards me in the gloom, and I could feel him studying my face as if trying to decide something. "There's been a lot of weird things going on lately. I know it sounds crazy, but I think someone's trying to kill me."

"And you think it could be that lady?" I wished I'd paid closer attention to her. "Have you called the police?"

"No! I mean, no. It's just been a series of strange things." He looked away from me, back to the side mirror. I didn't say anything, wondering if he was going to elaborate. He didn't. The windows began to fog up, and I switched on the defroster.

"Okay, so where do you want me to take you? I could circle around to the bookstore—she's probably gone by now."

"Do you think you could take me home? It's not that far, and I'd be happy to pay you for your trouble."

I thought of Addie, home alone and scared. Argh. "I guess. If it's not too far. And don't worry about it, I don't need to be paid."

"It's not far, just up off Washington," he said. "And really, I insist. I appreciate you going to the trouble."

I didn't want to point out that I'd not been given much of a choice. He gave me directions, running us through downtown. Traffic was light, which was just as well considering I could hardly see the street. I followed a pair of red taillights as we made our way past empty office buildings and deserted parking lots, using them to guide me since I couldn't see where the lane markers were.

Tension radiated off him, fueling the stress I was already experiencing from terrible driving conditions.

"So, you've never seen that lady before, but you think she's trying to kill you?" I normally don't like to pry, but he'd kind of foisted himself on me, so I didn't feel so bad.

He took a deep breath. "I'm not sure. I actually think it might be my mother."

"Wait, you think that lady is your mother?" I considered stopping the car and shoving him out right here. Famous writer or not, this guy was wacky.

"No, no. I think my mother might be angry enough to...I don't know."

"You think your mother might be angry enough to try and kill you?" I know I sounded skeptical, but really. Mothers don't usually get angry enough to kill their children. "What did you *do*?"

"This book." He patted his bag. "This book has a chemist in it, and well, she's a chemist."

The rain hissed under my tires as I drove.

"That's it? She's a chemist and you wrote about a chemist, so now she has to kill you."

"Okay, it does sound stupid when you say it that way, but it's not like that. She is a chemist. A pharmaceutical chemist, and she's recently been asked to head some high-level government task force." He reached over and touched my arm. "You can't tell anyone about this, okay?"

Since I had no idea what he was talking about, it didn't seem like that would be a problem. Although, Evan would be agog at this. "O-kay," I said slowly.

"I didn't know anything about that, and the chemist in my book has nothing to do with her. At all. I made this character up. But I guess someone she works with read my book and told her about it. And I guess they're worried that what I have in my book might mess the whole task force thing up for her."

"But still, that's kind of out there."

"You don't know my mother. She's capable of anything."

"Capable of killing her own child?" I could hear the disbelief in my own voice.

"Anything is expendable in the name of research." He sounded like he was reciting doctrine.

"Even her child?" Maybe he had a mental disorder. I glanced sideways, trying to see his face, but he was turned away from me.

"You don't know my mother. If I'm getting in the way of something she deems important—I think I could be expendable."

I stopped at a light, nearing the turn to Allen Parkway. The red reflected against the windshield, and one of my wipers squeaked as it raced side to side, trying to clear the water.

"Okay. But I'm sure she'd understand that this book has nothing to do with her. I mean, how long does it take you to write a book? This task force thing probably wasn't even on the radar while you were writing this, right?"

"No, it wasn't. I actually just found out about it. She's been calling me because they want to set up a time to talk to me. I guess it's all part of the clearance process."

"Who does the clearance for that? The FBI?"

"Yeah. But just because I didn't know about it ahead of time doesn't mean it wouldn't be a concern for them." The light turned and I eased a wide left, still following the helpful tail-lights. He sighed. "My chemist isn't the best person. He steals trade secrets, that kind of thing."

"It's fiction, though, right?" This all sounded rather melodramatic. Then again, this guy *was* a thriller writer. "And she probably won't get to head this task force if she kills you either, so there's that."

He gave a half laugh. "But if someone else actually did it"—he paused—"if someone else actually killed me and they couldn't prove she was involved, then I wouldn't be a problem for her anymore."

"If you could just hear how you sound."

Suddenly the rain that had been bad became overwhelming. I couldn't even see ten feet in front of the car. I gripped the steering wheel, hunching towards the windshield as if getting my face closer to the glass would magically help me see. The rain lashed the car, the noise nearly drowning out the sound of my heart pounding in my ears. If ever I understood the phrase "white knuckle," it was now.

"Wow. I don't think I've ever seen it this bad," Lander said.

"Yeah, me neither." I'd slowed to ten miles an hour and I flipped on my hazard lights. Another flash of lightning illuminated the bayou to the right of the road. It had spilled out of its banks and was creeping over the park area and running trails. It would cover the road before the night was over. Heck, probably before the hour was over.

We inched along in the right lane, my neck muscles working themselves into knots. Just ahead, I could see the Federal Reserve Building and the dim red dot of a stop light.

"I think we need to get off the road," I said. "Maybe pull into a parking lot or something until it lets up."

"I think there's a parking area up ahead," said Lander, his voice echoing the stress in my head.

Orange construction barrels suddenly popped into view as my wipers sluiced the water from the glass and I hit the brakes and steered left to avoid them. I could sense more than see Lander bracing one hand on the dash while the other clutched his seat belt.

"Yeah, we need to find a place to pull over," I said, my voice sounding slightly hysterical even to me.

"Is there anyone behind us?" he asked, swiveling around and trying to see through the rain. "If no one's coming, I'd say we turn left at the light and wait it out on a side street. I think we'd be better off getting to higher ground."

I peered into my side mirror, but the rivulets of water running down the surface rendered it useless. Glancing over my shoulder, I caught a flash of movement in the lane to my left.

"Yeah, I think there's a car," I said. The crush of metal on metal cut me off as something slammed into the left rear panel of my car, knocking us over the curb, past the construction barrels and onto the sidewalk. I gripped the wheel and jammed my foot on the brake, trying to stop our momentum towards the brown water churning just ahead.

Details registered in frozen flashes of time—headlights reflecting against the rain, a slick of mud on the sidewalk, tree-tops rising from the raging depths of the overflowing bayou. The antilock brake system on my car kicked in, and we shuddered to a stop, the front wheels skidding off the edge of the sidewalk onto the muddy grass. I thought I might throw up.

I took a shaky breath and turned towards Lander. "Are you alright? Geez, I didn't even see him." His face was ashen in the dim light. The second hit came almost immediately. This one wasn't as hard, but suddenly the car began to move forward as an engine revved behind us and I realized we were being pushed towards the water.

I screamed this time. At least I think it was me. My cries echoed off the windows as we slid forward, the car edging towards the flowing water. My foot jammed so hard against the brake I thought I might push it all the way through the floorboards.

Lander grabbed the parking brake and jerked up, but we continued our relentless slide towards the bayou, the wheels now skidding on the muddy slope, ever closer to the water. It roiled just ahead of us, like an angry river, brown and turbulent, rising quickly and carrying chunks of debris in its wake.

I felt paralyzed by fear, my body locked motionless while my brain accelerated, frantically searching for a way out. The headlights eked out a feeble glow against the driving rain and I scanned for anything that could help stop our progress. There was nothing. The steady, deadly pushing from behind continued to drive us down the bank. I cranked the steering wheel to the left, hoping I could turn us alongside the water and keep us from going straight in, but my wheels were in mud now, the water lapping at the front bumper.

And suddenly we launched.

I'd taken a Duck Boat Tour in Boston once, and for a split second it felt the same—a gentle drift into the water and a slight bob. But unlike the Duck Boat Tour, the front end of the car dropped forward and water began streaming in around our feet. The current was strong and we swept sideways for several yards before stopping.

Seconds felt like hours as the water closed around us and we sank into the murky depths. Beside me, Lander flailed at the passenger-side door and I watched as if removed. We'd tilted forward but had mercifully lodged against one of the submerged trees. Water raced past the windows while our air pocket inside began to slowly dwindle.

Movement returned to me with a panicky convulsion, like a person zapped alive by the paddles of life. I undid my seat belt and threw my weight at the door, useless against the powerful current. Pain jarred my shoulder, a harrowing reminder that I was still alive, but maybe not for long. The water was flowing against the driver's side, and I knew we'd never get out this way.

A thought bubbled through the terror in my brain, pushing through the fear—my window basher. I'd kept a seat belt cutter/window-breaking hammer in the map pocket ever since I'd gotten my first car. This was Houston—we tended to flood.

My hand reached down, fingers uncoordinated, grasping fat-fingered into the pocket. At first I didn't feel it and my breath turned into fast panicky gulps. The water crept to the console now. Lander had turned sideways and was trying to kick his window out.

I reached down again. It had to be there. I never took it out. I tried to will myself calm. My fingers brushed hard plastic and I grabbed the little hammer, wrapping my fingers tightly around it. *Don't drop it, don't drop it.* If I dropped it, we would die. I had no doubt about that now.

I grabbed Lander's shoulder.

"Here! Break out your window, we'll never get out this side." I reached for his hand and pressed the tool into his fingers when I found them. He felt for the pointed steel side and shifted closer to the window.

"Be ready to come out right behind me," he shouted. "I'll try to help you, but that water's running hard. I think we're hung up on a tree. Try to hold on to it so you don't get swept away, and work your way up."

The water was to my chest now. Dread filled my heart as he

readied the hammer. I didn't want to die. I didn't want to drown. I didn't want to get torn apart by a bayou that was out of control. But staying put meant dying. At least getting out gave us a chance.

I didn't hear the crack of glass, but suddenly Lander was pushing out through the passenger window. Foul brown water rushed in through the opening, and I scrambled, not wanting to be left behind. He tried to reach for me but was gone before I could grab ahold of his hand. I filled my lungs with air and tried to follow.

As soon as I was through the window, raging water tossed me like a baby's sock in the spin cycle and I felt myself being pulled and tugged in all directions. Fear shot through me as I squinted into the dark, churning water. I wasn't sure which way was up, and my chest began to burn with the effort of holding my breath.

I'm a good swimmer. I've always been a good swimmer, but this was unlike anything I'd ever faced. Survival instinct kicked in, and my legs began trying to propel me. The headlights on my car were still illuminated, pointed down into the murky depths. It wasn't as deep as I thought, but I was no match for the power of the current.

Suddenly my head shot above the surface and I sucked in greedy gasps of precious air. I barely had time to close my mouth before the water dragged me under again. Within seconds I caught on a tree. The branches snagged me by the shirt and I was able to break the surface again, gasping in more air, more tired this time.

I reached out an arm and wrapped it around a wide trunk, a torrent of water pinning me to the tree. I caught my breath and inched up as high as I could, rubbing a hand over my eyes to clear my vision. I wasn't far from the bank, but I doubted I could swim the short distance against such a violent onslaught, and the bayou was continuing to rise. Even as I watched, the water rose slightly and I inched farther up. Fear prickled along my skin and my muscles felt suddenly fatigued. I didn't know how long I could hold on. My tree felt sturdy, but what if it uprooted?

As if through a tunnel, I thought I heard my name.

"Jessie! Jessie!" I squinted towards the bank. A dark shape ran back and forth in short bursts—Lander running in circles like a dog trying to pick up a scent.

"Lander! Over here!" My voice sounded feeble, but suddenly he stopped moving and stood peering out towards me.

"Where are you?"

I waved one hand, arm still wrapped tightly around the tree. "Over here!"

He stood staring out into the dark. The rain had let up slightly, and while the thunder still rumbled, it was from much farther away. The worst of the storm seemed to have passed, but that didn't help me much in my current predicament.

I looked towards the bank, trying to judge how far downstream I'd traveled. Surprisingly, I could still see the back end of my car several yards up. Unfortunately, it was directly upstream from where I perched, and I prayed it wouldn't come loose from its position before I could get out of its path.

I realized Lander was yelling at me.

"What?" I shouted.

"The trees," he shouted, waving an arm at me. "There's more trees. Can you find a branch that's coming this way? I think you can hold on and make it to the next tree."

From my position against the trunk, I felt along under me with my right foot. I didn't feel anything solid. About a quarter way around the trunk, I saw a heavy branch above the surface of the water, heading towards shore.

"Right there," Lander was shouting. "That branch will get you to the next tree."

I squinted into the darkness. Lander was right— there was a

grove of crepe myrtles between me and the bank. But could I make it tree to tree without being swept away? They looked so fragile, and I was so tired. I took a deep breath and then another. If only the water wasn't moving so fast.

It was warm for May, but I felt chilled and my teeth began to chatter. Or maybe that was the fear. At any rate, I needed to do something. I had no idea if rescuers were on the way, but most likely not.

I inched around the trunk of the tree, reluctant to loosen my hold.

"Go slow," Lander hollered from the shore. "Hold on tight and keep coming this way."

Easy for him to say. I studied the branch, trying to create a visual path. If I could hold on and inch my way over, the next tree was only about five feet away. Taking a couple deep breaths, I finally unhooked my right arm from the trunk and reached for the branch.

Just as I loosened my hold, the water nearly pulled me under, dragging at my legs, and I panicked, throwing my arms around the trunk again. Bark tore at my skin, but I barely noticed. Vertical was better than horizontal. I could hold on by hugging this tree, but I couldn't see that I would be able to make it across that branch.

"You can do it," shouted Lander, a veritable one-man cheer-leading squad.

"No, I can't," I cried back. "I can't. Go get help."

"Just wrap yourself around the branch and go slow. You can do this. I promise."

Tears blurred my vision and I blinked them away in frustration. Why wouldn't he just go get help? A couple more deep breaths and a spark of anger flickered to life inside me, replacing the despair that threatened to overwhelm. Why wouldn't he go get help? This whole mess was his fault. He'd basically carjacked me. He'd put me in a dangerous situation just by getting in my car when he knew someone was trying to kill him. Whoever'd pushed us off the road was probably the one who was after him, and now here I was in the middle of a raging bayou, possibly going to die, and he wouldn't even go call 911.

I shimmied a little higher up the trunk, then swung a leg over so I was sitting on the branch, still hugging the trunk. I was farther above the water but no closer to shore. I took a couple more deep breaths, trying to calm myself, before sliding backwards along the branch until I was flat against it, wrapping my arms and legs tightly around and straddling it like a bear cub with a fear of heights. The water rushed under me, brown rapids splashing up. It would have been better if the branch was thicker, as I felt myself sliding to the side. Inch by inch, I made my way backwards towards the next tree.

Lander called encouragement from the bank, doing little more than irritating me further. Maybe there was a reason someone was trying to kill him.

Once I backed into the next tree, I couldn't figure out how to shift from my now semi-secure position. This was like a gym class nightmare. I'd never liked this kind of stuff in elementary school, and making it critical to saving my life didn't make me like it any better. I finally managed to hook a leg around the crepe myrtle trunk and return to my upright tree-hugging position. I was much closer to the bank than I'd expected.

"You're doing great!" Lander said, waving an arm as if he could pluck me from the tree. Unfortunately, I didn't see any more convenient branches for me to traverse, so I settled for yelling at him.

"Yeah, now what?" I shouted, trying to see my next steps. "Just go get help, okay? Why won't you just go get help?" I was pretty sure I needed a helicopter, strong guys and a basket that would whisk me to safety and deposit me in my front yard since even if I got out of the bayou, I had no car.

"You're just about there," he said, moving along the shore again. "Look, it's not that deep. Come down the trunk a little bit and I'll bet you can touch bottom."

I looked down at the rushing water. "I don't know," I said.

He took a tentative step off the bank towards me, holding one hand around a slim tree trunk. Plunking forward, he landed in hip-deep water and struggled to hold on as the water nearly bowled him over. He finally got himself upright and semi-braced between two small trees before reaching out a hand towards me.

"Okay, come on," he said. "I got you. Just try to find the bottom."

I slid a little down the trunk, feeling more skin come off my inner thighs. If I didn't drown, I was going to be at risk for a nasty infection. God only knew what kind of pathogens were floating around in this water.

Water pushed against my back as I lowered myself. I waggled a foot, trying to find bottom, but still didn't feel it. The muscles in my arms were beginning to shake with fatigue and I slid farther into the depths, praying I could touch bottom.

I finally felt hard surface under my foot, but the water reached nearly to my chest. This would be difficult to walk through in a still swimming pool; moving this fast, it was impossible.

"Grab my hand," Lander shouted. He leaned forward, one hand clutching a thin sapling and his legs spread wide between two more.

I reached out a hand, but even stretching, we were too far apart.

"I can't reach."

"Come on. We've got to get out of here," he said, as if I was obstinately keeping him from his plans. "Look, just jump. Jump upstream a little so that I can grab you when the water pushes you this way."

I didn't see any way around it. I didn't think this would go well, but I didn't have any better ideas and I wanted to be on firm ground. I turned and pushed off, grabbing for Lander's hand.

As soon as I let go of the tree, the water whisked me away like a beach ball in a tidal wave. Fighting not to go under, I flailed like a classic drowning victim—arms flapping at the surface, feet fighting to find something solid. I gulped air and held my breath, expecting to be pulled under but mercifully landing in a thicket of small trees and bushes, which acted as a filter that I was too big to pass through.

I grasped at the tangle of branches and trunks, trying to right myself, before finally washing up close enough to the bank to be able to drag myself out of the water. I threw myself into the mud on my hands and knees, nausea washing over me.

My heart pounded as if I'd just finished a marathon and my arms felt like rubber noodles, barely able to support my weight. I spat into the dirt, trying to clear my mouth of the bayou water that I'd ingested. I'd seen a news story once about the nasty things that flowed into the bayous in these kinds of floods, and I spat a few more times for good measure.

Lander raced to my side, slipping in the mud and going down on one knee.

"Are you okay?" he asked, reaching a hand toward my shoulder, then pulling it away quickly as I glared at him. I reached up and pushed limp wet strands of hair off my face.

The streetlights from Allen Parkway cast a dim yellow light across this part of the park, and I could see that Lander didn't look much better than I felt. His hair was plastered to his head, the jaunty ruffle gone, and brown goop stretched across his cheek like he'd been spackled with baby poop. I felt a gag reflex burble up in my throat and I looked away.

"What?" he asked, putting a hand to his face. "*What?*" He felt the slime and brought his fingers down to peer at them in the dimness. "What is that?" He took a tentative sniff at his hand, then rubbed it convulsively on his jacket. "Ugh. What *is* that?" He ripped his jacket off and began rubbing his face with the inside lining like he was trying to scrape his skin completely off the bone.

That made me feel perversely better about him. I struggled to my feet and tried to take stock of myself. Cuts and scrapes ran down both legs as well as my arms. A section near my ribs felt sore as if I'd been sucker punched, and I had a pain on the side of my head that, when touched, felt swollen. I had no idea where that had come from.

My clothes disgusted me, and I wanted nothing more than to peel them off. My feet squelched in my shoes, and I sat back down to remove them and pour out what water I could. I didn't even want to think about my car.

"We need to find a phone and call the police," I said, slipping my feet back into still squishy shoes.

"No, we can't call the police," he said. His face was mottled from scrubbing and I refrained from pointing out there was more brown stuff up near his hairline.

"What do you mean, we can't call the police?" I asked, lurching to my feet. "Someone runs you off the road and tries to kill you—you call the police. That's how it works."

He looked away, belatedly taking in our surroundings. "We need to get out of here," he said, lowering his voice. "They're likely to come back and make sure we're dead. If they find us here, we won't get a second chance."

"All the more reason to call the police!" I shot back, my voice rising.

"Shhh." He closed the distance between us and ushered me farther along towards some overgrown bushes. We were still below street level, hidden from view by the incline. I hesitated, uncomfortable following him to an even more remote area. Then again, if he wanted to kill me, he could have just left me in the car.

I pulled farther away but followed him, just out of reach.

"Lander. We need to go get help." I'd modified my tone, trying to sound soothing. The tone you'd use when trying to talk a five-year-old into going to the dentist. "Someone tried to kill us. They nearly succeeded. We need to call the cops."

"We can't. I can't have the police involved until I know who's doing this. You don't understand."

"No, clearly I don't." I was getting aggravated. "Look at my car. It's totaled. You know that, right? At a minimum, I'm going to need a police report for the insurance. Not to mention, *we nearly died*."

"Look, I'll take care of it. I'll get you a new car. I just—" He cut off with a huff. "Please. Trust me on this."

We were at an impasse. A slight wind had picked up and I shivered again, my clothes clinging to me in sodden folds.

"Well, I need to get home," I snapped.

"I'm sorry," he said. "I'm really sorry I got you into this." He started to hold out his jacket for me, then remembered the goop he'd wiped off onto the lining. "Sorry."

"Can we at least go somewhere and call for a ride?" I asked. Then I realized my purse was in my car. With my cash. And credit cards. And my phone. "Then again, I don't have any money with me anymore."

It was then that I noticed he still had his messenger bag slung over his shoulder and resting behind his hip, dripping a steady stream down his backside.

"Oh," I said, staring at it. "You managed to get your purse out. I didn't."

"It's not a *purse*."

"Well, it's more than I've got."

We stared at each other.

"I need a minute to think," he said. "I can't go home. They'll probably be checking my house to see if I got out of there." He looked towards the bayou, then rubbed at his hair, agitated, and began mumbling to himself.

I could tell him one thing—he wasn't coming to my house.

Then a thought struck me. I took a few steps up the embankment and poked my head up to see where we were.

"Look, we're not that far from my friend Evan's house," I said. "I mean, we're maybe a mile or two. But it's walkable. We could go there and he could take me home. And you... well, you can figure your mess out. I need to get home."

Apparently, it was better than anything he'd come up with and we started walking. The rain had stopped but it was windy and I felt cold, the skin on my fingers wrinkling up like raisins. It was probably only a little more than a mile, but it took a lot longer than it should have because every time a car came along, Lander insisted we duck behind a parked car or dash up someone's driveway and hide behind a bush. By the time we reached Evan's street, I was a mass of jangly nerves.

Evan's was the first house in off Montrose, just behind a small shopping strip. There used to be a Mexican restaurant on the corner, but it had closed a few months ago. It had been one of the primary attractions that drew Evan to the property. His porch light was off, but I could see light glowing behind the bedsheet that was acting as a curtain across the front window. To say he'd bought a fixer-upper was a bit of an understatement. Lander followed me up the sagging steps, so close I could feel his breath on my neck.

As I reached out to ring the bell, Lander grabbed my arm.

"Are you sure this guy's okay?" he whispered. He had the look of an animal about to bolt wildly into traffic.

"Good grief, he's fine," I said. "He's one of your biggest fans."

I hit the button. Evan's dog, Henry, raced to the door, his bark piercing the air. We stood for a couple of minutes, listening to the dog go wild.

"He's not home," Lander said. "Let's get out of here. I have a bad feeling."

He was really starting to freak me out with this stuff. Finally, footsteps thumped to a stop, and I saw a small slit of bedsheet being raised at the window.

"Evan, it's me," I said, waving my hand. He didn't move from the window but continued to stare at us. "It's me, Jessie," I said. "Oh, and I have Lander Jones with me."

The door flew open and Henry raced out, flying around our ankles in joyous circles. "Hey, Henry," I said, kneeling down to pet him. He sniffed around me, fascinated by my new smells. I didn't even want to know what he was picking up.

Lander was nearly dancing up and down beside me with nervous energy.

"Can we come in?" I asked Evan, standing back up.

"What happened to you?" Evan asked, staring at me with a strangled look. He sniffed at us, drawing back and wrinkling his nose. "And why do you smell like that?"

A car turned the corner and I thought Lander was going to hit the ground. I pushed past Evan and grabbed Lander by the sleeve.

"We need to come in," I said, pushing Lander to the side, out of sight of the doorway.

Evan ushered Henry inside and shut the door behind us. We stood awkwardly in the light of the overhead bulb and stared at each other.

"What are you doing here?" Evan asked, suddenly brushing at his hair and looking down at his ratty T-shirt. "I mean, it's awesome! Like, Lander Jones at my house." He looked around the cluttered living room and kicked a Diet Coke can under the couch.

"Someone ran us off the road into Buffalo Bayou," I said, swatting at an itchy prickle coming from inside my shirt.

"What? Are you kidding me?" Evan asked. "Are you okay?"

"We nearly died." I pulled the neck of my shirt forward and peered down, reaching in to pull out a nasty-smelling leaf. "And my car is in the bayou."

"It's like one of your books or something!" Evan said, his eyes alight with excitement.

"I need a ride home. And we still need to call the police and file a report," I said, looking pointedly at Lander.

He turned away, peering towards the darkened kitchen. "I can't stop you from calling the police," he said. "But I would really rather you didn't."

"My car is underwater. We nearly drowned. I think it's customary to report that. You know, so they can catch who did it!"

Evan's head whipped side to side watching this exchange. "You're wanted," he said, looking at Lander. "You can't call the cops because you're wanted for something."

"No, I'm not wanted. As I was telling her, someone is trying to kill me, and until I know who, I don't know that I can trust the cops."

"Sounds pretty paranoid to me," I mumbled. "Look," I said, turning to Evan, "I need a ride home."

He hesitated, looking from me to Lander and back. "What about you?" he asked Lander. "Do you need a ride home too?"

"Actually, I don't think I can go home until I figure this out." He squinted a little and looked down at his feet. "I don't suppose

I could stay with you for a few days until I get this sorted out? I mean, I don't even know you, so no one would ever find me here. I'd actually feel kind of safe."

Evan lit up like he'd just won the lottery. "That'd be great! Yeah, sure! Of course you can stay here." Then he faded a few watts. "But I don't have a guest room set up. I just have the couch." He gestured towards a plaid nightmare that I'd spent the night on a few months ago.

"Good luck with that," I said. "Word to the wise, you're going to end up on the floor one way or another. You're better off putting the cushions on the floor starting out. At least that way you won't get hurt slipping off."

Lander glanced toward the window, then at the couch. "It looks good to me."

CHAPTER THREE

E van drove me home after pointing Lander towards the shower. I could tell he begrudged every minute away, like he was missing out on the adventures that Lander and Henry might be having without him. When we got to my house, he didn't even get out of the car. I felt fortunate that he stopped completely and didn't make me jump out and roll.

He drove away before I realized that my keys were at the bottom of Buffalo Bayou, still stuck in the ignition of my car. Fortunately, I have a keypad that opens my garage door. I was standing in front of it, trying to remember my code, when a hand grabbed my shoulder. I whirled around as a light clicked on, nearly blinding me. In one reflexive move, I jerked my arm sideways, connecting with the light and sending it crashing to the driveway.

"Hey, whoa! What are you doing?"

It was Larry, my next-door neighbor. I knew this from his voice because my vision was still impaired by the dancing yellow lights.

"Geez, Larry. What are *you* doing?"

"I'm patrolling," he said, bending down to retrieve his flashlight. "This is an expensive flashlight. If you broke it, you're going to have to pay for another one." He shook it a couple of times, turned it over and clicked the button. The megawatt bulb snapped to life, blasting his face in a yellow burst.

"Patrolling what?" I remembered my code and turned to punch it into my keypad. The garage door groaned open.

"There's been an uptick in crime recently. I'm being a good neighbor. You're welcome."

"Okay," I said, moving into the garage. "Have fun."

"You look like crap," he said as I hit the button, shutting him out. I had a house key hidden under a paint can and I brushed away a cobweb as I lifted the can.

Forty pounds of black-and-white fur hurtled at me as I pushed into the kitchen, ecstatic that I was finally home. I sank to the floor and rubbed my fingers through Addie's soft fur, comforted by her wild kisses against my face. It didn't take long for her to discover my new fragrance, reminding me I needed to go decontaminate myself.

I kicked my shoes into the garage, grabbed a trash bag and headed for the shower. Moving my bathroom rug aside, I spread the trash bag wide and stepped onto the black plastic. Peeling my clothes off one item at a time, I let bits of debris fall around my feet directly into the bag. Brown leaves and twigs had washed through my clothes and stuck to my skin like confetti in a rainstorm.

The inch-long squirmy black bug that crawled out of my underpants nearly did me in. I threw myself into the shower, letting the hot water wash over me while I scrubbed at my skin with a washcloth and a bar of soap until I was nearly raw. Cuts and scrapes sprang to painful awareness as the soap hit each opening, but the pain was almost a relief—a validation that I was alive.

I stayed under the hot stream until it began to run cool. By the time I dried off, slathered myself in antibiotic ointment, and put on a pair of baggy pajamas, I was exhausted. Addie had watched all this from the middle of my bed, head resting on her paws, her expression concerned.

I took her downstairs and fed her while I heated up some soup. In spite of the May heat, I craved comfort. I tried to ignore the thoughts popping up about everything I was going to have to do to try and get my life back in order. I needed a way to get around. I needed a new car. I would have to replace my license, credit cards, insurance cards. New house keys, keys to my grandmother Frances's house. And as a final affront, I'd had my favorite purse with me.

All of this because Evan wanted me to see Lander Jones with him.

I cleaned my soup bowl and dragged myself up the stairs, wondering how Lander would fare on Evan's couch. It served him right if he had a bad night, dragging me into this. Addie stomped in circles before throwing herself down beside me with a groan. Her presence comforted me, and as I turned out the light, I felt a little bad for Lander. Someone definitely had it in for him, and the way it looked to me, they were pretty close to getting what they wanted.

I had a restless night, bad dreams cut short by tender muscles that ached every time I moved. At five thirty I dragged myself out of bed and treated myself to an Advil. Random muscles hurt in places where I didn't even realize I had muscles. A couple of my scrapes were looking ominously red, and a bruise the shape of Indiana covered my right thigh. At least the bump on my head was down. Still sore to the touch, but hard to see.

I worked slowly through a series of gentle yoga stretches before heading downstairs to fire up the coffeemaker. Pulling out a pad of paper, I started making a list of all the things I had to address. Fridays are normally busy for me, as I visit my dog biscuit distributors, checking inventory, getting feedback, and offering free samples for their clients.

Realizing I had no car to get around in, I scratched "distributor visits" from my list and added "figure out transportation." In addition to my dog biscuits, I also did some dog walking to help pay the bills. I'd had no idea how hard it would be to start a business until I'd started this one last year. I used to work for an oil company, drudging away for a horrible boss, until one day I'd just quit and never looked back. The thought of having to go find another "real job" was what kept me moving and working the long hours that I did.

My dog clients were fairly close to where I lived, although not exactly walking distance. I really needed a car. I spent some time reviewing my bank accounts, my insurance policy and my business's earnings spreadsheet. This depressed me enough to nearly send me back to bed, but instead I refilled my coffee and added an extra dollop of oat milk to cheer myself up.

Truth be told, I did have an emergency fund. It was a trust fund my grandfather had set up for me. It was actually a hefty little thing, and I know it sounds weird, but—I didn't really want to touch it if I didn't have to. And also, I would have to go through a trustee to take out more than a little bit at a time, and buying a car would exceed my threshold. I didn't have time for that.

I should file a police report and contact my insurance company, though. More tedious things I didn't want to do. By six thirty, I'd finished my list as well as all the coffee. Things were coming into focus.

The rain had stopped although leafy debris stuck to the curb like sodden confetti after a rowdy carnival parade. The oppressive humidity had broken to what was a relatively cool day for May. I walked Addie, took stock of my biscuit ingredients, gathered the phone numbers for all my distributors, and started my first batch of peanut butter dog cookies. While they were baking, I showered, dressed and made it back downstairs in time to pull two trays of perfectly browned cookies from the oven.

I called Enterprise Rent-A-Car, made a reservation for one of the cheapest cars they had available on their lot, and asked if they could come pick me up. Unfortunately, I forgot that my driver's license was in my wallet somewhere in Buffalo Bayou. In spite of persuasive arguments on my part, as well as some full-on begging, they refused to budge on their requirement that I be able to produce a driver's license and proof of insurance. I hung up the phone in frustration. Where was I going to get a car?

I started up another batch of biscuits, trying to think of someone other than my grandmother that I could borrow a car from. If I told her my car was in the bayou, she would flip out, probably tell my parents, and that was going to generate all kinds of drama I wasn't interested in right now. And there was the matter of not having a driver's license. How in the world was I going to find time to go stand in line at the DMV? I could maybe do it online, but I needed a temporary one now so I could rent a car.

I punched the dough into a big ball and rolled it out on the floured counter. Addie retreated to the couch, where she lay with her head angled on the arm, half dozing, half watching for cats and neighbor dogs walking by. How nice to be so carefree.

The more I thought about it, the more I decided against calling Frances. She was as cool a grandmother as anyone could have, but she had her limits when it came to me being in any kind of perceived danger. Okay, fine, I'd been in actual danger last night, but that was last night and now I was fine. But she might not see it that way.

I was going to have to get Evan to take me to the DMV. I mean, this whole thing really was his fault. Okay, maybe not exactly his fault, but enough of his fault that he could at least give me a ride.

I whipped out dozens of little bone-shaped biscuits and popped them in the oven. I didn't want to go to the DMV. I just needed to get my purse back. It was probably still sitting in the back seat, and maybe the water had gone down enough that I could retrieve it. It wouldn't help my car predicament, but I would save me the trouble of replacing my license and credit cards. Plus, I loved that purse.

I booted up my laptop and sent Evan an email.

"Can you come get me and take me to where my car is? I need my purse."

Impatience ran through me as I waited for his reply. I gave him two minutes, then grabbed my home phone. I'm probably one of the few remaining people in North America who still has a landline, but it's the number I use for my business.

I struggled to remember his work number, but it finally came to me and I dialed.

"Hey," I said when he picked up. "Did you get my email?"

"Uh, I did, but I'm at work."

"Yeah, I know, but I need a ride."

The silence stretched on.

"Evan?"

"Don't you just have another purse you can use?" he asked, sounding exasperated at my unreasonableness.

"My license, credit cards, insurance and everything I need is in that purse." I could hear him clacking his keyboard. I sighed. "Look, I wouldn't bother you, but I can't even rent a car unless I have a license and insurance."

"Fine. But I can't be gone long, I have a meeting later."

We agreed that he'd come now so that he could get back to work and I could get to my dog-walking rounds. I pulled the last batch of biscuits from the oven and set them to cool.

I was standing on the curb when he squealed to a stop in front of my house. I'd changed into some old shorts and a ratty T-shirt in case I ended up having to wade into the bayou again. I'd also put on my shoes from yesterday, the damp, sludgy stench wafting up with every step.

"What is that smell?" he asked as I slid into the car.

"What smell?" I buckled my seat belt and pretended I didn't know what he was talking about. He turned the car around and headed north towards Allen Parkway. I cracked my window a smidgen.

"Lander called me at work just before I left," Evan said. "He heard on the news that they found your car and they're reporting that the driver is missing. They're bringing in dive teams to search for your body."

"Oh, great," I said, thinking I should have just called the police last night like a normal person. Meanwhile a cold chill ran up my spine at the thought of divers looking for my body.

"Yeah, it is great! He said that's best case, because now his assailant will think the two of you are dead."

"They didn't say my name on the news, did they?" I had visions of Frances and my parents freaking out thinking I had been washed away and drowned. I hoped the police hadn't contacted them. This was a disaster.

"No, I don't think so. At least he didn't say that."

"I guess I'll have to explain what happened."

"No! You can't tell the police what happened. You heard Lander. How do you know they're not in on it?"

"Oh, for Pete's sake," I said, looking out at the lush green lawns of River Oaks as they flew past my window. "You sound as paranoid as him."

"Jessie, you don't understand. He was telling me some stuff last night..." He trailed off, glancing over his shoulder before shifting lanes. "You just don't know. It sounds bad. Like seriously, I'm afraid they're actually going to get to him."

"Well, what am I supposed to say? Oh, yeah, I drove into the bayou and then just went home. Call off the search team."

"Yeah. Say that."

"Someone ran me off the road! I could have been killed. I nearly *was* killed."

"Lander was almost killed too, and there's someone out there ready to take another crack at it if they find out he's still alive. He's working really hard to figure out who's doing this. He asked if we could sit down tonight and let him bounce some thoughts off of us."

"What good's that going to do? We don't know anything."

"His next-door neighbor is coming over too. Lander thinks maybe some new perspective would help. We don't have any preconceived ideas. What do you say?"

We'd reached Allen Parkway and were sailing along the curvy lanes towards downtown. The Waugh bridge underpass showed remnants from last night's flooding—water marks crept up the concrete support walls, and leaves stuck in bands where the flood line had reached. But barely a puddle remained on the road.

"We went off on the other side up near Taft," I said. "I'm not sure if you'll be able to turn around or not."

It wasn't hard to find the location. Two police cars, a tow truck and a crowd of people marked the spot where I'd gone off the road. A news van angled across the sidewalk and a cameraman panned the action near the bayou. From our vantage point at the light, I could just make out the back end of my car.

Evan pulled away from the light, his eyes riveted on the scene. He bounced gently off the curb as a horn sounded behind us. We inched along in the left lane as he looked for a place to turn around, but a median strip blocked us from doing a U-turn.

"I don't think there's anywhere to turn around," I said as the car behind blasted past us on my side with a long honk and a finger wave.

"You sure?" Evan asked.

"Pretty sure. I think we're just going to have to go downtown and turn around."

"Nah." Evan slowed even more, then gunned his car up the curb onto the grassy median. Several more horns blared as we were now blocking lanes coming and going. The ground was soft from the rain, and for a moment I thought we were going to get stuck. The tires spun a few times before we shot across and into the outbound lanes, headed back the way we'd come.

I patted my chest, trying to calm my heart as Evan pulled to a stop behind one of the police cars. He shut off the engine and we sat in silence looking out across the unfolding scene. Two cops peered into the windows of my car, which was nose down the embankment, stopped from sliding further only by a small grove of trees that had conveniently wrapped their branches around the wheels and undercarriage. The bayou had ebbed back to its banks, leaving my car as exposed as a dirty, naked baby.

The same funk that had covered my clothes last night mottled the white paint, and water seeped from the interior. The passenger window was gone, probably several miles downstream by now. My breath caught in my throat looking at it, feeling how close our escape had been.

"Good, it looks like I should be able to reach my purse," I said, trying to focus on the positive and not get overwhelmed by delayed emotions. Evan didn't notice the little break in my voice. He had pulled his phone from his pocket and was snapping away like a tourist at the Grand Canyon. We walked closer to the crowd. They were snapping pictures too and I felt like a slacker for not wanting to join in. I really didn't need any reminders of this.

Closer to the bayou, police walked up and down the bank, presumably looking for my body. I could see additional police cars parked farther down, and a few more on the other side.

"I should probably tell them they can quit looking for me," I said, not wanting to become the center of attention. I wished the news crew would leave.

"That's unbelievable," Evan said, finally looking at me. "You're lucky you got out of that." He gave me a pat on my shoulder and a little shake. Evan's version of a comforting hug.

"I know."

"Someone's not kidding around."

"I know."

I bit my lip and made my way towards the closest officer. I really didn't want to draw attention to myself, but when I told him that was my car, he hollered to all the searching cops to pull it back, the owner was here. That set the news crew into high gear and they raced across the mucky ground towards me.

"Look, I don't want to talk to them," I said in a low voice to the officer. "I really just want to see if I can get my purse out of the car. I need my license and insurance."

"We're going to need to get some information," he said, giving me the side-eye. He was probably looking for hangover signs. Crap. Could they charge me with anything for having been nearly killed? I really couldn't prove I hadn't been drinking this long after the event.

"Someone ran me off the road last night." I looked towards the rear end of my car seeing signs of damage even from over here. "You can see the damage on the back. There should be more on the left rear quarter panel."

We'd moved away from the crowd, and he signaled the news

crew back, giving a little finger flick to another officer, who led them towards the sidewalk.

He walked me along a grassy strip, upstream of the muddy trail my car had left. The tread marks only went partway down the embankment, disappearing where we'd gone waterborne and had begun to float. There were no other signs of our journey, unless you counted the crushed trees.

Another officer joined us and they both pulled out note pads. Evan lurked behind, clearing his throat every few seconds as if trying to warn me against mentioning Lander's involvement in this.

"Why don't you run us through what happened here?" the first one asked me after he'd taken down my personal information for the record.

"Sure. Well, you know how bad the weather was last night, right? Um, I had gone to a book signing—" At this point, Evan went into extended throat clearing until both officers looked over at him.

"Sir? Are you okay? Perhaps you should wait over there."

"No, no, I'm fine," he said. "Just a tickle or something. Allergies, you know?"

They both stared at him, unblinking, until he began to fidget and then finally pulled out his phone and started scrolling down the screen as a distraction.

"You were saying?"

"Yes, so I went to this book signing, and on my way home it was raining like crazy. I was going slow because it was so hard to see, when someone hit me. At first I thought it was an accident. You know? I mean the rain was so bad, and there were these construction barrels that just, like, popped up out of nowhere. But then they hit me again. And I ended up going up over the curb." I turned towards the street looking for marks but couldn't see any signs from here. "And then they followed me up on the curb and basically rammed me again until my car went into the water."

They pivoted from me to my car to the ground around my car and back to their notebooks.

"Why would someone do that?" Officer One asked.

"I have no idea," I said, halfway expecting to be tackled by Evan.

"No idea?"

"No idea."

"Had there been any traffic issues? You know, a dispute with another driver on your way home? You did mention it was hard to see."

Well, here was an out.

"I guess it's possible. It really was hard to see."

"Did you get a look at the car at all? The driver? Anything?"

I closed my eyes and tried to picture it. You always wonder why witnesses are so unreliable. You find yourself thinking, what are you, kidding me? You don't know if there were three gunmen or two? You can't tell if the car was blue or red? You didn't see if the person who snatched your purse was a tiny man or a big woman?

"I really didn't see anything. I mean, I caught a glimpse of a vehicle, but it was literally just a glimpse."

"Could you tell what color? What make or model?"

And now I understood all the other lame eyewitnesses. I grimaced. "Maybe dark? Maybe big?"

I heard Cop One give a small sigh. Yep, another lame eyewitness. He pointed his pen at my car. "We'll see about paint transfer. And we should be able to tell something based on where the impact damage is."

"Oh, cool," I said, wondering if Houston had the spiffy crime labs like on all those TV shows. Somehow, I doubted it, particularly since the victim was still standing and breathing.

Evan pointed his phone at my car, and I could hear the tiny fake whir as he snapped picture after picture.

"Sir? Step back, please." Cop Two gestured at him. "Were you with her last night?"

"No. Well, I was with her at the book signing." At this he stopped and looked stricken like he'd let his own cat out of the bag. "But I went home in my own car."

"Is this your boyfriend?" Cop One asked.

"No," Evan and I said in unison. "We're just friends. We used to work together," I added. They glanced over towards Evan's car. No dents, dings or scratches. No marks where he could have rear-ended someone and pushed them into the bayou.

"Do you think I could get my purse out of my car?" I asked. The tow truck driver was beginning to unload a chain rope, throwing it down and stretching it out towards my rear wheels.

"Sure."

Cop Two was peering at my muddy car. "I notice you broke out the passenger-side window?"

I felt Evan tense up beside me. I should really come clean—tell them the whole story. Like I'd said to Lander last night, if someone's trying to kill you, you go to the police. That's what they're there for.

"The water was hitting my window. I don't know, it just seemed like it would be easier to get out on that side. You know, go with it, not try to push against it." They both nodded and took a couple more notes, then one walked with me to the car.

Our feet squelched on the grass as we got closer, and an odor wafted from the broken window like a cracked diaper pail.

"I guess that's pretty much totaled," I said, feeling a pang. It was a little like losing a friend. I'd been through a lot with this car. But even if the engine wasn't ruined, which it had to be, nothing could get that stench out.

"I would imagine," he said. "I hope you have some good

insurance. Where's your purse?" he asked, poking his head into the empty window.

"Should be in the back seat." I slid over next to him, trying to see in the window. He reached in and unlocked the door, pulling it open with a small jerk. It gave a little sucking sound, and a trickle of brown water ran out. He stepped back and we both peered in.

There wasn't as much bayou debris as I'd expected, but the windows were fogged over with evaporating water, and the smell made us both turn our heads.

"Gross," I said, holding a hand in front of my nose. I held my breath as I leaned in and caught sight of my purse in the back seat. "There," I said, pointing to the officer. "My purse is right there." I noticed the book I'd bought last night, its pages bulging with water. No sense taking that with me.

He reached in, trying to keep the funk away from his uniform, and snagged the edge of my purse between two fingers. It dripped water as he pulled it towards us, and held it out for me.

"Thanks," I said, taking it gingerly and holding it well away from myself. I set it on the ground and pulled the zipper back, revealing the contents pretty much just as I'd left them. Well, except for the smell and filthy water. I pulled my wallet out first. License, credit cards and cash all there. Hand sanitizer, makeup, small package of Kleenex, all ruined. I set them aside and scrabbled for my phone. Gone. Then I remembered dropping it in the footwell when Lander had startled me getting into my car.

"I think I dropped my phone on the floor," I said. The cop made his way around to the driver's side and opened the door. His sinuses must have been ruined by now because he leaned in and reached around until he pulled the small phone out and held it up. He also pulled my keys from the ignition.

"Here you go," he said. I took the keys while he gazed at the mud-covered phone. "Yeah, I think this is ruined too." He made his way over to me, hit the power button and we both watched the screen hopefully. Nothing. "Sorry," he said, handing it over.

Another wave of sadness washed over me. All my contacts. My texts. My photos.

"You shouldn't have tried to turn it on," said Evan, suddenly appearing over my shoulder. "You should have taken the battery out and then put it in dry rice."

"Great, thanks," I said. I gathered up all my items and tried to think if there was anything else I needed to get out of my car. Addie's seat belt harness was in the back seat, but I wasn't about to let that touch her sweet skin ever again.

The officer asked me if he could see my license. He took down some information, then gave me a number I could use to get a copy of the official police report for insurance purposes.

The tow truck driver was hooking up his chains, which distracted the news crew completely. Evan and I made our way around the far side of the crowd and left before they started dragging my car up the embankment. It was just too painful to watch.

CHAPTER FOUR

Evan dropped me off at the nearest rental car agency, where I secured the cheapest ride I could—a bright yellow two-door Kia Rio. It looked like a lemon drop on wheels. In spite of being a nonsmoking car, the tiny interior reeked like a smoking lounge that someone had gamely tried to cover up with a pine-scented chemical spray. Add my bayou shoes and water-logged purse to the mix and it was a heady combination indeed.

I cracked the window and headed home, stopping at an AT&T store. The guy behind the counter held a polite hand in front of his nose as I dropped my phone on the counter.

"I need a new phone," I said.

"I can see that." He used a pen to push my phone back towards me. We haggled only long enough for him to realize I truly wasn't going to buy his most expensive phone. I already had a plan, and I just wanted something similar to the smelly thing lying dead between us. I was out in thirty minutes and heading home to change for my dog walking rounds.

I tended to think of my dog walking as a temporary boost in cash flow until my biscuit business took off, but the truth was, I loved this part too. No matter what was going on in my life, my dog clients provided a steadying calm. I wasn't sure I could ever give up this aspect of my work. I currently had six dog clients, each one of which got thirty minutes of walking, playing or cuddles.

The day flew by with long moments where I forgot about the accident, only to have it resurface with a feeling of dismay. By the time I got home, I was hot, sweaty and ready to relax. My new phone dinged while I was in the shower. I stuck a hand around the curtain and checked the message from Evan, telling me to come over at six. I'd totally forgotten about his brainstorming invitation.

By six, I'd fed Addie, left her a stuffed Kong and was pulling into Evan's driveway. A yellow cab pulled to the curb as I got out, and a white-haired gentleman leaned in to pay the cabbie.

"Hello," he said as he straightened up and smiled at me. He was slender and nattily dressed in pressed blue slacks and a crisp mint-green button-down. His ears curved ever so slightly forward under neatly clipped hair, giving him an engaging elfin look, and wrinkles along the sides of his mouth indicated decades of good humor. He clutched two puffy plastic grocery bags in his left hand.

"Hi."

"Am I in the right place?" He looked around. "I'm looking for a friend of mine."

"Are you the next-door neighbor?" I asked, hitting the remote and locking my car. We watched the yellow cab drive away.

"I am," he said as we approached the porch steps. He lowered his voice. "William Wagner. And you are?"

"Jessie Gallagher," I said. "I'm a friend of the homeowner here and I was with your neighbor last night." We shook hands and walked to the front door. I glanced towards the street, a slight paranoia creeping back. William put a gentle hand to my back and ushered me across the porch, the boards creaking under our weight. The living room windows, normally covered by a bedsheet, now also had aluminum foil and newspapers covering every last inch of glass. I rang the bell and heard Henry skitter to a stop in front of the door before launching into an earsplitting salvo of barks.

"Ah, a watch dog," said William, brightening at the noise.

"I don't know about that," I said, leaning my head towards the door. Besides the dog, I didn't hear the normal thudding of feet that precipitated Evan's arrival at the door. "I wonder where they are."

I rang the bell again and cast a nervous glance around the yard. Finally, the door cracked open two inches and I saw Evan squinting out.

"Hurry up! Hurry up!" he said, opening the door about two more inches and waving a hand at us. "Get in."

I pushed the door open far enough to slip inside with William right behind me. Evan shoved the door closed with a bang and clicked the deadbolt. Then he leaned down and pushed a rubber doorstop towards the slim gap at the bottom of the door.

"There, that should do it," he said. The doorstop popped sideways and fell against the worn hardwood floor.

"Hey," said Lander, materializing from the kitchen. "I'm so glad you could come." He included me with a glance, but he made his way to William, and the two men exchanged a warm hug.

"Thank heavens you're okay," said William. "I was so concerned when I didn't see you get home last night."

"I should have called you, but by the time we got here and got settled it was so late. And I thought it would be safer for Evan to call you from a different phone."

I lit on the cell phone in his hand. "Is that your phone? Did you have that with you last night? How is it not ruined?"

"It was in my bag in an inside pocket that has a pretty good seal." He caught the look on my face. "I guess yours was ruined? I'll get you a new one."

"I already replaced it," I said.

His phone might be okay, but Lander looked a far cry from the polished author he'd been at the bookstore. He appeared to be wearing the same clothes from last night, although he'd lost the blazer.

"Seriously, Evan? You couldn't give him clothes to change into?"

Evan looked from me to Lander, his cheeks reddening and his mouth gaping slightly.

"It's fine, it's fine," said Lander. "I showered, I'm clean, it's all good." I thought of the black bug crawling out of my underwear.

"Evan, get him some clothes. That's just nasty. I was in that same water. Believe me, you need new clothes."

William held up the grocery bags. "Here you go. Not knowing exactly what's happening, I assumed you might want a change of clothes. I wasn't sure what to bring. I just grabbed a few things."

Lander grabbed the bags and peered inside. "This is perfect," he said. "You don't think anyone saw you go into my house, do you?"

"I watched for a long time to make sure there was no one around that I could see, and I went in through the kitchen."

"That's great," said Lander. "If you'll excuse me, I'll be right back."

Evan was fussing around the kitchen, the banging a dead giveaway of a sudden snit.

"How's it going?" I asked, sidling in.

"I thought it was going fine," he said, putting a dish away with such vigor I thought I heard a crack.

"Look, I'm sorry. I wasn't trying to be critical," I said. "It's just, seriously, that water was really nasty. I feel bad that he had to stay in his gross clothes."

"Well, I feel bad now too," he said, slamming another plate on the pile. The doorbell rang, mercifully interrupting us.

Lander popped out from the bathroom, looking transformed in a white T-shirt and khaki cargo shorts.

"Is that the pizza?" he asked, his voice barely above a whisper.

"Let me check," Evan said, moving towards the front room. He made his way to the front window and pulled back a tab on the newspaper that was taped to the glass. "Yeah," he said. "I'll go out and get it."

Lander handed him a couple of bills and Evan scraped himself through a gap getting through the door.

"That doesn't look suspicious," I said as Evan pulled the door closed behind himself.

Lander shook his head. "Yeah, I tried to tell him to act as normal as possible, but..." He trailed away.

"Evan's not exactly a master of subtlety," I said.

William paced the dim living room, watching Lander as he moved.

"Lander, what can I do?" he asked. "We need to get a handle on this. Don't you think it's time to go to the police?"

"Look, let's just eat and then we'll talk through it," Lander said quietly.

Evan reappeared, trying to fit two pizza boxes through a six-inch gap. He finally turned them sideways, pulled them through the crack and kicked the door closed.

"You guys hungry?" he asked, sounding a tad less upset. Although I noticed he didn't include me in his look.

Evan had bought his house several months ago but didn't have much furniture yet. Most of his money had been going for necessary repairs. At least he had a new roof if not a dining table. He had set up a card table and four folding chairs on the far side of the living room, where he set the pizza boxes down before heading to the kitchen for drinks.

I trailed along, rounding up paper plates, napkins and silverware, while he grabbed four beers from the refrigerator.

No one said anything about the mangled pizza when we opened the boxes—we just scraped the cheese off the box and put it back where it belonged. Even though it wasn't yet late, the covered windows made the room dark and the lone bulb hanging from the ceiling barely had enough wattage to light the floor below.

We hunched over our plates as if no one had eaten in a week, the scent of cheese and tomatoes filling the room with a comforting aroma. In spite of the food, tension filled the air and everyone kept glancing side to side as if expecting armed intruders to come bursting in at any moment. Evan and Lander shoveled pizza into their mouths so fast, I started getting concerned I wouldn't even get a second slice. This was normal behavior for Evan, but I could only guess that Evan hadn't thought to leave any food for Lander. I certainly wasn't going to bring it up, though.

"You didn't really tell me what happened last night," William finally said as he slowly cut his second slice of pizza into bite-sized bits.

Lander took a drag of beer, washing down a wedge of crust. "There was a woman at the bookstore. She works for my mother."

"What?" I asked. "Who?"

"The fan club president," Lander said.

"You never said she worked for your mother," I said.

"We didn't get that far last night," he started to say.

"He didn't know right away," Evan cut in, clearly excited to be in the know. "She was hanging around to have her book signed. Remember?" His pizza flapped sideways as he waved a hand. "Anyway, she kept hovering like she was waiting for us all to leave."

"She *was* waiting for everyone to leave," said Lander. "She was the last one in line. I could tell she wanted to be last—sometimes people do that because they think they'll be able to have some one-on-one time or something." He shook his head. "It's so awkward sometimes. Anyway, I was getting that kind of vibe off of her. I mean, like uncomfortable, but not scary."

"You said it was kind of scary," said Evan.

"Not at first. I mean, it was just like, ugh, another woman going to try to bond on a deeper level or something."

Oh brother.

Lander had the grace to look embarrassed. "I know how that sounds," he said. "It's not how I meant it. But once she was the only one at the table, she asked me to sign her book, and when I asked what name to make it out to, she said 'to your number one fan.'"

Evan was nearly bouncing in his chair. "Like the movie! Remember that Stephen King movie? It sounds just like that!"

Lander pushed a bit of crust across his plate. "Yeah. That's what I thought when she said it. It creeped me out."

"She looked like that crazy character too!" Speaking of crazy characters, Evan was nearly shouting now, although I can't deny a prickle of unease had run across me when Lander said it.

"So how did you find out she works for your mom?"

"I guess I looked at her funny when she said that, and then she got all, I don't know, giggly or something. So, she said, okay, how about 'To Nell, your number one fan.' And then she told me she knew a lot about me because she worked with my mom, and she said my mom was really *peeved* at me. *Peeved*. She kept saying that. And making this weird high-pitched laugh. It was so creepy."

"And that's when you ran out of the store and she chased you?" I asked.

"Kind of. She started digging around in this big bag she had. She said she had something for me and, I don't know, I kind of panicked. With everything that's been going on, I thought maybe she was going to pull out a gun and kill me right there."

We sat for a minute in silence. It would have sounded outright insane had we not then been shoved into a raging bayou and left for dead.

"I'm afraid I'm the only one here who doesn't know what happened next," said William. "Although, judging by your appearance, I may not like what I hear."

Lander took another sip of beer. "I pushed her book back at her, grabbed my bag and ran out. That's when I kind of hijacked Jessie here." He reached for another slice of pizza. "I thought if she could take me home, I'd have you drive me back to the bookstore today to pick up my car. But on the way to my house, someone forced us off the road and into Buffalo Bayou."

William's fork dropped to the table. His mouth fell open and he stared at Lander. "Into the bayou?"

"Yeah."

"In that storm?"

Lander shifted in his chair. "Well, yeah, but we're fine."

William turned his gaze to me, taking in the scrapes still visible on my arms before reaching out to cover my hand with his own. "Thank God no one was killed." I flashed to the water churning outside the car windows, and my heart did a sudden flop of remembered fear. William gave my hand a gentle squeeze before turning to Lander.

"Lander, I know we've talked about this, but it's time you

went to the police. This is too much. It's not just about you anymore. Not that that isn't enough. I don't want to see anyone get hurt." His voice broke. "Or killed."

"I appreciate your concern, you know I do," Lander said. "But you also know I can't go to the police. I can't."

"No, I don't know that," William said. "What I do know is that you need help. You can't face this alone."

"I'm not alone," Lander broke in. "Actually, I'm probably safer right now than I've been in weeks. No one knows I'm here. How could they? I'm at a total stranger's house. Someone who has no connection to me."

"Well, he has a little connection to you," I said. "I mean, we were both at your book signing last night. That's a connection."

"True, but it's minor. You're still virtual strangers. There wouldn't be a way for anyone to connect me to you."

"Except whoever ran us off the road."

Lander and I stared at each other across the table.

"Okay, let's start there," he said. "This is why I wanted everyone here tonight. To help me think this through and see what I'm missing."

I took another slice of pizza and wiped my greasy fingers on a paper napkin. "Outside of what happened last night, and the fact you think your mother is trying to kill you, I get the feeling I know the least about what's going on," I said. "I mean, no offense, but I'd never even heard of you before yesterday."

Lander laughed, the first genuine laugh I'd heard from him. "I never thought I'd be so happy to meet someone who's never heard of me," he said.

Lander and William gave us a brief history of the trouble Lander had been up against. I think Evan had heard bits of it last night because he nodded at various intervals. They tag-teamed the story, each stepping in to offer a detail here or clarify a point there. Apparently, it had started, near as they could tell, a few weeks ago, when Lander had begun having a string of unfortunate incidents. At first it had just seemed like a run of bad luck—a bad bout of food poisoning, a blowout while he was driving. He thought someone had been in his house at one point because he felt like things were just slightly out of place in his home office.

"Someone broke into your house?" I asked.

"No, that's the weird part," Lander conceded. "The doors were locked, no obvious signs of entry."

"Are you sure someone was in there?"

"I couldn't prove it," he said. "Things were just slightly off. It's like when you feel someone else's energy. I know it sounds crazy. I know this whole thing sounds crazy."

Actually, the whole thing gave me cold chills.

"Lander changed out the locks after that," said William. "Just to make sure."

"Did anyone else have a set of keys?"

"Well, my ex-wife used to live there. And my best friend had a copy. Not that he ever used it—I just gave him a set for emergencies when we first moved in. And William had the old keys and now the new keys." Evan looked sideways at William, obviously suspicious.

Lander carried on with his narrative, his inflection flatter than I would have expected for this kind of story. Last week he had nearly been run over while crossing the street after dinner. The driver hadn't stopped.

"So, you really think your mother is behind all that?" I asked. "Did she have keys?"

Lander and William exchanged a look.

"No," Lander said. "But I told you about the task force." William gave a small sigh and looked away. Even Evan didn't seem overly on board with this theory. "It's complicated. It's not just the task force." He fiddled with his beer bottle. "Look. It goes way back—like, I don't think my parents ever really wanted me."

William folded his paper napkin, his fingers running nervously along the crease. "Lander, we've talked about this."

I tried to think of a polite way to ask my question. "Okay, so a lot of kids aren't planned. But, not for nothing, that was what? Thirty-some years ago? They waited till now to try and get rid of you?"

"I'm just trying to make you realize that the typical mother-son bond isn't exactly what you're thinking. My mother's career means everything to her. My father's the same. And my sister, she's what they wanted in their offspring. A science, math, technology savant. Me? I was like some foreign exchange student they hadn't asked for and didn't want. I don't have anything in common with any of them."

I took another bite of pizza, trying to decide if this had anything to do with anything. He could sense the skepticism.

"Okay, here's the thing. My mother is ruthless. When I was a kid, she took me to the lab with her once. I guess she was trying to get me more interested in what she did." He paused. "She was working on something where they were doing product testing on rats." I grimaced, definitely not wanting to hear this story. "And it was awful. I remember crying when I saw the rats, and what was happening. She got angry at me. She told me that sometimes you have to make sacrifices in the name of progress."

"And now you're the rat?" Evan asked.

"This task force is a *huge* deal for her. It's progress," Lander said.

"But again, you don't know that your book is going to stand in her way," William said, sounding as if they'd covered this topic ad infinitum. "You still haven't done your FBI interview. You have your notes. You're a writer. You make things up. And really, I would think the FBI would consider her killing her son a bigger issue than a fictional chemist." Just what I'd said last night.

"Do you really think she ran us off the road last night?" I asked.

Lander sighed. "I don't know. Maybe not. But she could have gotten someone else to do it."

"Maybe we should make a list," Evan said.

"That's an excellent idea," said William. "We need to keep an open mind."

Considering I didn't know anything about who would want to kill this guy, an open mind wasn't going to be hard for me. Evan trotted off to the kitchen, where we could hear him rooting around and slamming drawers. He returned with a tattered notepad and a pen and held them out to me.

"Your writing is better than mine," he said as he took the last slice of pizza. He dropped the second empty box to the floor, where Henry had been patiently waiting. Tail wagging, the little dog flipped the lid up and positioned himself in the middle of the box, where he went to work snuffling up the remaining cheese and crust crumbs.

I took the notepad and pen, turned to a clean page and wrote at the top: *Lander Jones.* Just beneath I started a section for *Suspects.*

"Okay, your mom first. What's her name?"

"Cecilia Jones. Her friends call her CiCi." I wrote it down and made a note for motive. I felt ridiculous even writing it.

"Okay, who else?" I edged my pizza closer and took a bite.

"There's your ex-wife," William said. "I can envision her trying to kill you."

"I know you never really liked her, but I don't think so," Lander said slowly. "In fact, if anything, I think she might want to get back together."

"She's remarried," said William. "Don't you usually reconcile *before* getting remarried?" He motioned for me to write it down.

"What's her name?" I asked, adding *ex-wife* to the page.

"Annalise," said Lander. "Yeah, I don't think it's her. I get the feeling she's thinking about leaving him."

"Okay, what about her husband, then?" asked Evan. "Maybe he wants to kill you for trying to get her back."

"I'm not trying to get her back."

I wrote down *ex-wife's husband*. "What's his name?"

"Dick DeLuca."

"Dick DeLuca!" said Evan. "The lawyer? I love that guy's commercials. 'Have you been injured in a wreck? Does someone owe you money? Call Dick DeLuca 1-800-THE-DICK. I'll get you what you *De-Serve!*'" He had the inflection down perfect. I rolled my eyes. Worst commercial ever.

"Yeah, that's him," said Lander. "I don't know why she ever married him."

"He does have a lot of money," said William.

"So do you," said Evan to Lander. "I mean, his commercials are great, but he's got that slicked-back hair and he seems kind of sleazy. I can't believe she would take him over you."

"Well, I didn't have a lot of money when we were married," said Lander.

"What about him?" I asked. "Any reason he might be after you?" My pen was poised over the paper. "It seems a stretch, but maybe Evan's right. What if he thinks your ex is going to leave him and try to get back with you? Maybe he thinks it would hurt his reputation. You know, big manly lawyer and all. Male ego?" It sounded highly improbable.

I wrote Dick DeLuca down anyway. It wasn't like we had a very big list.

"It seems unlikely," said Lander.

"Do you have any stalker fans?" I asked. "Outside of the fan club lady?"

"Oh! Oh, yeah! Write her down," said Evan. "You saw how crazy she was." He tapped his finger on the paper. I thought of Evan trying to tip her out of her chair.

"You said her name was Nell?" I asked. *Fan Club President, Nell*, I wrote.

"Yes. I don't know her last name."

"Maybe you could ask your mom since they work together," said Evan.

"Any other fans that you've noticed?"

"A demented fan would be the hardest to track," William said, removing his glasses and rubbing the bridge of his nose. "You have millions of readers. Unless someone reached out directly and identified themselves, I'm afraid we'd have an impossible task working out who it could be, or what their motivation is."

"Crazy people go after celebrities all the time," Evan said. "I still think it was that lady from last night. You saw her," he said, looking to me.

"Yeah," I said slowly. "But you were just as excited about sitting in the front row as she was." I looked at my list. "So, we've got your mother, your ex-wife, your ex-wife's husband, and a crazy fan, including but not limited to the fan club lady." There was no way we were going to figure this out.

The darkness grew around us as we hunched in our folding chairs, traffic noises breaking through the silence. I could hear someone's watch ticking and a plane hummed high above the house. My nerves were more frayed than I would have expected and the paper-covered windows contributed to a feeling of claustrophobia.

"What about that friend of yours?" William's question broke the silence, and Evan and I both jumped in our seats.

"Seth?" Lander looked up and stared at William. "I don't know. Why would you think of him?"

"I'm not sure. It's just the way you've talked about him for the past year. It seems as if he's making a lot of bad decisions."

Lander stared at William, half-focused. "I haven't actually talked to him in a while. Like in months, now that I think about it." He frowned. "Last time we talked, he said he was having trouble at work. I don't know what, I guess I wasn't really listening."

"How would killing you help your friend?" I asked.

Evan picked up the pizza boxes from the floor and carted them into the kitchen. "Anybody want another beer?" he called. No one did.

"It wouldn't," Lander said. "I mean, maybe it's hard for him seeing my books do so well when he's not doing that great." He sounded doubtful.

"You said something else once," said William, taking a tiny sip from his bottle. "Something about him wanting to use your characters in a game?"

"Oh, right," said Lander. "I forgot about that. Yeah, he's bothered me for a long time about letting him use my characters in a video game he wants to develop."

"That would be awesome!" said Evan, sitting back down. "Are you going to do it? I would totally buy that."

Lander tapped a finger on his bottle. "No," he said. "I won't let him use my characters or anything else from my books."

"Why not?" Evan's voice wobbled between reverence for anything Lander said and disbelief that Lander might thwart something so awesome.

"I'm not comfortable giving up any creative rights. I feel I owe it to my readers."

Evan stared at him as if trying to process how he felt about this.

"Good for you," William said. "This is your work, not anybody else's."

"But a video game," Evan said weakly.

"I still don't see how having you dead would help him," I said. "Unless it doesn't, but he's just angry you said no."

"Even if I was dead, the copyright goes like seventy more years."

I added *Seth* to my list. Silence descended again. Henry had gone to sleep under the table, his head resting on William's shoe.

"So, what do we do now?" I finally asked, shifting against the hard folding chair. I was losing interest. Hard to have an opinion when you don't know any of the people involved.

"If a stranger is behind this, we're going to have trouble," William said. "But perhaps we could start trying to rule people out. We have to assume that whoever forced you off the road last night will have damage to their car. So maybe we start there?"

"Great idea," Lander said. "We'll start with checking the cars. That should be easy."

We spent a few minutes debating the best way to do this. William's car was in the shop and Lander's car was still at the bookstore, or maybe towed by now. He also sounded reluctant to leave Evan's house and risk being found. Which left Evan and me.

"Well, no one knows us," I said. "And I'm driving a rental, so I'm even more anonymous. Maybe tomorrow we can do some drive-bys and take a look."

"I haven't forgotten," said Lander. "I will get you a new car."

I started to object, feeling odd about having a stranger buy me a car. Then again, he was the reason I'd totaled mine.

"I'm hoping my car will be ready tomorrow," William said. "Maybe we can split up the list."

The energy in the room picked up.

"We could start tonight," said Evan. I'd never seen him this buoyant. I myself wasn't feeling quite so great about the whole thing. I could still smell the bayou water in my sinuses, and the fear that had imprinted on my psyche when my car had started its decline into the water had made this less exciting and more traumatic. But at least Evan was having fun.

"You know, I actually have a lot of work I need to do," Lander said. "I'm way behind. My editor has been on me to get this draft in." He rubbed his hands over his face.

"There's another one coming?" Evan practically vibrated with excitement. "Like, you're almost done with the next one?"

"I'm supposed to be, but I'm really behind. I hate to ask this" —he looked over at William—"but I need my laptop. Is there any way you could go to my house and get it for me? Along with my notes?" William hesitated, and I remembered he'd arrived in a cab. "Oh, right, your car is still in the shop."

Evan looked at me. "Jessie could go. She could take William home and then bring your laptop back?" I noticed that he hadn't volunteered to run this errand.

Lander spun his fork in perfect circles over his knuckles, obviously trying to think of another option. "I've already imposed on you way too much." My eyebrow shot up in spite of my best efforts. I'd nearly been killed doing him a favor.

William pushed his paper plate towards the center of the table. "I can just call a cab and go. The driver can wait for me, then I'll come right back."

"No, don't be ridiculous. I'll be happy to go with you," I said. Okay, happy might be an overstatement, but I did like William's gentle energy.

"Wonderful. I would be delighted with your company," he said. He turned to Lander. "Laptop and notes? I assume your notes are on your desk? Anything else?"

He agreed to gather some additional clothes before gently

rousing Henry off his shoe. I pushed the notebook to the center of the table, and we rose to leave.

"I can't tell you how much I appreciate this," Lander said. "I'll make it up to you."

It sounded so simple.

CHAPTER FIVE

I t was almost fully dark when William and I slipped out of Evan's door and headed for my lemon-drop rental. I scanned the street, looking for anyone suspicious, but the twilight made it hard to discern a bush from a lurker. I fumbled trying to find the lock switch as William buckled his seat belt.

"You've known Lander for a long time?" I asked as I made my way north on Montrose.

"Yes, he's been my neighbor for, oh, must be seven or eight years now." Traffic was heavy, typical of a Friday night in Houston. "He got me through a rough time." His voice wobbled. "After my wife passed away."

"Oh, I'm sorry," I said.

"It's been years and I still miss her every day. When Lander moved in, I was..." He paused. "I was not doing well." I checked my mirrors again. "He was newly married and I was newly widowed, but somehow we became friends. I don't even remember how it happened. He just kept coming around and slowly I made my way out of the wretched fog that had engulfed me." He was silent for a minute. "It was a good day when he moved in."

"So, you know his ex-wife, then?"

"Annalise. I do to an extent. She wasn't as interested in visiting as Lander was. He had just had his first book accepted by a publishing house, but it wasn't even in print yet. He wasn't confident in his writing, and he would come over and ask my opinion on things—ideas and such. I'm a retired English teacher, so somehow it just seemed natural."

I looked in my rearview mirror again, trying to decide if the car behind me was following us or just going the same way. I moved into the right lane and it shot past me.

"Annalise seemed frustrated from the time they moved in. She didn't like the house. She didn't want to work. I guess she thought being married to a writer was going to be more glamorous than it actually was." He gave a small laugh. "I think she gave up too soon, because it wasn't until after they split up that his books took flight. It doesn't surprise me that she's been calling him."

"Do you think she really wants to get back together with him?"

"I don't like speaking ill of folks, but Annalise likes money. There's no question of that. And, of course, I have no way of knowing, but I suspect Lander is more financially desirable now than the chiseler she's married to."

We were cruising into the Heights, and I slowed down to look for a cross street. "Where do I turn?" I asked.

William gave me directions while I made additional turns, going several blocks out of the way and watching all the cars around us to see if anyone was following. I moved slowly down the dark streets, finally pulling over a couple streets away behind another car, cutting the lights but leaving the engine idling.

"I don't see anyone following us," I said, still feeling uneasy. William was quiet, looking out into the still night.

"This has been really difficult," he finally said quietly. "Lander is like a son to me. I couldn't bear for anything to happen to him."

I looked at his profile in the dark. He seemed smaller somehow, and I felt a rush of concern.

"We'll figure this out," I said. "I do wish he would go to the police, though. Based on what happened last night plus everything you guys told us tonight, this person's not giving up. They're just getting more serious about it."

"I'm so thankful you kids weren't hurt or killed last night," he said softly. "And it's selfish, I know, but I'm glad you and your friend are helping out. I've been so worried, but he won't let me talk to anyone about it."

"Well, if we can make sure no one follows us, he should be pretty safe at Evan's. I mean, what better place to hide than with a total stranger?"

The front door opened on a house one door up, and a middle-aged woman stepped out, holding a small dog. She set him down on the grass, then looked around, stiffening as she spotted our idling car.

"I guess we ought to get moving," I said, shifting into drive and flipping on the lights. "Before one of the neighbors calls the cops on us." We made a few more circuitous turns before he directed me to our destination.

"This is my house right here, and Lander's is just there."

It was a quiet little street, tucked away almost like an alley. William and Lander's houses sat side by side, relatively isolated from their neighbors. An overgrown lot next to Lander's looked like a wildlife sanctuary for possums and raccoons. Across the street was a chain-link fence surrounding a windowless cinder block building. It appeared to be a warehouse or some other commercial building.

"Wow, it's so private back here. Like your own little corner of the world. I had no idea this street even existed." I pulled onto a narrow strip of straggly grass by the chain-link fence and shifted into park. "Is it okay to leave my car here?"

"Sure, this is fine. Come on in. I have Lander's key, but it's inside."

We made our way across a neat little stretch of yard to the front porch. In the dim light I could see a handful of bats swooping and circling near the treetops.

"It's like you're in the country here even though you're right in the middle of the city."

"So far, it's an undiscovered little place," he said as he fit his key into the lock. "But the way the development is going, it won't be long before we're surrounded by high-rises."

He opened the door, flipped a switch and ushered me into a tidy little living room that probably looked exactly as it had when his wife was alive. Two recliners sat side by side, separated only by a small coffee table. Doilies graced the arms, the ones on the bigger chair showing more wear, but neatly aligned. A small stack of books rested on the table within easy reach, a television remote nearly hidden by the pile. Lamps dotted the room, casting a warm glow over everything.

"I love this," I said. "This is maybe the coziest room I've ever seen." William's face lit with a genuine pleasure.

"Thank you," he said. "I have a biased fondness for this house. I may just be an old fuddy-duddy, but I find it peaceful." William moved into the kitchen and pulled a key ring from a small hook near the back door.

"You ready?" he asked. "I don't want to keep you any longer than needed from your evening."

"You're not keeping me from anything," I said. "If it weren't for the fact we met under these circumstances, I would say this was one of the better evenings I've had in a long time."

He smiled and ushered me out the back door and down

shallow steps. We crunched across a crushed gravel driveway, past a detached garage towards Lander's house. A long porch ran the length of the side and continued on around the front. William led the way through the dark to a side door.

"He always goes in this way," William said. "Through the kitchen. This won't take long." My new cell phone bleated from my purse, the ringtone loud and unfamiliar. I fished around trying to find it, finally grasping the beeping, vibrating thing before it went to voice mail.

"Hello?"

"Jessie? I've been calling you all day. Why haven't you picked up?"

"Hi, Mom," I said, stepping back down the porch steps into the yard. I held up one finger towards William, indicating I'd be right there. He nodded and let himself into the house. "Sorry, I was really busy today, and I had an issue with my phone. It died and I had to get a new one. Is everything okay?"

"Yes, everything's fine," she said. "I just wanted to let you know that your father and I are going to Dallas tomorrow morning. Your father landed a new client and they've invited the partners and their wives up for dinner."

"That sounds nice," I said as the lights flicked on in Lander's house.

"The reason I called," my mother continued, "is, well, I think your grandmother has been acting strange, and if you have time tomorrow, I think it would be good if you'd check in on her."

Now she had my attention. "What do you mean acting strange?" My grandmother, Frances, had been one of my best friends growing up and we were still close.

"Nothing I can really put a finger on," she said. "She just seems a bit, oh, I don't know, secretive or something."

"That's weird," I said. "Frances is usually so direct."

"I know. I'm sure it's nothing, but with your father and me

going out of town, I just think maybe it would be nice if you two could spend some time together this weekend. I know you've been busy with your..." She trailed off. "Your dog things."

My mother had still not gotten over me quitting my oil and gas job to make dog biscuits and walk other people's hounds.

"I'll come over tomorrow and check on her," I said. I glanced at Lander's door, but William hadn't come out yet. "Look, Mom, I've got to go. You guys have a nice trip." I disconnected and slipped the phone into my purse.

I would have thought William would be back out already. He must be picking out clothes. Moving towards the door, I tried to hush the whispers of unease flitting through my head as I tiptoed up the steps. William hadn't shut the door all the way, and I peered into the kitchen. Even in the dim light, I could see that it was designed for a real cook, not the takeout junkie I imagined Lander to be. I pushed the door open a few more inches, hoping to see William trotting around the corner with Lander's belongings.

"William?" My voice was barely a whisper. I held my breath, listening, my ears nearly ringing with exertion. "William?" Why couldn't I say it louder? Why was I still standing out here? Just go in and check on him. I took a step into the kitchen when a rustle from somewhere in the house made me freeze.

"William?" I called louder this time, loud enough to be heard. I felt a sudden shift in energy, a sense that someone was listening for me too. I stood rooted, fear nailing my feet to the boards beneath them. If he was okay, why didn't he answer me? A slight scrape sounded closer and I turned and fled into the yard.

Rational thought evaporated and I raced heedless across the backyard, towards the empty lot. In the far reaches of my mind, I thought of William, and a peep of concern tried to slow me. But the fear was stronger. I'd nearly died last night, and the conviction that I would die now if I didn't flee was primal, driving me into the darkness.

My breathing was loud as I crashed into the underbrush, branches brushing my face and pulling at my hair. Maybe I could get through to the next street. It wasn't until my foot caught on something, and I crashed to my knees, that I stopped. Curling into a defensive position on the ground, I turned to look behind me. Nothing. I curled tighter and pressed in between two bushes. Was someone there?

I tried to stifle the ragged gasping that broke from my throat. I hadn't gone as far as I'd thought, and I pushed farther back, soft branches giving way and closing around me. It reminded me fleetingly of an evergreen tree I used to play under as a child, where my grandmother and I would have tea parties.

The thought calmed me, if just for a second, and I gazed out into the dark yard. From my position, I could no longer see the door to the kitchen; instead, I was looking at the opposite side of the house. A light in a window towards the front of the house cast a weak yellow beam onto the bushes below, but I was too far away to see in.

What if William had had a heart attack? What if he had fallen or suffered a stroke and I was just sitting here letting him die? I edged my hand into my purse, trying to find my phone, when a flash of movement caught my attention. A shadow raced across the front yard towards a large stand of sago palms and disappeared. I stared unblinking where I'd seen the figure, trying to distinguish what was palm tree and what was person, but the darkness was too deep. Had I really seen something? I clutched my phone, wanting to call for help, but knowing that turning it on would light up my position like a spotlight.

I don't know how long I sat motionless, muscles tensed to flee but getting stiff in the evening air. I listened for noises. I watched for movement, but it was still and silent, the only sound distant road traffic.

If I had seen someone run across the yard, they could have made their way to the street and be gone by now. Or they could be circling around, preparing to come at me from the side. That thought revved up the fear that had just started to settle. I had to do something.

Slowly moving my limbs, I untangled myself and moved inch by inch out from under the bushes. Pins and needles shot through my right foot, and it was all I could do not to hop up and stomp my way to the middle of the yard to work them out. Instead, I moved slowly, trying to silently ignore the discomfort. Maybe William had already picked up the computer and was sitting in his kitchen, wondering where I'd run off to.

But I knew better. He'd be worried enough about me to come looking for me. Unlike what I was doing for him. I moved faster, leaves rustling underfoot. I paused, hoping that no one was nearby listening.

When I drew even with the window, I stood on my toes and tried to peer in from my place behind a tree. About fifteen feet of yard separated me from the house, and I couldn't make out anything in the room besides a slice of wall and ceiling. A row of low bushes ran along the side of the house, too sparse to offer me a hiding place.

I sank behind a new bush, tears of frustration and anger at my own cowardice threatening to come. I pulled my phone out, dimmed the screen and dialed Evan.

"Jess?" he said, picking up on the first ring. "What's taking you so long? Lander needs to get to work."

I choked on a sob. "Evan? I don't know what happened to William." My voice barely registered as a whisper.

"What?" he said. "I can't hear you." Because he couldn't hear me, he was yelling. I held a hand over the phone.

"He went in to get the laptop and I think someone was in there. He hasn't come out."

"Well, go see what he's doing!" A tear trickled down my cheek. "Hold on." I could hear him talking to Lander.

"Jessie?" Lander had taken the phone.

I sniffed as quietly as I could. "Lander? I think something happened to William. I'm afraid to go in."

"Don't go in. We'll be right there."

Several times during the wait, I tried to work up the courage to look in the window. Or go over to William's house. Or do what I really needed to do—go into the house and help William if something had indeed happened to him. And in my heart, I knew something had. I debated calling 911 but waffled, immobilized by uncertainty.

It was nine minutes before Evan's car skidded to a stop at the curb. The headlights went off, but it idled in the street, windows up, doors closed. I wasn't sure if I should make a run towards the car, but I had a fear they wouldn't recognize me and would hit me with a taser or whatever other kind of weapon they might have found around Evan's house. My phone bleated in my hand.

Where r u? the text read.

I broke from my cover and raced across the yard. Evan and Lander stepped out just as I reached them, both holding their doors as if ready to jump back in at the slightest whiff of danger. I felt like the victim of a disaster, ready for a metallic blanket, a cup of hot coffee and a warm hug. Instead they both stared at me, like little kids looking for an authority figure.

Lander moved first, shutting his door quietly and coming around to the driver's side, where we huddled in a small knot.

"I'm glad you're okay," he whispered. "But why did he go in alone?"

"My mom called just before we went in. I stayed outside to take the call."

"You couldn't tell her you'd call her back?" Evan asked. I stared from one to the other as heat flooded my cheeks and my stomach rolled over.

"I'm sorry," I said as tears rose. "I'm sorry."

Lander pressed his lips together. "No, it's not your fault. It's mine. I should have never sent you two over here. I'm going in to see..." He trailed off and squared his shoulders. "To see if everything's okay with William."

"You know it's not okay," Evan said. "He's not answering his phone. I'm coming with you."

The two of them made their way up the drive towards the kitchen door. No way I was staying out here by myself. I trotted after them, wiping away my tears. At the back door, Lander looked through the glass before using a knuckle to push the door open.

He inched into the kitchen with Evan and me right behind him like an ill-timed conga line. My nerves crackled with hysteria, and I had to fight the impulse to grab Evan's shirt as if we were going through a Halloween fun house. Instead I clutched my purse strap, needing something to hold on to. This is the part in movies where I usually have a pillow in front of my face, ready to hide when the scary thing jumped out.

We passed through the kitchen, pausing to listen. I could hear a slight whistling from Evan's breathing and the soft tick tick tick of a clock somewhere in the house. I didn't hear anyone, besides us, moving. Lander glanced over his shoulder at us, then motioned us forward with a jerk of his head. A narrow, dark hallway led towards the back of the house, but we turned into the living room and shuffled quietly across, our destination, apparently, a well-lit room just across the wide foyer.

I picked up a candlestick off a table as we went by, disappointed that it wasn't as heavy as it looked. Evan saw what I was doing and grabbed its twin.

Lander pointed a finger to draw our attention towards the front door, which stood slightly ajar. I guess I *had* seen someone run out that way. He nudged it slowly closed before glancing over his shoulder at us. Across the foyer, we bunched against the wall like reluctant HPD rookies going in for our first drug raid. Lander's gaze swept our candlesticks and I wasn't sure if it made him feel better or more frightened that we were his backup.

He turned to the doorway and slowly leaned around the corner. I hunched behind Evan, squinting as if that would help protect me from a sudden gunshot.

"William!" Lander raced into the room and we pushed in with him. William lay sprawled on a thick rug, his glasses askew on his face and blood pooling beneath his head. "Call 911," he shouted at us. I dropped my candlestick and dug furiously in my purse, but Evan had picked up a phone on the desk and was already hitting buttons.

"William. William." Lander leaned over William's prone figure and felt his neck. "He's alive! We need an ambulance now!"

Evan babbled into the phone as I raced towards the kitchen to get ice and towels and whatever else I could find. I didn't know what I was looking for, but I couldn't stand to be in the room. William might be alive, but I wasn't sure how long he was going to stay that way. What if he died because I'd left him there unaided for so long?

I pulled a bag of frozen corn from the freezer, then raced towards the back of the house, only briefly wondering if someone might still be here. From the closest bedroom, I grabbed a quilt off the bed, then found some towels in a bathroom and ran back, shoving the whole pile at Evan. He was still on the phone and let it all fall to the floor.

"I don't know," he said. "I don't know. Could you please just hurry?" His voice cracked and he jammed the phone against his ear, staring unblinking at Lander and William.

Lander knelt beside his friend, holding William's limp hand against his chest while smoothing the hair off William's forehead with the other, like a mother comforting her feverish child. William's hand looked small and pale in Lander's, skin crinkled and nearly translucent, the bones looking as fragile as a bird's. Lander murmured soothing sounds and I looked away from the intimate scene.

Sirens sounded in the distance and I pulled open the front door and galloped into the night, ready to flag down the emergency personnel. An ambulance and a police car arrived within seconds of each other and I motioned them in like a coach urging a player home at the bottom of the ninth.

"Hurry. Hurry. Hurry," I intoned, the words like a mantra. "Hurry. Hurry. Please." Two paramedics pushed past me with a gurney, emergency equipment piled along for the ride. They bumped up the front step and raced into the study. I stayed put, aware that there wasn't a lot of room left in the small room. Or that was what I told myself. He needed room to breathe. They didn't need someone else sucking up all the oxygen.

A police officer made his way more slowly up the walk, doing a visual sweep of the yard before approaching me.

"What happened here tonight?" he asked, trying to sound kind. I knew someone was going to ask me that and I had no idea what to say. But his eyes were cold and I found myself withdrawing into myself.

"I'm not sure exactly." I hugged my arms against my chest. He poked his head through the front door assessing the scene. A breeze washed across my face. It was a nice night, warm but not oppressive.

With a burst of squawking radios and rattling gurney, the EMTs ran their cargo towards the ambulance with Lander racing along the side. Evan followed in the rear, breaking from the parade and moving towards his own car. And suddenly they were gone, leaving me alone with the officer.

He wandered inside and I followed after him, feeling like an awkward hostess. He knelt beside the blood on the floor, looking appraisingly at the stain. I don't know what it told him, but it told me that William had lost a lot of blood.

Lander's study looked like it belonged to a famous thriller author. I wondered if he'd ever been featured in *Architectural Digest*. The desk itself was an ergonomic wonder of sleek black material with wide telescoping legs, allowing it to go up and down. His chair was equally ergo, a black mesh affair with levers sticking out all over. But it was the room around the desk that drew the attention. Along the walls, framed movie posters show-cased dark-cloaked spies, guns and the occasional grim Russian city. Shelves behind the desk featured action figures that jock-eyed for room amongst the books. Against the wall, a small pirate chest rested, and I wondered what it held.

The officer walked behind the desk and peered at the action figure collection, stopping here and there to lift one up and inspect it closer. I sure wished Lander had stuck around. I wasn't comfortable being alone with these obviously valuable things.

"Nice collection," I said. He'd seemed to have forgotten that I was there because he jumped a little, then set down the Spider-Man figure he'd been looking at.

"You live here?" he asked, stepping out from behind the desk.

"No, I was just here to pick up some stuff for the owner." He brought out a small notebook and stood expectantly. We stared at each other.

"And the owner is?"

"Lander Jones," I said, running a finger up and down the strap of my purse. We stared some more. The name clearly meant nothing to him and I wondered if I could wrap this up quickly by deferring to Lander to make a statement. "Yeah, he went with the ambulance. I think he could tell you what happened."

"Why don't we start with you telling me what happened?"

"Well, I'm not sure. I was outside taking a call when William fell. So I don't actually know what happened." I glanced around, looking to see if there was a bloody weapon indicating that he'd been conked on the head, or if it was conceivable that he'd fallen and hit his head on the desk. It seemed the less I could say, the better.

I could tell he was uncertain whether this was a bad accident or whether he should call in the crime scene guys. Being Friday night in Houston, they were probably pretty busy. His radio finally decided it for him. A dispatcher, squawking through static, called with a code I didn't understand. He took a moment to take down my name and phone number, then left me as he race-walked to his squad car. In seconds, he peeled away from the curb, kicking up a spray of gravel and turning on his sirens.

I closed the front door behind him and snapped the lock shut, unease resurfacing. Lander's laptop still lay on the desk. I didn't know if he would want me to pick it up for him, or if he would just be coming back here after...after he left the hospital. My stomach rolled over again. I'd text Evan in a few minutes and find out which hospital they'd gone to.

Meanwhile, I picked up the laptop and slipped it into a worn canvas computer bag that lay slumped next to the desk. Then I shoved in a Moleskine notebook and a manila folder overflowing with papers. I wasn't sure what notes he'd wanted, but these were the ones he was going to get. I slung the bag over my shoulder, picked up the quilt, towels and frozen corn and took a moment to throw them back in their respective places.

It was as I went into the bedroom to replace the quilt that I noticed the broken window at the far side of the room. The glass had been smashed, apparently to unhook the lock, then raised. Jagged shards littered the floor, their edges glinting in the overhead light. Humid air drifted in through the gap—nothing solid to wall out the menacing darkness beyond.

I had considered gathering some clothes, as William had been planning to do, but the urge to flee took over instead. Hustling to the kitchen, I looked around for William's keys. I didn't see them, so I slipped the lock shut and pulled the door closed behind me. Not that it mattered what with the open bedroom window.

The lights from William's house glowed cheerfully in the dark, and I dashed across the yard towards his back door. I'd already failed him once tonight; the least I could do was lock up his house. The door was cracked open, and I reached in, turned the lock and pulled it closed behind me. Locking up was one thing—I wasn't going to go through looking for intruders. I ran around front and ensured that door was locked too before bolting for my car.

I slid in, tossing my bags onto the passenger seat and making sure the door locks were down. I'd thought this street was so cool, being off the beaten track as it was. Now it felt creepy and isolated. I turned around in William's driveway and headed for bright lights and crowds.

I found a convenience store a few blocks away and pulled into the parking lot. Cars zipped in and out and a small group of teens gathered at the end of the sidewalk, sharing a pack of smokes and looking tough. I pulled my phone out, hesitating before shooting a text off to Evan to find out where they were and get an update on William. *Oh, William—please, don't be dead. Please, don't be dead.*

Ding. My heart flopped over. William wasn't dead. I blew out a breath I hadn't realized I'd been holding. They were at a hospital about two miles away. I wanted to go home and forget this whole evening. Instead, I told Evan I'd be there in a few minutes.

I drove past restaurants that I'd been to with Frances, wishing that was where I'd been tonight. It took only minutes to arrive at the hospital. I parked on the street outside and sat in my car, composing myself.

I hate hospitals. Even when it's for happy occasions like new babies, I still hate hospitals. Just the smell that assails you as you walk through the door causes me to hyperventilate. Make me walk past rooms where people are moaning, and I'm likely to sprint out the nearest fire exit or pass out on the floor. It's a real crapshoot which way it might go.

Fortunately, Evan was on a bench outside. He was staring at his phone, the bright screen lighting up his face in the dark, as he scrolled through baseball scores. I sat down next to him.

"Hey," I said. "How's he doing?"

"He's upset. I mean, that could have been him tonight."

It took me a second to realize he was talking about Lander.

"Oh, Lander. Yeah. I meant how's William doing?"

He flicked off his phone, plunging us into darkness. "It doesn't sound good," he said softly. He looked off to the side and I found myself looking too. "Maybe we should get inside," he said. "At least there's more people in there."

I took a moment to decide whether I wanted to risk my life out here with a crazy killer on the loose, or go into the hospital. Evan walked in through the automatic doors, cold air billowing out in a gust. I jogged along after him, Lander's bag banging on my hip. I followed him down a long corridor to a small waiting room lined with hard plastic chairs. He slumped into an orange seat and I sat down on the attached yellow.

"Lander said he'd come out after he talked to the doctor. He wants to talk to you but he can't have his phone on in there."

I shifted the bags on my lap, cradling them against my chest like an anxious subway rider. A television angled in the corner, tuned to a news show, volume muted. A big-haired anchor was talking while video footage of a rally, or a protest, or maybe a rabid mob played out beside her. I tried to read the captions, but the signal wasn't good and static flicked across the screen.

In the far corner, a family gathered, looking as much at home as if they were in their living room. Four kids sat on the floor playing cards, while a fifth lay curled with his blanket on a chair, placidly watching his siblings and sucking his thumb. Mom sat next to the youngest, absently rubbing his back, while a set of grandparents sat on the other side, staring quietly into space.

Three chairs down, an older man sat leaning forward, his hands pressed together between his knees as if this pressure alone was keeping him from flying to pieces.

We waited for what seemed like forever. Ten feet away, a set of automatic doors, wide enough to pass rolling beds through at full speed, opened to a long white hall, presumably leading to the areas where they did things to people. I tried not to think about it, but every time the doors crashed open, I nearly leapt from my chair. Finally, Lander shambled around the corner and plopped down in a chair across from Evan. He drooped like a flower that had been pulled from its pot.

"How is he?" I asked, my voice sticking in my throat.

"They've got him stabilized, but they want to transfer him to the medical center. He's got a lot of intracranial pressure and they need to get in and relieve it." He leaned forward and put his head in his hands, kneading his skull like he wanted to crush it. "They feel that the neurology department down there would be better equipped to handle this."

Evan and I glanced at each other, unsure what to say. "He's going to be okay, though, right?" I finally asked.

Lander looked up at me, his eyes red with misery. "The next

twenty-four hours will tell us a lot." He bowed his head. "I should have never let you guys go over there. First last night and now this." His fingers gripped his hair.

"Lander, this wasn't your fault," I said softly. "It was mine. I should have never let him go in by himself. If I'd gone in with him, this would have never happened." I looked away. "And I should have gone in right away to check on him when I realized something was wrong."

"It's not your fault," he said. "It's not your fault at all."

I ran my finger across his computer bag, wishing I felt that was true.

"Look, I know this is a stupid question," Evan said softly, "but someone did this to him, right? He didn't just fall and hit his head?" I flashed to the shadow I'd seen run from the house.

Lander looked up. "Yeah, I considered that when I saw him lying there." His voice was low, barely a whisper, and Evan and I leaned across the space. "I guess he could have hit his head on my desk, but from what I could tell he was injured on the back of his head." His hand reached up, touching his own head in an approximation. "Maybe he was pushed, or maybe someone hit him with something. But the front door was open. There's no way this was an accident."

"I didn't see anything laying there, like a weapon," Evan said.

I thought back to picking up the quilt and corn. I hadn't noticed anything either. At least not on the floor.

Lander put his head back down and started pressing on his skull again.

"Well, whoever was in there got in by breaking a window in the bedroom," I said.

"My bedroom?" he asked, looking up.

"I guess? Gray bedspread?"

"Yeah, that's my room."

"So this could have been a regular break-in?" Evan asked. Even he sounded doubtful.

"Or someone was trying to make it look that way," said Lander. "At some point I'll have to see if they took anything."

I shifted his bag off my lap and held it out. "I got your laptop, a notebook and a folder full of papers that was sitting there. I wasn't sure what else to grab."

Lander grasped the strap like it was a lifeline. He pulled the bag towards his chest and held it like a traumatized toddler would hold a teddy bear given at the scene of a tragedy.

"Thank you," he said.

"I didn't get any clothes," I added.

"That's fine. I don't care."

"So, Jess. The window is still open?" Evan asked.

"Yeah, I didn't really see that there was anything I could do to fix it."

"Look, I've got all kinds of stuff in my garage," he said. "I'm pretty sure I've got some plywood. Why don't we go board it up? At least then they can't get in again."

It crossed my mind that if William... if William wasn't okay, Lander's house would be a crime scene, but I didn't want to think that, much less say it. And I really didn't want to go back to Lander's house either. Then again, it would get me out of this hospital and make me feel like I was doing something constructive.

CHAPTER SIX

L ander had been adamant about us not going, but in the end he handed over his keys. They were getting ready to transport William, and the concern for him overrode everything else.

I followed Evan back to his house, glad to be leaving the hospital. It felt like weeks since I'd left here, and the familiarity of Evan's house was comforting. Henry's reassuringly solid little body was even more comforting, and I spent several minutes on the floor with him, trying to hold his wriggling body still while Evan ran around looking for the tools he thought we'd need. Henry finally settled into my arms and I centered myself by stroking his fur and breathing in his warm doggie scent. I slowed my breaths, timing them as I ran my fingers down Henry's soft side. *One, two, three, four. One, two, three, four.* By the time Evan was ready to head out to his detached garage, I was feeling more level.

I hadn't been in his garage since he'd first bought the house, and it looked like he hadn't done much to clear out the junk left by the previous owner. But in the end, he was right—he had several pieces of stained-looking plywood resting against one of the walls. I wasn't really sure which size we'd need, so we loaded three of various dimensions into Evan's Jeep and headed out. All the good work I'd done getting myself calmer evaporated as we approached the darkened house again. Evan pulled into the drive and right up near the kitchen door. It took an effort of will to get out of the car.

"Let's go check this window," Evan said, sounding remarkably unfazed. Somehow his lack of unease made me feel a little bolder and I followed him, although not before picking up the hammer he'd left on the back seat.

"Wow, this is nice," Evan said as he walked into the kitchen and flicked on a light. "Look at how nice this kitchen is. Look at those appliances." I'm sure he was comparing them to the seventies-era appliances he had.

"Yeah, but he's sold like ten million books, right? It should be nice."

He gave a little sigh and ran his finger over a sharp-edged quartz countertop. The house was quiet, but I found myself listening, straining to hear anything other than the sound of our own breathing.

Evan wandered slowly around the house, looking as if he was on a museum tour. When we got to the study, we both stood in silence, the blood on the rug a grim reminder of why we were here.

"Do you think he'll be okay?" I asked.

"I hope so," Evan said. "I just don't understand why anyone would want to do this." He looked around, seeming to notice the action figures for the first time. "Wow, look at all this stuff." He picked up a small green-caped figure reverently, poking a careful finger against its chest. "I'll bet these are worth a fortune. Maybe you guys did interrupt a burglary."

I moved over towards the little pirate chest as he put one figure down and picked up another. The chest was fairly simple, about two and a half feet wide with a gently rounded top. The wood was weathered and dark and if it weren't for the faded green carved parrot on the front, I might have wondered if it was real.

"Look at this," I said. Evan glanced over, less interested in the chest than the Hulk action figure he was holding now. I raised the lid, halfway expecting to see a pile of gold doubloons. Instead there was only a folded fleece blanket. "Well, that's disappointing," I said, closing the lid again. "Hey, do you want to go take care of the window? I need to get home."

He set the Hulk back in its place and we backed out of the room, both careful to avoid the blood. I wondered if we should clean it up, then thought maybe we shouldn't, in case—well, in case the police needed to do a more thorough investigation. I took a deep breath. William was going to be okay. He was.

The warmth and humidity had crept through the back of the house, infusing the rooms with a feral scent. Evan poked his head through doors, doing a cursory search before crunching across the glass in Lander's bedroom. Walking over to the window, he held up his hands to get an idea of size.

"Okay, I think that one piece of wood we brought should cover this pretty well," he said. I was going to clean up the glass while he went to his car, but as I saw him turn down the hall, I followed after him instead.

"I'll, uh, just come with you." He started to say something, then changed his mind and nodded.

I'd like to say it was an easy task, but in spite of living in a hurricane hotspot, neither one of us had ever boarded up a window before. And, I guess, generally people board them up from the outside, not the inside. After a couple of false starts, we finally just got the biggest board and I held it while Evan tried to hammer through it to the trim beneath. Some of the nails made it through, but they missed the trim and weren't long enough to hit the wall. Others, he hammered through where it was just window beyond. Finally, after much banging, he got enough nails through the board and into the trim to hold the plywood in place. I hated to think what it would look like when Lander took the board off, but at least the hole was closed for now.

When we finally finished boarding the window, Evan forayed into Lander's closet, pulling clothes from hangars and shoving them into a suitcase he found. He added a pair of sneakers before emptying out a couple of dresser drawers. He piled in about a month's worth of clothing before grabbing everything that he could find from the attached bathroom. I wondered just how long he thought he would have Lander living at his house.

I got home a little before one, exhaustion washing over me like a toxic fog. Addie ambled down the stairs to greet me, her excitement no more than half-speed. Steering her towards the back door, I took her outside for a final break. The air was clear and stars twinkled above, shining brighter than the city lights that normally diminished them. A slight breeze drifted across the patio, bringing the smell of cigar smoke.

"Hey, girl next door," said Larry from the other side of the fence. "Why you out so late? Aren't you usually in bed at eight?"

"Hey, Larry," I said, stifling a sigh. "I was out." I snapped my fingers at Addie, trying to get her attention. She needed to hurry up with her business, but she seemed fixated on a scent.

I could hear him take a puff of cigar. "Ooh, hot date? I gotta say, I've never been sure you like men. You're kind of, what's the word? Cold?"

"Addie, c'mon. Hurry up." She finally squatted and I opened the door.

"You're not leaving me, are you? Come over and have a drink with me. Get to know a real man."

I ushered Addie in and shut the door with a hard click.

As tired as I was, sleep was a long time coming, but I must have finally drifted off because when I awoke it was almost six. I had to think about what day it was before realizing it was Saturday and I didn't have to get up. Rearranging my pillow, I resolutely resettled myself. I wondered if William was okay. Had he made it through the night? I flopped to the other side. *Don't think about it. Don't think about it. Go back to sleep.*

Addie's rhythmic breathing was calming, but my brain had engaged and sleep had departed. I got up and stood under a hot shower, trying to work the kinks out of my sore muscles. The spray hit my scraped skin with a teeth-clenching sting, and muscles that had been sore yesterday felt even stiffer today. Last night's stress had tightened my neck like a vise, and it felt like the muscles were at least two inches too short as I turned my head from side to side. I worked my way through some yoga poses and deep breathing and finally resorted to a muscle-heating cream. I was moving and smelling like someone three times my age.

Firing up the coffee pot, I tried to plan my day. It was too early to check on William. I needed to do some biscuit baking. I needed to go see Frances. Mostly, I wanted to curl up on the couch and binge-watch something stupid. Instead, I forced myself to walk Addie before settling onto the couch with a giant cup of coffee. Addie hopped up beside me and we sat in peaceful silence. It's possible that I might have drifted off after I set my cup down, because the ring of my phone jolted me more than the caffeine had. I tried to suppress the feelings of dread surging in my chest before I had anything concrete to feel dreadful about. I fumbled with the phone, still unfamiliar with its layout, but recognized Evan's number. I finally managed to connect.

"How's William?" I asked.

I could hear his sigh through the phone. "He's hanging in

there. I guess they did something, some surgery or, I don't know, something to try to get rid of the pressure around his brain, but he's still unconscious. The doctors told Lander that might be a good thing. I think they said something about putting him in an induced coma or something."

"That doesn't sound very good," I said. We sat silent for a moment. "How's Lander doing?"

Evan's voice dropped lower. "He just got back about two hours ago. He looks pretty bad, but he said he wants to go over to his parents today and check their cars. Figure out if his mom actually had something to do with this or not. I think he just wants to feel like he's doing something."

"I can't imagine his mom hitting William over the head," I said.

"Yeah, well, we don't know her, do we?" Fair point. Evan said he was going to make breakfast and asked if I wanted to join them. It sounded good to me, and I said I'd be right over.

Lander cracked open the door when I got there. Evan wasn't kidding when he said that Lander looked pretty bad. His previously jaunty hair now drooped over his forehead, but not enough to cover his bloodshot eyes. Or the purple circles beneath. His mouth had a grim set that seemed foreign to him.

"Hey," I said for lack of anything meaningful to say. I bent down to rub Henry after I'd squeezed inside.

He glanced quickly out the door before closing it behind me. "Hey. Thanks for coming."

"I guess William is..." I hesitated. "Stable?"

"Yeah. He's at the medical center now. He's getting the best care in the world. It's just a matter of waiting, I guess."

"I hate to even ask this," I said, "but do you think whoever did this—well, do you think William's safe? I mean, what if whoever attacked him figures out where he is?" The thought of an unconscious William lying helpless in a hospital bed while someone slipped unseen into his room to finish him off nearly made me hyperventilate.

"I hired private security for him," Lander said. "He's in the ICU, so it's harder to station a guard than if he was in a private room, but I finally convinced the head nurse that he needed protection." He rubbed a hand across his eyes. "She was sweet. I guess she felt sorry for me."

"Does she know who you are?"

He looked embarrassed. "No, thankfully. I don't think anyone did. I think she thought I was his grandson or his nephew or something. She said she'll keep an eye on him too, and make sure that access is limited."

We shuffled into the kitchen, where Evan stood whipping a batch of eggs with a fork. Butter smoked in a pan on the ancient stove and the toaster popped with the ferocity of a spring-loaded missile launcher. Two waffles flew out of their slots and onto the counter. I felt Lander start beside me.

"Could you grab those and put in a couple more?" Evan asked me. "The plates are right there."

He certainly looked the most energetic of all of us. He poured the eggs into the pan and stirred them with a flourish. Within minutes, we were back at the card table with a reasonably decent breakfast in front of us. The extra coffee that Evan provided, along with the sugar from the syrup, boosted my energy, and even Lander started looking a little more alive.

"So, you're going to see your mom today?" I asked Lander as we carried our plates out to the kitchen.

He set his plate down with a thump. "I need to do something. I need to find out who's behind all this." His voice had an edge.

"Are you just going to drive by and look at your mom's car? Or what's the plan?" I asked.

He glanced at Evan, then at me. "Well, I need a ride over," he said.

"I'll take you!" Evan piped up. "I'll go!"

Lander semi-smiled. "I think I need to do more than drive by. If my mom's not behind this, we need to find out a little more about that lady that works with her." I thought about the fan club lady's face as she beat on my passenger-side window, her mouth open as she yelled, the rain plastering her hair to her skull. I was doubtful it was either of them, but I guess we'd see.

It didn't take much to convince me to ride along. The other things on my list could wait. Lander gave Evan directions and we made our way west, past the 610 loop and towards the Piney Point Village area.

"Wow, look at these houses," Evan said, looking side to side. "This is as nice as where your parents live, Jess."

The properties were indeed massive, a collection of new-build blending in with older midcentury ranches that sprawled across wide lots. Tall pines and expansive live oaks shaded the grounds. Yard crews were already getting started and the sound of leaf blowers roared through the air, a necessary annoyance if you wanted your yard to look like a park. We wound our way through curvy streets at Lander's direction, until he finally pointed to a newer-looking three-story Georgian with a yard so pristine I had to wonder if they kept someone on staff to run out and snatch up any leaf that dared fall. We pulled to the curb and stared out. The garage was off to the side, but even from here I could tell the doors were down.

"Well, let's get this over with," Evan said, shutting down the engine. This was the kind of neighborhood where the most extreme crime they saw probably involved stolen packages.

"So, what are we going to say again?" I asked, as if we'd come up with a plan more detailed than just showing up.

"I don't know," Lander said, poking a stiff finger against the doorbell. It felt weird that he was ringing the bell on his own parents' house, but I guess they didn't have the kind of relationship where he just popped into the kitchen periodically, looking for leftovers.

The bell chimed in the interior recesses and was immediately followed by a furious chorus of barks. The barking came closer and I could hear nails scrabbling on the floor just out of sight. Anyone afraid of dogs would probably be halfway down the path by now, but in spite of the enthusiasm of their guard duties, I could tell these guys were no more than knee-high.

It took about two minutes before the door swung open to reveal a woman in a dark pencil skirt and white blouse mostly covered by a black rubber apron. Similar black rubber gloves covered her arms almost to her elbows, and a pair of goggles were pushed up on her head. Two white Scotties fell all over each other as they darted forward one at a time to take a sniff before retreating to resume their barking.

"Faraday! Dalton! Sit!" she shouted to no avail. "Lander, this is a surprise." She looked at Evan and me curiously before extending an arm, inviting us in. "They won't hurt you," she yelled over the barking. I hoped the dogs would settle down because it was going to be tough to have any kind of conversation over this din. I kicked myself for not bringing biscuits with us; had I known they had dogs, I would have brought a whole bag.

"Hi, Mom," Lander said, leaning down to rub a finger on one of the dog's heads. "Sorry to just drop in like this."

"It's no problem," she said, still giving Evan and me the once-over.

"They're so cute," I said in my fussiest dog voice, kneeling down to see the dogs. "Hi, guys." The dogs backed up a little and reduced the full vocal onslaught to a series of muted woofs.

"These are my friends, Evan and Jessie," Lander said. "This is my mom, Cecilia Jones."

"It's nice to meet you," said Mrs. Jones. "My friends call me CiCi." The slight emphasis on *friends* made me wonder what we were supposed to call her.

Evan and I murmured our hellos before she caught sight of her black rubber gloves and gave a small laugh. "Oh goodness. Could you just give me a minute? I'll be right back."

Evan stared at her as she made her way down the hall. "What is she wearing?" he whispered, turning to Lander. "It looks like she could be dismembering bodies back there."

I gave a small shudder. It kind of did. "She has a home office," Lander said, "although I can't imagine they'd let her bring her experiments home."

"Yeah, imagine if the FBI task force found out about that," Evan hissed. "Your book would look pretty harmless then, wouldn't it?"

She returned, minus her rubberized accessories, using both hands to smooth her hair.

"I apologize," she said. "I wasn't expecting company. I was trying to clear a clogged drain that your father has promised he would fix for days." The outfit seemed a bit excessive for drain clearing. Then again, I'd read the warnings on those bottles. They did make it sound like you were likely to lose an eye, have your skin burned off or die of fumes just opening the container. She turned to Lander. "Come in, come in. To what do I owe this visit?"

She led us into a bright kitchen with French doors that led out to a startling blue pool. Opening the door, she let the two dogs outside, where they raced past the pool towards an expanse of vivid green lawn.

"Lander, you look..." She paused, choosing her words. "Tired. Is everything alright?"

We all stared at her, trying to discern the meaning behind her words. Was she concerned as a mother? Or was there a little surprise that he was alive at all?

"Everything's fine," he said, fidgeting with the strap on his messenger bag. I'd noticed he'd brought it, bulging with his laptop and whatever else he had tucked in there. Whether he was intending to get some work done or it was more of a comfort item, I wasn't sure, but I was amazed that it didn't still smell of lingering bayou. "I had a book signing the other night."

"I heard," his mother said. "My admin is certainly a big fan of yours."

"Yeah, she was there," he said haltingly. "She mentioned she worked for you."

"Can I get you all some tea?" she asked, pulling a kettle from an industrial-sized gas stove and turning away to fill it at the sink.

"That would be nice," I said when the guys didn't respond.

"What kind of tea would you like?" She began pulling mason jars full of loose dried leaves from a cupboard. "I have chamomile, tulsi, hibiscus, peppermint, nettle, lemon balm."

I looked over at Evan. He was watching this with the look of a dental patient observing instruments being placed on a tray. As she pulled out four stainless steel tea balls, he began snatching at Lander's sleeve and shaking his head side to side.

I stepped over to look at the jars. "This is cool," I said, picking up the jar marked tulsi. "Do you grow and dry these yourself?"

"I don't," she said, giving me a smile at my interest. "I generally buy online. Although, if I ever have time, I would like to give it a try."

"Me too," I said, setting the jar down. "I'll try any of them."

"Gentlemen?" she asked, turning to Lander and Evan.

"No. None for me. Thanks," said Evan. Her dark brow shot up.

"I'm going to do a blend for you two. Lander, you look like you need some astragalus." She pulled a jar full of beige powder from the cabinet and twisted off the lid, spooning some of the powder into two of the tea balls. Then she pinched bits of dried leaves into all four, mixing in varying amounts from different jars. As the kettle began to shriek, she plunked them into over-sized mugs and poured the steaming water over each.

"We'll just let them steep for a few minutes," she said. "Why don't we go sit down, and I'll bring them in shortly." It sounded more like a command than a question, so we shuffled into the family room and sat. I perched on the edge of a cream-colored sofa while Lander plopped into an oversized armchair near the window. Evan had been following close behind him and he looked panicked as he realized he couldn't sit with Lander without actually sitting on his lap. He finally joined me on the couch, sitting so close that his leg pressed up against mine.

"Move over," I said to him under my breath. I pointed towards all the room farther down, but he ignored me.

"This is nice," Lander's mother said. She stared at us, seemingly immune to the discomfort that Evan and I were experiencing. "So, you had a book signing. That must have been exciting," she said, turning towards Lander.

"I guess you could say that," he said. I thought about the assault that had nearly drowned us both and I watched his mother for any telltale signs of culpability.

"Were there many people there?"

"It was packed!" Evan said, finally finding something he could contribute.

"Oh, you were there too?" she asked, turning her intense gaze on him. He scooted over even closer to me, nearly knocking me from my perch.

"Yes, we were both there," I said when Evan didn't respond. "There really were a lot of people there. We were packed like sardines. Evan sat next to, I guess she's your admin? She's quite the fan, I have to say."

"Trust me, I know," Mrs. Jones said. Her delicate sigh conveyed her feelings about that. She glanced over at her son. "Half the time when you have a new book out, I can hardly get any work out of her."

"Did you know she's the president of his fan club?" I asked.

"I was unaware you had a fan club," she said to Lander. "Although it doesn't surprise me. She never stops with the questions. *What was Lander like as a child? What's his favorite book? Does he like cats?*" She'd suffused her voice with a breathless pitch that was probably a fairly accurate impression. "If she wasn't so good at managing my schedule and keeping everything on track, I would seriously consider having her transferred to someone else."

"Her name's Nell?" asked Lander.

"Yes, Nell. Nell Rey."

"How long has she been working for you?" Lander asked.

"Why? Are you interested in her?" She smiled. "I'm sure she would love to hear that."

"No, no. Nothing like that," Lander said, tapping a finger against the rolled arm of the chair. "I was just wondering. She seemed really, I don't know. Intense?"

"Like the Stephen King movie," said Evan, chiming back in.

"The Stephen King movie?" asked Mrs. Jones looking confused. "I'm not sure I follow."

"The one with that writer who had the stalker fan? Remember?" Evan's cheeks were getting pink but he was on familiar ground here. "*Misery!* That's it. Don't you remember that?"

Lander's mom glanced over at him. "You think my admin is

stalking you?" She sounded slightly skeptical but not completely.

"No, not really," he said. "She just seemed—"

One of the dogs began barking at the back door and Mrs. Jones excused herself to go let them in.

"You need to go check her car," Evan whispered, leaning across me to get closer to Lander. "See if it's smashed in from where she hit you guys."

Lander heaved himself up from the chair and we followed him into the kitchen, where his mom was fussing with the teacups.

"Where's Dad?" Lander asked, moving over to a far door. He opened it and stuck his head through. I could see the dimness of an unlit garage beyond. "And where's your car?"

"What are you doing?" his mother asked. "If you must know, your father took my car in for a little work. It was due for service."

Mrs. Jones finished removing the tea strainers from the cups and began handing them out. She shoved one across the counter towards Lander before peering into the others and handing one to Evan and one to me. The last one she picked up and curled her fingers around, blowing softly on the surface. She seemed oblivious to the fraught silence and sideways looks we were giving each other.

The dogs had found a squeaky toy and one of them raced through the kitchen, skittering on the tiles while the other gave chase.

"Did you want to go sit down?" she asked. "Or are we just going to stand here while I try to discern the true purpose of the visit?"

We followed her back into the family room and resumed our seats. I blew on the hot liquid, taking in a floral scent from the steam. I'd be sweating in minutes. We really should have come up with a better plan.

"Your dogs are really adorable," I said, reaching out to pat one as it ran by. "I've heard Scottish terriers are pretty feisty. But these guys seem really sweet." When there's nothing else to talk about, get people to talk about their dogs.

"Oh my heavens, feisty is a good word. It's a good thing they have each other, or they would drive me to drink." She smiled the first real smile I'd seen since we arrived. "You know dogs?"

"I have a Border collie mix myself, and I do some dog walking too."

Her full-on gaze was a little intimidating, like she was studying a specimen. One of the dogs suddenly ripped through the toy's seam and they both set upon it, pulling stuffing out and shaking it side to side.

"Faraday, Dalton, stop. Leave it. Leave it!" she said, setting her teacup down and standing to retrieve the toy. "Well, they were bred to hunt and kill vermin," she said calmly as she gathered up the fluffy stuffing. "Boys, stop." They raced away with dangling shreds.

From the recesses of Lander's bag, his phone began to bleat. He lifted a side pocket and pulled it out, staring at the screen. The look on his face was so odd that my heart turned over.

"Is it the hospital?" I asked in a low tone.

"No." He swiped the screen and the chime stopped as his mother reappeared. She looked at me oddly like maybe she'd heard my question, but before she could say anything, a phone in the kitchen began to ring. Lander's sudden anxiety was nearly palpable, and Evan and I exchanged a look.

"Sorry," I whispered. "I didn't think."

"What's going on?" asked Evan. I could feel him tense up beside me.

From the kitchen, we could hear Lander's mother sounding

aggrieved. "Yes, of course I remember you," she snapped. "I'm not senile." There was a pause. "Yes, as a matter of fact, he is." Lander looked like he was about to bolt through the back windows. He shook his head side to side, slipped his phone into his bag and stood up.

"Come on," he said. Evan was on his feet, ready to dash down the hall as CiCi came back into the room.

"Lander, it's for you. It's Annalise." She held out a cordless phone, poking it at him until he reluctantly took it.

How did she know he was here? CiCi sat down, gesturing to Evan and me to sit. Lander walked into the kitchen, holding the phone as if it might explode in his hand.

"Well," Lander's mom said, picking her cup back up. "How's your tea?"

I took a sip before answering. "It's very good," I said. "What did you blend?"

"For you I combined hibiscus, lemon balm and chamomile." I was trying to hear past her to what Lander was saying in the kitchen.

"What did you want?" He sounded oddly flat.

"How about you?" CiCi was addressing Evan now.

He looked into his cup, his nose slightly wrinkled. "It's kind of cloudy," he said. I glanced over. It did look different than mine.

"Try it," I said to him. "I'm sure it's good."

"Where?" I heard Lander say from the other room. A pause. "No, where did you run into him?"

Mrs. Jones said something else, but I was focused on Lander and I didn't catch it. Evan's leg began a nervous jiggle next to me, and I had to stop myself from doing the same.

Mrs. Jones sighed before trying again. "So, you two are friends of Lander's?" It took an effort not to shush her into silence. How were we supposed to hear Lander's conversation if she was going to insist on polite chitchat?

"We haven't known him long," I answered, trying to split focus between her and Lander. I took another sip of tea, deciding that Lander would fill us in on his conversation and maybe I should be using my time to get some information from his mom. I had a sudden inspiration. "Oh, let me ask you something. Are your dogs afraid of thunderstorms? My dog is so scared of them, and that storm that blew through Thursday night was horrible. I was hoping to be home from the book signing before it hit, but I didn't make it in time, and I felt so bad that she was alone for that. I wish there was something that actually helped with the anxiety."

She patted her chest. "That *was* a bad one. Dalton is frightened of storms, but Faraday isn't. Although even Faraday shook a bit during that one."

"So you were here with them?" Could I be any clunkier with my questions?

"I got home just as it started," she said, one eye narrowing as she assessed me.

"That's good," I said, trying to sound more normal. "Do you know of anything that can help? I've tried some of the herbal remedies and things like that, but none of them really work."

She smiled. "You've actually come to the right place. Wait right here." She put her cup on the coffee table, her heels clicking on the floor as she disappeared down the back hallway.

"I think she poisoned my tea," Evan whispered to me. "Look at it. It's all cloudy."

"She did not poison your tea," I said. "I've been drinking mine."

"Yours wasn't cloudy like this." He swiveled around like he was looking for something. "Geez, they don't even have any plants." Before I could stop him, he lifted the back part of the couch cushion and poured his tea out.

"Omigod, Evan! What are you doing?" He shoved the cushion back in place just as we heard Mrs. Jones tapping towards us.

"I make this for Dalton myself," Mrs. Jones said, approaching and holding out a small dark glass vial.

I felt a fake, overly bright smile break across my face. It was all I could do not to turn and stare at the couch. I was sure the tea would be spreading and any minute we'd hear the drip drip drip of liquid onto the hardwood floor beneath. "What it is?" I asked, taking the cool glass in my fingers.

"It's a tincture of my own blend of calming herbs and a minute dose of canine antianxiety medication. It really works well. You're welcome to try it."

"Thank you so much," I said. "I really appreciate this." I was talking too loudly now, hoping that if the tea did start to drip, I would drown it out.

"You should probably put an antibiotic cream on those scrapes," she said, gesturing to the reddened patches on my arm. I tucked them against my body and squeezed my legs together, hoping she wouldn't notice the ones on my thighs.

"I will," I said brightly. "I wonder where Lander is."

As if on cue, he appeared, holding the phone out to his mother. He looked over at Evan and me. "Are you guys ready to go?"

Mrs. Jones tilted her head and stared at him. "While it's always nice to see you, Lander—heavens knows we don't see much of you—was there anything in particular you were looking for this morning?" she asked. To be fair, this had been a freaky kind of visit.

"No, I just wanted to stop by. I haven't seen you in a while.

Oh, and your admin said you were peeved at me? I meant to ask about that."

I thought I heard a liquid drop plop beneath Evan and me.

"Well, thanks so much for the thunder drops," I said loudly. "I really appreciate the help." I stood and Evan popped up next to me.

She looked from us to Lander. "I'm not sure this is something we should discuss in front of your friends. But I need you to schedule that appointment that I've been leaving you messages about."

"Right. Right, yeah. I got your messages. I'll see what I can do," Lander said. He shifted his bag and turned to us. "You guys ready?"

"Lander, one more thing," she said. "Do you still see that friend of yours? What was his name? Seth?"

Lander turned back towards her. "Yeah, we're still friends. I haven't seen him in a few months, though, I guess. Why?"

She gave Evan and me a pointed look, then flicked a glance towards the door.

"Oh," I said. "Lander, we'll just wait for you outside." I heard another drip. This time his mother cocked her head as if she'd heard it too. I set my cup down on the table next to Evan's empty one and gave him a shove. "Thanks again."

The dogs scampered along with us towards the front door, stopping at the threshold. I hurried down the front walk towards Evan's car. Sometimes going places with Evan was like traveling with a kid. I could only imagine what CiCi was going to think when she discovered her tea-soaked sofa.

CHAPTER SEVEN

"What was that about?" Evan asked as he peeled away from the curb.

"Which thing?" asked Lander.

"Your wife calling?"

"And what did your mom want that she didn't want us to hear?"

There was a rustling from the back seat. I glanced over. Lander was digging through his bag. He extracted a notebook and pen, flipped the book open and began scribbling notes.

"Sorry, hold on," he said. "I want to get this down."

Evan drove slowly through the quiet streets, reversing direction multiple times and backtracking down streets we'd already traveled, before finally heading towards his house. Lander closed his notebook but kept it out as he fiddled with his pen. I couldn't believe he wasn't getting car sick—I know I was.

"Sorry," he said. "I just wanted to get as much down as accurately as I could. Sometimes you remember the gist but forget the details."

"How did your wife know you'd be at your parents?" Evan asked.

"Ex-wife, and I have no idea," Lander said. "She had some story about how she'd run into my friend Seth and she said he seemed messed up and she was worried about him. I guess he lost his job. I knew he was having work issues, but I didn't realize he was out of work entirely. She said that was why she was trying to reach me." He sounded skeptical.

"And you don't believe that?"

"Not really," he said. "I mean, Annalise couldn't stand Seth when we were married, so I find it hard to believe she would be worried about him after all this time. And for all she knows I'm in close touch with him." He paused and I could hear his pen scratching against his notebook again. "Not to mention, she's a terrible liar, and not very quick on her feet. It actually sounded like she was trying to make up an excuse to talk to me."

"It's weird she would call your parents' house," said Evan, slowing for a light.

"She said she hasn't been able to reach me."

"Hard to reach a dead guy in a bayou," said Evan. "I think she was just checking to see if you're alive."

"And your mom was asking about Seth too?" I asked. "I mean, suddenly he's popping up in all kinds of conversations."

"That actually makes more sense, although I think she's off track. But it's like I told you—it's all about her task force. She's concerned because Seth and I got in trouble a lot when we were in school. It's dumb, but she always thought he was a bad influence on me. Like it was his fault that I didn't do well in school. His fault that I sucked at math and science. His fault that I barely graduated."

"But look how great you turned out," said Evan.

"Well, she is your mom," I said at the same time.

"Yeah, the reality was, I just sucked at school. And I hated it. Seth didn't cause any of that."

"How does that relate to her task force?" I asked.

"I don't see how it does," he said. "I told you, she's just really obsessed about this. She wanted to know if he turned out to be a respectable, functioning member of society. Her words. Just in case the FBI decides to explore that avenue." This seemed as far-fetched as Lander's conviction that she was trying to kill him. Maybe far-fetched thinking ran in the family.

We rode back to Evan's mostly in silence. Besides getting some anti-anxiety dog drops that I had no intention of giving Addie, I didn't see that we'd netted much from that visit. I left Evan's with no clear idea of what the next steps would be. Honestly, besides hoping that William would be okay and figuring out my car mess, I was pretty sure my involvement was done.

Pulling into my driveway, I saw Larry lying in a mesh lounge chair in his front yard, wearing nothing but a Speedo. His white belly rose over the red fabric, and kinky hair puffed out from the high-cut leg openings. I hit my garage door opener and looked directly ahead.

"Hey, neighbor!" he shouted. I turned up my radio, feigning that I couldn't hear him. From the corner of my eye, I saw him toss a beer can into his yard before reaching into a cooler and pulling out another one. "Hey, I want to talk to you."

I turned the volume up higher. As soon as the door was up, I hit the gas, my tires squealing on the concrete as the car shot into the garage. Before I had a chance to close the door behind me, Larry had hauled himself from his chair and padded barefoot into the garage, still holding his beer.

"Hey, Jackie!" He leaned forward and tapped on my window. "I was talking to you."

Gathering myself, I turned off the engine and pushed open the driver's door in a sudden move, forcing him to step back. "Geez, you nearly hit me," he said, taking another gulp of beer and letting out a loud burp. I got out of the car and looked away so I didn't have to see this vision up close.

"You know my name's not Jackie, right?"

"Really? Whatever." He waited.

I finally looked at him. "What did you want?"

He swiveled a hip side to side, his attention clearly elsewhere, before reaching down and adjusting the leg of his Speedo, exposing even more hair. I looked away again.

"Ow. I guess now I know what it means when someone says they've got you by the short hairs." He laughed and poked my arm to make sure I got the joke.

"I'm busy. I need to go in," I said. Addie gave a sharp bark from inside.

He gave a little pout, then sucked in his gut and ran a finger down his chest. "I need a favor." I stared at him without blinking. I learned how to do this from Addie. "Look, it'll just take a minute." He held a hand up to cover another burp, clearly trying to be on his best behavior.

I sighed. Might as well move this along. "What?"

"I need you to rub some oil on my back. I have a date tonight and I want to be tanned up." He sucked his gut in again. "Looking good, right?"

"You mean sunscreen?"

"No, baby oil. I want to be a golden brown that she can't keep her hands off of." I realized the sheen I'd been looking at was indeed oil, not sweat like I'd originally thought.

"No one does that anymore. Do you want to get skin cancer?"

He tossed his head and ambled out of the garage. As he got to the driveway, he reached around to where his suit had buried itself in his crevice, slipped a finger under the elastic and snapped it in place on his butt. "Come on, it'll just take a minute. I mean, what else are you doing?"

I considered closing the garage door and racing inside, but

knowing Larry, he would just lean on my doorbell, getting oil all over the place until I came back out. I followed him across the driveway. He settled himself facedown on his lounge chair, waving a hand towards a bottle of baby oil buried in the grass. Picking it up, I dribbled a line of oil down his back, then used the bottom of the bottle to smear it side to side.

"Your hands are cold," he said. "Doesn't surprise me. Warm 'em up on Larry. Come on, get in there and really rub."

"Look. Do you want me to help you or not?"

He settled into his chair, grinding into the mesh and treating me to a butt wiggle.

"That's it." I threw the bottle at him and headed towards my house.

"Where you going? It was just getting good."

I hit the button on the garage door, wondering why I'd gotten stuck with this guy as my neighbor. Other people got neighbors that they liked—helpful folks you could borrow sugar from, or watch football games with; people who would pick up your mail if you were traveling or bring you soup if you were sick. But I didn't get any of those people. I got Larry.

After a quick lunch, I changed into a lightweight long-sleeved shirt and a pair of capris to hide my scrapes, and headed to Frances's with Addie. A quick peek out the window revealed that Larry was gone. I still hadn't replaced Addie's seat belt and I debated leaving her home, but she loved seeing Frances so much that I decided to risk it. Last night had been terrible, nearly overshadowing my mother's words about Frances acting weird. But now that I was thinking about it again, I was getting an uneasy feeling. I hadn't heard from her as much as I usually did. In fact, I tried to think of the last time I'd talked to her and realized it had been at least a week. Or was it more?

Frances lives in a tidy guesthouse in my parents' backyard. By backyard, I don't mean your standard fenced-in plot that barely holds a concrete pad for your air conditioner and a small space for a grill. No, my parents' backyard is more like an acre of prime real estate in the middle of River Oaks, one of the most expensive areas in Houston.

The guesthouse had been a later addition, built as my grandfather had started having health problems. Now my grandmother lived there alone, far enough away from my parents to be independent, but close enough that someone could traverse the distance in ten seconds if they ran really fast. I loved the house. It was comfortable and cozy, and if it wasn't in my parents' backyard, I would want to live there myself.

My tires crunched on the drive as I rolled in, Addie perched on the console, whining with excitement. My parents' longtime gardener's truck was in the driveway, which was surprising, because Rafael usually didn't work on the weekends.

The yard looked immaculate—wide expanses of perfectly cut grass leading to a frame of boxwoods that ran along the back of the house. Lines of variegated liriope swayed in neat rows with small mounds of begonias adding a pop of color in front. The pool sparkled in the sunlight, its azure blue inviting in the hot sun. Another month or so and the water would be bathwater warm, but right now it would still be refreshing. I berated myself for not bringing my bathing suit.

As soon as I opened Addie's door, she surprised me by bolting out of the car and dashing around the side of the guesthouse. I trotted after her, guessing she'd spotted a squirrel and decided to give chase.

"Addie, no! Addie!" Frances's voice carried a note of panic and I picked up my pace, racing around the side of the house. I nearly fell over a roll of wire mesh fencing while dodging three more that lay just beyond. A new row of fence posts had been planted in measured intervals, stretching about twenty-five feet back from the guesthouse and maybe fifteen feet from side to side. Rafael knelt beside one of the mesh rolls, unwrapping the label. His face looked as guilty as if I'd caught him having inappropriate relations with my grandmother. Frances stood in front of a wire cage the size of a large dog kennel, ineffectively trying to keep between Addie, who darted side to side, and three young chickens who were frantically trying to break through the back of the cage to get away from the terrifying beast.

"Addie," I said sharply, clipping a leash to her collar and pulling her back. "Leave it." I knelt beside her, holding her trembling body. Her ears pricked forward and her eyes narrowed as she stared at the chickens. She licked her lips expectantly and I tightened my grip. Had I been a chicken looking at this, I would have died from fright. "Come over here," I said, dragging her away.

Frances bent towards the chickens, clucking softly. "It's okay, girls. It's okay." She wore lightweight overalls tucked into garden boots, set off perfectly by a straw hat with a floral bow streaming down the back.

Finally convinced that none of the chickens were going to die of fright, she turned to me, anger and embarrassment intermingling on her face.

"Jessica. I didn't expect to see you today. If you would have let me know you were coming..." She trailed off and moved around towards the front of the house. I followed, keeping a tight hold on Addie as she kept trying to flip around and make her way back to the chickens.

"I'm sorry I didn't call. Mom called me." I paused, trying to consider—was that really just last night? "Last night to let me know they were going to Dallas. I've been busy and I know I haven't called in a while, so I thought I would just drop by."

"Your mother needs to not be so nosy," she said, opening the door and ushering me in. "She told you to check on me, didn't she?" We'd walked in without her noticing my bright yellow rental car. She must be miffed.

"Well, I don't think she was being nosy, exactly," I said, getting ready to unhook Addie's leash. "There's not anything else in here that I need to keep Addie away from, is there?"

"No." We made our way to the kitchen, where we spent most of our time. Frances washed her hands at the deep sink, then pulled a stainless-steel bowl from a bottom cupboard and filled it for Addie.

I sat down at the table. "She just said you'd been acting a little strange and she thought I could look in on you," I continued. "And I wanted to come see you anyway. It's been a while since we got together."

She pulled a pitcher of iced tea from the refrigerator and poured us each a tall glass before slicing a fresh lemon garnish. Sliding into a chair across from me, she pulled her hat off and ran a hand over her hair.

"Are you going to tell your mother about this?" She took a drink and wiped daintily at the sweat on her upper lip with a napkin.

"They don't know about the chickens? How do you think they won't notice this?" I gestured towards the window where Addie stood braced, her front paws resting on the sill. She vibrated with excitement, a low whimper whining through the air as she watched the feathered things strut around their cage.

"I don't think either one of your parents has been behind this house in decades."

"This house hasn't been here for decades."

"Don't be smart, you know what I mean." She took another sip of tea and glanced out the window. A small smile lit up her face.

"Chickens," I said. "Why chickens? You could have gotten a cat like normal grandmothers do."

"What would I do with a cat?" she asked, turning and giving me a bewildered look. "I never took to cats. You know that."

"What about a dog?" Addie banged the window with her nose and let out a sharp bark, causing both Frances and me to jump. "Addie, get down. Come here." I snapped my fingers for emphasis, but her focus was laser sharp. Pushing back my chair, I went and looped a finger through her collar, pulling her back.

"I've been doing some research," Frances said, sounding moderately proud of herself. "I was going to plant a small vegetable garden out there, but then I went to that nursery over by Memorial Park. The day I was there, they had someone doing a class on backyard chickens. And before you knew it, here I am."

"Chickens." I took a long drink of tea, the lemon tart on my tongue. "It seems like so much work."

"What else do I have to do with my time?" She wrapped both hands around her glass and stared down into the liquid. "I have a lot of time."

"Frances. I'm sorry! I know I missed our dinner last week—"

"Jessica, no. You have your life to live, you're not responsible for entertaining me. This is something I want to do. Your grandfather's been gone awhile now, and I think I've done pretty well, but lately... well, lately I just haven't felt like working on charitable campaigns or going to ladies' day luncheons at the club."

"What about painting? You used to love to paint." Pangs of guilt and worry were breaking out behind my ribs.

She smiled at me. "I've been thinking about that too. I might just pull my brushes out. But the chickens, I don't know how to explain it. When I saw them fluffing their feathers and prancing around that enclosure, I was captivated. I enjoy watching them. And the way they interact. The lady at the nursery said that they get to know their owners and they like to play. Not to mention the fresh eggs."

I had to admit she looked happier than she had in a while. My phone buzzed in my purse and I pretended not to hear it, knowing how much Frances hated the intrusiveness of modern technology.

"Well, if it's what you want to do, then great. Let me know if you need any help. I'd be more than happy to come over and help out with whatever needs to be done."

She pushed away from the table and pulled another glass from the cupboard as my phone buzzed again against the side of my purse. "I'm going to take Rafael a glass of tea. It's hot out there today." She clinked a few cubes into the tall glass and poured tea to the brim. "You go ahead and check that phone of yours. I'll be back in a minute."

As soon as she left the kitchen, I pulled my phone out and checked the screen. Even via text, I could hear how jacked up Evan was. Apparently, he and Lander had decided to go check out Annalise's car for body damage tonight and they wanted to know if I'd like to go along. Frances came back in, gathered up the glasses and put them in the sink.

"Was that something you need to take care of?" she asked, gesturing to my phone and sounding hopeful.

"No, no, it was just Evan. He's got a friend staying with him and they're thinking about going out later. They wanted to know if I wanted to go too."

"Well, that's very nice!" she said. "I think it's wonderful how close you are with your friends." She stared at me expectantly before flicking a glance towards the window.

"You and I haven't gone to dinner in a while," I said, trying to figure out if she was trying to get rid of me or hoping for a dinner invite. "Do you want to go out tonight?"

"While you know I love seeing you, Jessica, I think you should go out with your friends. You and I can catch up when it's not so busy." She glanced out the window. "Rafael and I have a lot to do, and we need to get the coop set up before it gets dark. Apparently the girls have a twilight bedtime."

We hugged goodbye before I leashed Addie up and headed out, thankful that Frances was too preoccupied to walk me to my car. When I looked back, she was looking over Rafael's shoulder as he used a drill to attach something to one of the posts. I was pretty sure my parents were going to notice the chickens, and equally sure that they weren't going to be overly thrilled.

CHAPTER EIGHT

Now that Frances had given me the boot, I had to decide if I felt like chasing after a woman I didn't even know in another half-baked attempt at unraveling Lander's mess, or spending a relaxing evening on the couch with Addie. Most Saturday nights I went to dinner with Frances and still get home early enough to relax and enjoy my solitude with Addie. God, I was becoming pathetic. I tried to think of the last time I'd had a date and had a small panic attack when I couldn't even remember.

I was back at Evan's house at six, having wasted half an hour trying to figure out what to wear. Evan had mentioned we needed to be ready to get in anywhere, so I assumed we weren't just going to be looking at front-end car damage. I have to say, so far I was not impressed with Evan and Lander's detective planning skills. In the end I'd finally settled on a black miniskirt, studded black tank top, and flat black sandals with decorative rhinestones that wrapped around my ankles. I shoved a cropped cardigan in my oversized bag in case I needed a cover up for a fancier place, and I tied a hot pink scarf around my neck as an afterthought.

Evan's mouth fell open when he opened the door.

"What?" I asked, pushing past him. Henry bounded over, as delighted to see me as if I'd been gone for years.

"You look great," said Lander, coming around the corner from the kitchen. I felt a rush of pleasure. It had been a while since I'd been on the receiving end of an appreciative look from a man that wasn't wearing a hard hat or pushing a lawn mower. I really needed to work on my life.

Evan recovered enough to close the door and his mouth. His version of *get in anywhere and blend in* consisted of his everyday work wear—wrinkled khakis and a blue button-down. At least he'd tucked his shirt in. Lander sported black jeans and a dark gray shirt. The sneakers kind of ruined the look and made me think that Evan had forgotten to pack more than one pair of shoes. At least he wasn't wearing the waterlogged pair from Thursday night. He'd taken some time with his hair. It stood nearly on end before flopping to the side, held in place by some magic goop. Overall he looked better than he had this morning. I was guessing he'd gotten a nap in.

"Thanks. You guys look pretty sharp yourselves." Evan was still staring at me like he'd never noticed that I was a girl before. "What?" I asked him again. "Are you going to stare at me all night like that? Geez."

"No, I've just never seen you dressed like that before," he said, flushing and turning away.

"So what's the plan?" I asked, hoping that they'd actually come up with something more productive than driving around.

"We're going to go by Annalise and Dick's," Lander said. "If they're home, hopefully we can check out both cars at once."

Evan gave Henry a biscuit, a neck rub and a kiss on the head before locking up. We piled into Evan's car, where Lander insisted on riding in the back seat so that he could drop to the floor if needed.

"Have you seen their house before?" I asked, wondering if he was more stalker-like when it came to his ex-wife than he wanted to admit. "I mean, do you know if we'll be able to see in the garage?"

"I've never been there, but Evan Google mapped it and you can tell from the street view that we'll be able to see the garage."

"What if the door is down?"

"Saturday night. We've got a decent chance one or both of them will go out." He sighed. "Or we'll be watching a closed garage door. I don't know. I feel like I need to do something."

We weren't even a mile from Evan's house and he was already turning into a fast-food drive-through line.

"This okay with you guys?" Evan asked as he pulled up behind a rattling pickup truck. When he'd mentioned we'd pick up dinner, I'm not sure why I thought it might be something better than fast food.

"Sure, whatever," said Lander, slumping down and doing a quick visual survey of our surroundings. Another car pulled up behind us, and I could feel his tension level increase as we became trapped in line. His stress was contagious and I found myself trying to estimate if Evan's Jeep could get over the six-inch curb and across a narrow stretch of yaupon hollies that penned us in on the right. I was guessing we could do it if we had to.

"We didn't get a chance to talk about it, but do you think we can rule your mom out now?" I asked.

"I don't know about that," Evan said as he pulled closer to the truck in front of us, trying to see the menu board. "She seemed pretty scary. I can understand why you think she's trying to kill you. Heck, I think she might have been trying to kill me too."

I wondered if she'd noticed the tea stain yet. I know I was never going over there again.

"Yeah, I'm not sure we can," Lander said. "I mean, we didn't really find anything out."

"Well, she did indicate she was home Thursday night. I asked her about the storm and the dogs and she said she was home."

"Yeah, but she could have lied," said Evan. "And her car wasn't there. Seems pretty suspicious she just *happened* to be having work done." I was still having a hard time picturing Lander's mother ramming us from behind and shoving us into a raging bayou.

The pickup truck in front of us belched a cloud of diesel as it inched along. I was getting a sinking feeling that our expedition tonight was going to be as fruitful as this morning. Well, I could always go home and watch a movie with Addie, because I wasn't sure which was more pathetic—driving around following strangers and acting like we could solve a mystery or hanging out with my dog.

"Okay, so your ex-wife. It's weird she called your parents' house acting like it was so important she get in touch with you, but then her reason sounded pretty lame."

"Yeah, she said she'd been trying to reach me and she did actually call my cell a couple of times last night."

Evan looked back at him. "You didn't answer?"

"I had my phone turned off."

"She didn't leave a message?"

"No."

"So she could have been checking to see if you were alive," I said, trying to think through this. If she'd been the one to shove us in the bayou, maybe she'd called his phone later to make sure there was no answer. Creepy.

"Hey, what do you guys want?" Evan asked as the pickup truck lurched past the menu board and towards the payment window.

"Burger and fries is fine," said Lander, wrestling his wallet out of his pocket. "And a Diet Coke, please."

"That's fine," I said, reaching for my purse.

Lander peeled off some bills and handed them to Evan. "Here, I got it."

Evan pulled to the menu board and squinted at the options.

"I'd like three super value meals," he shouted at the box. "And two Diet Cokes and a regular Coke."

"I don't think you need to yell," I hissed at him.

"Sorry, could you repeat that? I didn't catch your order," squawked a tinny voice that broke on every other word. Evan grimaced at me.

"Three super value meals. Two Diet Cokes and a regular Coke," he screamed. My parents could probably hear that in Dallas. Lander had slumped down even further, only about two inches of his head now sticking above the window. The box screeched some static at us, and we drove forward to the window.

Evan passed a large white bag back to Lander and handed me a pulp fiber carrier with three giant drinks wedged into the slots. I balanced it on my lap as Evan pulled onto the street and headed west. He held a hand toward Lander, motioning for food, and Lander passed him a paper-wrapped burger and a cardboard container of fries. The smell of fries filled the car and my mouth began to water.

"Do you want yours now?" Lander asked me as he edged up to a sitting position, pulled a fry from the bag and bit off an end.

"I'll take the fries now. Maybe I'll eat my burger when we get there." I exchanged a drink for the fries and settled Evan's drink in the center console. We were heading down Westheimer, traffic clogging the narrow, curved lanes. The right lane was so pitted with potholes that I tucked the fries between my knees and picked Evan's drink back up in an attempt to keep the liquid from sloshing out like pool water in an earthquake. Evan was alternating between watching where he was going and picking through the food in his lap.

"Stop!" I shouted as we sped towards the back end of a sedan stopped at the light ahead. My right foot stomped the floorboard in a wishful attempt to slow us down, and I squeezed my eyes closed. Or almost closed. I could still see the taillights getting closer through a wall of lashes. Evan slammed on the brakes, the wheels squealing on the pavement as we skidded to a stop just inches from the bumper. I was thrown forward as my seat belt tensioner kicked in, snapping me against my seat. The drinks weren't so lucky—the lid on one popped off as I squeezed it too tight, and brown liquid rose in an arc, splashing across the dashboard and down my legs.

There was silence in the car as we all took stock.

"Gee, sorry about that," Evan said as he leaned forward and picked up his half-eaten burger from where it had rolled onto to the floor between his feet. Smashing the bun back in place, he peered at it closely before picking a hair off and taking another bite. A horn sounded behind us, and I looked up to see the light had turned and the cars ahead had moved on. Evan started up again as if nothing had happened.

I looked over to see how Lander had fared. His drink was intact, his bag had slid to the floor and he appeared to be practicing some deep breathing exercises. No doubt he was considering the irony of hiding out with Evan to keep himself safe from an unknown assailant, only to be nearly killed by Evan instead.

"Okay back there?" I asked setting Evan's drink in the cupholder. Now that half the liquid was gone, I wasn't worried about it splashing out anymore. My fries were contained, although a bit wet.

"Yep, yep. I'm okay." Lander handed me a stack of napkins,

and I went to work cleaning as much of the sticky liquid off as I could. I noticed Evan's gaze alternating between the road and the floorboard where his fries had scattered around his feet.

"Don't even think about trying to get those," I said, shoving the sopping napkins into the second cupholder. "You just pay attention to your driving."

At Weslayan, we turned and headed south towards the Bellaire area. I finished my fries and wiped my greasy fingers on the sodden napkins. We were now just outside the 610 Loop, still heading west. Evan turned onto a side street and slowed as we made our way past yards shaded by overgrown live oak trees. Soccer nets, bicycles and yard signs congratulating the resident graduates indicated this was a very family-friendly neighborhood. It was definitely the kind of neighborhood where someone would surely call the police on three strangers lurking in a Jeep.

"Okay, it's that one on the corner," said Lander, leaning forward and pointing to an oversized monstrosity. Three stories of flesh-colored stucco rose above its closest neighbors, looking bloated behind wrought-iron fencing. Ornate columns flanked the front door, and matching pillars squatted on an upstairs balcony. The yard was dominated by palm trees that looked as if they'd been plucked from Egypt and planted around a gaudy fountain that burbled over four tiers of poured concrete.

We drove slowly by, the three of us gawking out the window. I considered Lander's house, then looked again. I wondered if Dick and Lander were as different as their house styles, and what exactly that said about Annalise.

"It's certainly fancy," I said, trying to be diplomatic. Frankly, it looked like something an Atlantic City mob boss would aspire to. "I'm guessing Dick DeLuca's doing pretty well."

"Well, I doubt he's doing better than Lander," Evan countered. "He hasn't sold ten million books."

"What's she like?" I asked. "Annalise?" I'd gotten a sense of her yesterday from William, and it hadn't been very flattering.

"Annalise is..." Lander paused. "Annalise likes the good life. She likes shiny things. She wants people to be impressed by her." He motioned towards the house. "She wants this. Actually, I would think she wants more than this. She likes money. It's as simple as that."

We'd come to a cul-de-sac and Evan was slowly turning around. He pulled up on a side street between the DeLucas' house and the house behind them. The driveway was about fifteen feet directly in front of us. A three-car garage was clearly visible from where we sat.

"Aren't we going to be too noticeable here?" I asked.

"Where am I supposed to park?" Evan asked. "It's not like there's a lot of cover around here." He cracked the windows, shut off the engine and began retrieving the fries from the floor. He picked through them, eating the ones he deemed salvageable and tossing the rest out the window. Done with that, he sucked up the last of his Coke and started jiggling the straw up and down through the lid. I held my drink, the ice cooling my hand as the condensation dripped off onto my lap.

I was having a hard time picturing Lander with someone like Annalise. I wanted to see her so I could get a sense of her for myself. "I know this is kind of a personal question," I said, "and feel free to tell me to mind my own business, but how'd you two end up getting married? It doesn't sound like she's, you know, very nice."

There was a silence from the back seat. Evan and I both turned to look at him.

"It was stupid," Lander finally said, looking embarrassed. "Seth and I were in Vegas for a Comic-Con convention. It was a few years after we graduated and she was there for a bridal shower with her sister and some friends. We'd all gone to school together, so it's not like we didn't know each other." He looked away. "Anyway, we got drunk and ended up married."

Evan snorted. "Are you kidding me? You got drunk and got married?" He sounded both amused and frightened, like this could inadvertently happen to him.

"Yep."

"Couldn't you have gotten it annulled?" I asked.

He shook his head. "If only," he said. "But the other thing about Annalise is, she's never wrong. She wasn't going to admit she made a mistake, so when we got home, we tried to make it work."

Evan stared at him. I couldn't tell if Lander was going up on his admiration scale, or down. "Wait, wait, wait. Let me make sure I understand this. You're in Vegas. You run into someone you went to school with and you end up *married*?"

"Pretty much," Lander said. "I don't actually remember the whole thing. But it's really easy to get a license and there are wedding chapels all over the place. Vegas is a disaster waiting to happen."

"Dude."

"I know. I guess she was pissed that her younger sister was getting married before she was, and the next thing you know, I woke up married."

Evan twisted his straw in a knot. I doubted he'd venture to Vegas anytime soon.

"It got worse when we got home," continued Lander. "Neither one of us really had any money, and we couldn't afford our own place, so she moved in with Seth and me."

"Okay, no offense, but as a female I can't even imagine that," I said.

"Yeah, it was about like what you'd think. Our apartment wasn't that nice. I was trying to write and was working nights as a security guard at an office complex. Seth was finishing his degree and working as a bartender."

"And Annalise did the cooking and cleaning?"

Lander laughed. "No. She was working for her dad. He owns a car repair place and she was doing the books. I mean, the whole thing was kind of surreal, like we were playing at being grown-up. She had this checklist, like what she thought married people needed to do. Get a joint account, buy a house, stuff like that."

The sound of a slamming door caught our attention, and the garage door on the DeLuca house began to rise.

"Everyone down!" whispered Lander.

I curled sideways, my head colliding with Evan's as we listened to the driveway gates squeal open. Lander inched his head up, like an alligator just breaking the surface of the water.

"I think it's Dick," he whispered. "It seems like he's alone, but it's hard to tell with the tinted windows." Evan started to sit up, but Lander shot out a hand and held him in place. "Hold on, he's just coming out."

"Could you see if Annalise's car was in the garage?" I asked.

"I don't think there was another car there, but I couldn't swear to it."

"What do we do?" Evan asked.

"I guess we could see where he's going," Lander said uncertainly.

"You don't honestly think he's doing this, do you?" I asked.

"Do you have a better idea?" asked Evan. He started the car and took off after Dick before Lander had a chance to change his mind.

"Go slow," Lander said. "We don't want him to spot us."

A shiny black Cadillac Escalade rounded the corner ahead of us and moved swiftly up the block. Didn't he see all the kid paraphernalia? As a lawyer, I'd think he'd be more concerned about the liability risk of running over a child. Two blocks later we hit a main thoroughfare and headed north towards the Galleria. Once we were in traffic, it was easy for Evan to maintain more distance.

In spite of the heavily tinted windows, it appeared that Dick was traveling alone. We kept up with him through the heavy traffic, but nearly lost him as he sped up to make a light. The car in front of us braked to a stop and Evan wheeled sideways into a tight gap and shot forward through the already busy intersection as horns blared. For the second time in the past hour, I braced for impact, muscles tightening exactly the way they tell you not to do if you're going to be crushed.

Evan calmly picked up his tailing duties while I flapped my top, trying to get air to my newly perspiring parts. Lander was practicing his deep breathing again.

"You know," Lander finally said, "not to complain, but I'm trying to figure out who's trying to kill me, and I would hate to die in the process."

Evan laughed, sounding a tad too giddy. "I got it. Don't worry. This is great!" He did a quick over-the-shoulder check before cutting into the right lane. "This is way easier than the time Jessie nearly got us killed. That time I ended up totaling my Mustang." He glanced over at me. "Remember that?"

"Uh, yeah. Hard to forget." I still felt bad about that. He'd ended up totaling his car while trying to get me away from a crazy man. Lander lapsed into silence, clearly not comforted by that exchange.

At Richmond, Dick hooked a left and headed west. Evan vibrated with excitement, the thrill of the chase adding to his caffeine buzz. It didn't take long to reach our destination. Dick was headed for Assets, one of the more upscale gentlemen's clubs in Houston.

"Oh yeah!" Evan said, slowing down as if he was going to follow Dick right into the valet line at the club.

"No, don't follow him in there, keep going!" said Lander. Evan swerved slightly and continued on.

"What do you mean, don't follow him?" asked Evan, sounding slightly put out.

"The three of us are really going to be really noticeable if we follow him in there. Look, just turn around when you can and pull in somewhere while we decide what to do."

Evan maneuvered into a deserted strip mall about half a block down from the club and turned around so we were facing the street. We could see most of the parking lot and the driveway. It looked like Assets was going to have a big night judging by the number of cars lining up to get in.

"Is it always that crowded?" I asked. No one answered me.

"So, what do we do now?" Evan asked.

"Did anyone see if he had damage to the front of his car?" I asked. "I mean, that thing is huge. He could have hit us and barely gotten a dent."

"I think he'd still have enough damage that we could see it," Lander said. He was leaning forward surveying the scene. "I can't tell for sure, but the car looks clean."

"One of us needs to go in and see if we can find anything out," Evan said.

"Oh, and which one of us are you proposing?" I asked.

"You can do it if you want to, but it seems pretty obvious I'm the only one that can go undercover for this," said Evan. I hated it when he was right.

Lander was leaning between the seats. "Okay, it's no surprise Dick's at a topless bar—I mean, that's pretty much his reputation, right? I think he met his last wife at one of these places."

"Annalise is a stripper?" Evan asked.

"No, the wife before Annalise. So why would Dick want to kill *me*?" asked Lander.

"Because he's afraid you're going to steal his wife back," I said. "Although judging from where he is, I don't know that he cares that much if you do."

"It makes no sense. There's no reason to try and kill me unless it's just an ego thing, and I don't see it. He'd just move on to the next one."

We stared at the club. Purple and white lights surged up a pole before flashing neon gold around the sign at the top: Assets Assets Assets. Pilots coming in from the west could probably read the sign from twenty thousand feet.

"I think I should go in," said Evan. "I'll just see what I can find out. I mean, we're here and all."

Judging from how well he had done during our investigation of Lander's mother this morning, it seemed unlikely that he was going to learn anything, but he was already shifting the car into gear and staring at me as if expecting me to get out.

"Wait. You don't think we're going to sit in this parking lot, do you?" I asked. "If you're going in, we keep the car, you can walk over."

"No one walks over to a club like that," Evan said, sounding incredulous at my stupidity.

"Okay, kids, settle down," said Lander, pulling open his door. "Evan, sorry, but she's right. If you're going in, we'll keep the car. I'm not going to sit exposed out here where anyone could get a shot at me." Suddenly I wished I was going in with Evan and not sitting here waiting for someone to "get a shot" at us. Evan grumped under his breath but unbuckled and slid out of the driver's seat. Lander slid in beside me. "Text us when you're ready to go. We might be driving around a little bit." Then he handed some bills out the window. "You're going to need some money in there," he said with a smile. "Have fun."

CHAPTER NINE

We watched Evan walk away looking both excited and apprehensive. He'd been right, though; no one else was walking in. I winced as he nearly got mowed down by two different vehicles as he made his way across the gravel lot.

"Now what?" I asked, still mesmerized by the traffic streaming into the topless club.

"I don't know," Lander said, adjusting the mirrors. "I don't want to go too far. I'm hoping he won't do anything..." He paused, searching for the right word. "Anything to make Dick suspicious. I should have told him to just hang back." He groaned, sliding his hands around the steering wheel. "Dick might be a sleazebag lawyer, but he can read people like a predator. I've heard he can get inside a witness's head and just rip them apart during trials. I mean, I don't know Evan very well, but I don't get the sense he's overly astute when it comes to people." He glanced over at me. "Don't be offended."

I laughed. "Social acumen isn't his strongest point."

"Maybe we should text him and tell him to forget it."

Cars continued to back up as the valets raced to move the line. "Look, there are a zillion people in there. I doubt if he'll even get close to Dick. I'm still not sure what he thinks he's going to find out, but I can't imagine anything's going to happen to him in there."

"You're right." He looked across the street, squinting. "I wonder if there's somewhere we could park that we could see the front better."

He pulled out of the parking lot and cruised along with traffic for about two blocks before turning around in an empty auto parts parking lot and heading back towards the club. He seemed antsy about getting too far away, and I began to wonder if I should be concerned about Evan too. Or maybe the restlessness wasn't a concern for Evan.

"I've been afraid to ask," I said as he pulled into a Store-Ur-Stuff parking lot directly across the street from the club. Bright lights lit up most of the lot, but Lander drove slowly towards the edge where it was darker. "How's William doing?"

He didn't say anything for a minute while he nosed into a space that gave us a clear view of the front door. We still had six lanes of traffic between us and the club, not to mention about another twenty yards to the front door, but short of going into the parking lot ourselves, this was as close as we were going to get. He put the windows down before shutting off the car.

"He's still in the ICU," he finally said softly. "So far he hasn't regained consciousness. The doctors said that that might be the best thing for him. Give his brain a chance to heal."

I plucked at my seat belt strap as emotion welled in my throat.

"I'm so sorry," I finally whispered. "I never should have let him go in alone."

"No!" he said, turning towards me in the dark. "This wasn't your fault, it was mine. I never should have asked you guys to go to my house. With everything that's been going on..." He took a ragged breath. "I just didn't think they would hurt anyone else.

God, I'm stupid." He turned away from me, his hands strangling the steering wheel.

"Yeah, well, I let him go in alone. And it's not just that. I heard something. And I ran away." Tears blurred my eyes as shame and loathing constricted my chest. "If I'd gone in instead of being a coward, I could have stopped it. I could have kept this from happening. Or at least I could have gotten him help sooner."

"Jessie, don't do that. None of this is your fault. We will nail whoever did this," he said. "And I want you to know how much I appreciate everything you and Evan are doing to help." We sat in silence for a few minutes, humid air filling the car like warm cotton batting. Shouts and laughter from Assets floated across the street, and we watched a group of guys, already drunk, spill from a Hummer limo before it even reached the door.

"Yeah, Evan's working hard to help figure this out," I said.

Lander reached into the back seat and pulled his bag forward. Fumbling inside, he extracted a pair of binoculars and held them up. "That's better," he said.

"Do you think we're going to find anything out here?" I asked, wishing I could take a turn with the binoculars.

"I don't know," he said. "It seems kind of unlikely, but I'm kind of wondering if Annalise will show up."

"Why would she show up?" I asked, surprised.

"If she's planning to leave Dick, I can see her trying to get ammo for a divorce." I wasn't a divorce attorney, but it seemed to me any good lawyer could make the case that she knew what she was signing up for.

We sat for a long time. I wasn't even sure how they could cram that many people into the building. Weren't there fire codes or something? By nine o'clock I was ready to go. Lander had given up the binoculars and I'd entertained myself watching all the men go into the club while he scribbled notes into a black notebook. I didn't know how he managed to see what he was doing since full darkness had descended a long time ago, but by tilting his page towards the window, it seemed he was going strong. I'd stayed quiet, not wanting to interrupt his train of thought, but my Diet Coke was working its way through me, and I knew it wouldn't be long before I was going to have to go find a bathroom.

Lander finally snapped his notebook closed and looked up, almost like he'd forgotten where he was. I don't know that I've ever had that kind of focus.

"What's happening?" he asked, slipping his notebook in his bag and rolling both wrists in opposing circles.

"Nothing that I can see." I handed him the binoculars and he scanned the parking lot.

"No sign of Evan?"

"Nope." I was thinking we might not see Evan again until closing time, and I wondered if Lander would be willing to take me back to my car. Or at least a bathroom.

He shifted in his seat. "I could use a bio break," he said. "Let's go find some facilities." He rummaged in his bag and pulled out a baseball cap. Jamming it on his head, he turned to me. "Can you tell it's me?"

"Most of the people around here tonight are probably seeing double, so I think you'll be okay."

He started the car and we drove until we found a McDonald's. In truth, we made several loops down side streets, stopped in parking lots, and scanned everyone around us before actually arriving at the McDonald's. I could feel his stress ratchet up as he weighed going in.

"Do you want to go in together?" I asked.

"Yeah. That would be great."

He looked around the parking lot before opening the door and slipping his bag over his shoulder again. It must be like his own personal therapy bag. I walked around the side of the car feeling paranoid myself. He moved close, ducking his head and looking out under the brim of his hat. He threw an arm around my shoulder and pulled me close, tucking his face in towards the side of my head. We shuffled together towards the brightly lit door. The restaurant was more crowded than I would have expected, but a quick glance around revealed that it was mostly groups of high school kids with a handful of drunk couples thrown in for balance.

A pasty-faced, lank-haired teen behind the counter called out to us as we headed for the side hall towards the bathrooms. "Bathrooms are for paying customers only!"

"We're gonna get something in a minute," I said.

"Yeah, you better," he said.

The ladies' room was the first door, and I disengaged from Lander's hold. "You going to be okay by yourself?"

"It would be embarrassing if I wasn't," he said, smiling. But in spite of the smile, he hunched into himself, looking like he was trying to be invisible.

"I'll meet you right here in a minute."

The lighting in the restroom was harsh. I squinted at my reflection in the mirror. My skin looked the color of a Kabuki dancer with a liver disorder. Leaning forward, I pulled down an eyelid to check for jaundice, but up close everything looked normal. Some of the scrapes on my arms looked the color of raw hamburger. I took a quick peek at my thighs. Same. I guess Mrs. Jones was right, I did need to put some more antibiotic cream on them. I'd thought this outfit looked cute on me, but clearly I was wrong. Although in this lighting I don't think anything would look good. I took care of business and was back in the hall in less than three minutes, but no sign of Lander.

I waited another two minutes before poking my head around the corner to see if he'd gone to the counter to order something.

Nope. I stood for a couple more minutes in the hall, feeling very uncomfortable. I hadn't checked on William, I had just waited, and look how that had turned out. Now here I was, not sure again if there was anything wrong. What if something had happened? But what if he was just, well, going to the bathroom?

I finally knocked but stopped myself just before saying his name. "Hey? Hey, uh you in there?"

The door swung open and he came out holding his notebook and a pen. "Sorry. I'm sorry. I haven't been in a fast-food bathroom in like, forever, and I'd forgotten how gross they are. I wanted to take some notes."

"You're taking notes on a bathroom?" I asked. "Seriously? I was freaking out that something happened to you."

"I'm sorry. I should have thought, but yeah. Those floors. The way your shoes stick in like one or two places, and then suddenly you're carrying that stickiness all over." He demonstrated by pressing his heel down on the tile. "Do you hear that?"

I looked at him like he was insane. "Yes. I'm guessing you should take those off when you get to Evan's." I might have to throw away my cute little sandals too. Gross.

"I want to remember the details," he tried to explain, then caught me sliding my feet across the tiles, checking for sticky spots. "Never mind." He shoved his notebook in his bag and we headed for the front. If we'd had any ideas of skipping out without ordering, the high school kid was still waiting for us.

"Bathrooms are for customers only!" he called out.

Lander sighed, ducked his head down and asked me, "What would you like?"

"I don't know. Some water, maybe?"

"I'm assuming you mean bottled?" the kid said. "As in you're actually going to buy something?"

"Three bottles of water, two chocolate chip cookies, a Big

Mac and a large fries," said Lander, stepping to the counter.

"Wow," I said. "Isn't Evan feeding you at all over there?"

"Actually the cookies are for us, the rest of the food is for him. I have the feeling he's going to need something to help soak up the alcohol when he comes out."

He handed some bills across to the counter and the kid counted out his change, ripped off a receipt and held it out. Staring at Lander, he did a double take.

"Don't I know you from somewhere?" he asked. "You look really familiar."

Lander froze beside me, but he kept his voice light. "I don't think so, but I get that all the time. I guess I just have one of those faces." He turned slightly away, looking out over the dining area.

"I don't know," the kid said. "I'm pretty good with faces. I think I've seen you before. Do you know Bill Doran? I feel like I've seen you with my dad."

"No, sorry," Lander said. "I'm gonna go grab some napkins." He turned away and walked over to pick up some napkins and ketchup packs. He was still fiddling with the plasticware when our order hit the counter. I reached over to grab the bag. What makes the smell of fries so irresistible? I undid the bag and snagged two off the top. Lander was already heading for the door.

"Do you ever go to the Greenstop Games?" the kid shouted over the counter. "I know I've seen you before."

Lander nearly ran for the car and I trotted along, hoping he wasn't going to take off without me.

"Wow, you really do get recognized," I said, slipping into the passenger seat.

"Yeah. Luckily a lot of people are like that. They think I look familiar but they don't know why."

"I guess a lot of people read your books. That's a good thing."

He started the engine and backed out of our space. "I don't think he was one of my readers."

"You never know," I said. "He certainly seemed to recognize you."

We returned to our parking place at Store-Ur-Stuff, where Lander cracked the windows and shut off the engine.

"How long are we going to wait?" I asked. "I mean, honestly, I think we're pretty much wasting our time here."

He sighed. "Yeah, I agree. We'll give him a few more minutes and then maybe you can text him to see if he's ready to go."

We ate our cookies, I ate most of Evan's fries, and we took turns with the binoculars again.

"I think I see Dick's SUV," Lander said after spending a long while studying the lot. "It was behind another big thing that's gone now. I can't see the license plate, but I think that's it." I reached out a hand for the binoculars, but he kept peering through them. "It doesn't look like there's any damage to the front."

My phone buzzed.

Where r yous guy?

"It's Evan," I said.

I was typing out my response when Lander said, "There he is."

I looked across the street and sure enough Evan stood on the sidewalk, swinging his head in exaggerated left and right arcs as if it had come loose on his neck. Lander started the Jeep and I deleted my text, replacing it with *We'll be right there.*

By the time we'd made it through the light, U-turning to reach Evan, he had sat down on the sidewalk and looked like he was about to lie down. I put down my window as we stopped.

"Hey, Evan. Get in." He looked up at me, surprised.

"Jess? What are you doing here?" Oh boy. I jumped out of the car and opened the back door.

"Evan, come on." Behind us a car honked as I reached out to pull him to his feet. "Get in." He heaved himself up and fell headfirst across the back seat. I slammed the door and hopped in the front.

"Hey, guys. Thanks. I wasn't sure how I was going to get home." His *s*'s were running together and the smell of alcohol, perfume and rancid grease radiated off him like a putrid fog. I reopened my window.

"How'd it go in there?" asked Lander as he slowed down to turn right. Evan slouched loosely, looking as if his bones had turned to gelatin.

"Good! Good," he said carefully, working to control his tongue. "I was right there with Dick." He flopped against the door as Lander turned the corner.

"You locked the doors, right?" I asked, looking over to Lander. He hit the button and they all locked with a click.

"That's great," said Lander as we pretended Evan wasn't struggling to right himself. "Were you able to find anything out?"

"Oh, yeah," said Evan. "I talked to him and everything." Oh boy. "He's a nice guy, ya know? He bought me a coupla drinks."

I turned in my seat. "Were you able to find out where he was last night? Or Thursday night?"

Evan squinted at me, probably trying to bring both of me into one image.

"We talked about a lot of things," he said, furrowing his forehead in concentration. "You know, I just love his commercial." He settled back and cleared his throat. "Have you been injured in an accident?" We'd stopped at a light and Lander turned to look at me.

"We'd better find out if he learned anything tonight because by tomorrow he's not going to remember."

"Call 1-800-THE-DICK!" Evan finished triumphantly

throwing an arm up in the air and colliding with the roof. "Ow." He brought his hand down and stared at his fingers.

"So, what else did you guys talk about?" I asked.

"Yeah, we talked about shtuff. But ya know, it was loud in there. Like, really loud. Hard to hear. And he was busy with the girls some." He reached over and gave Lander a poke in the shoulder. "You know. You know what I mean?"

"Yeah, buddy. I know what you mean."

"Oh, for God's sake," I said, turning around. "We sat here all night for this? For nothing?"

"It's not for nothing," Evan said, sounding injured. "I found out he's cheating on his wife. Er, your wife. Your ex or whatever."

We cruised in silence for a minute, trying to work out how that helped us. Or if it did.

"You're sure about that?" Lander finally asked. "As in more than getting a few dances at a club?"

"Well, I think he was gonna meet up with one of them after they got off." He laughed. "That came out wrong. Sorry, Jesh. You wouldn't believe in there..." He trailed off, staring out the window.

"Here, do you want a Big Mac?" I asked, handing him the bag.

He opened the bag and stared in. "That's nice. You're so nice. And you look nice. Those girls were pretty, but..." He reached a hand into the bag, trying to fish out the Big Mac. "But the paint. They have so mush paint on 'em. I can't remember who Dick's going out with." His forehead furrowed in thought, then cleared as he managed to snag the sandwich. "Big Mac. No, that's not her name. But he's goin' out with one of 'em. Tonight, I think. It sounds like he's cheating."

It sounded like he was cheating to me too, but did that have anything to do with someone trying to kill Lander? It sounded more like someone ought to be trying to kill Dick DeLuca.

CHAPTER TEN

I slept late Sunday morning. Well, late for me. I would have stayed in bed even longer, but by seven thirty Addie was lying beside me, licking her paws in a way that she knows drives me crazy.

"Knock it off," I muttered as she slurped at a paw, the wet, rhythmic noise loud in the still of the morning. I flipped onto my other side, turning my back to her and pulling the pillow over my exposed ear. There was a slight pause before she resumed. With a groan, I gave up and rolled over. She abandoned the paw and thumped her tail against the bed, shoving a nose into my face and rewarding me with a small snort. It's a good thing she's my favorite dog. I reached out a hand to rub her belly.

I thought about last night. Had we learned anything? Not really. So Dick DeLuca was messing around on his wife. Maybe. I wasn't really sure how reliable Evan's observations were, and I couldn't see how that would have anything to do with someone wanting to kill Lander.

Outside of the fact that I was really worried about William, I kind of just wanted to move on from this drama. There are times you get mixed up in things that you have to deal with, and then there are other times where it's really not your fight. This felt more like that.

I knew Evan would likely be out of commission for much of the day, and that was okay with me. I really didn't feel like chasing any more people around, asking lame questions and getting nowhere. Frankly, if Lander didn't know who was out to get him, I wasn't sure why he thought Evan and I would have any clue.

I spent a relaxing morning with Addie. We went for a long walk before it got too hot, followed by a leisurely breakfast and a pot of coffee. Wondering how Frances was doing with her chickens, I made a trip over there to check on them as well. This time, I left Addie at home.

When I arrived, I found Frances out back, much as I suspected I would. She stood next to a wooden chicken coop, her head bent as if eavesdropping on the inhabitants. She looked up as I came around the corner.

"Jessica! How lovely to see you."

"Hi, Frances. I wanted to see how the first night with your chickens went."

She motioned me towards a small gate near the corner of the house. I lifted a latch, swung it open and made my way in, astonished at how much they'd accomplished after I'd left. The fencing was impressive. Six-foot posts supported three horizontal boards with mesh wire stretched between. The weave was small enough to keep predators out and chicken heads in. This did not look like a temporary hobby. I could not imagine what my mother was going to have to say about this.

"This is amazing," I said, turning in a circle. "And look at this coop. It's so cute." The coop was adorable. A tiny wooden building perched on small stilts stood in the shade of an oak tree that had been enclosed by Rafael's fencing. Painted white, it looked like a Cape Cod house for tiny people. A ramp ran down from one side to an enclosed run that extended under the house itself. Screened windows let air in from both sides. Frances looked pleased at my reaction. "I can't believe you got guys got this all done yesterday."

"Well, Rafael's son came over later to help finish it up," she admitted. "I guess I should have made sure it was set up before the chickens arrived, but it all just happened so fast."

"Speaking of," I said, "where are the chickens? In the coop?" I moved towards a window and leaned my head closer, much as she had been doing when I arrived. When I didn't hear anything from within, I tried to peer into the dim interior.

"Yes. I'm supposed to keep them in there for at least twenty-four hours," she said. "But it's just so hard. I want to see them."

"You know my mother's going to freak out when she sees all this, right?"

She looked slightly uneasy. "Well, it has turned out to be a bit more of an undertaking than I expected." She took a couple steps back, poked a toe at some loose straw and looked around. I was going to say something about how much work this seemed, but she'd been pretty touchy about that yesterday, so I refrained. Still, I couldn't help but notice how tired she looked. Normally when I saw her, we were going out to dinner or the symphony or maybe a museum. Today in the bright light, the signs of age that were less noticeable in the kind lights of the indoors were more pronounced. My heart turned with a thud, not wanting to think about Frances aging.

"What time are they getting home?" I asked.

"Probably late this afternoon," she said. "It's entirely possible they won't notice this. At any rate, what does it matter? I live here too." She sounded slightly defensive and I felt a rush of protectiveness.

"It looks like you've got a great setup here," I said. "But honestly, I don't know the first thing about raising chickens."

"I don't either," she said. "But they're having a backyard chicken class next weekend at the feed store, and Rafael knows quite a bit about them."

I hoped my mother wouldn't ruin this for her, because in spite of looking tired, she had an air of excitement that had been missing for a while. We made our way inside, leaving our shoes at the door. I texted Evan while Frances went to wash up, wondering if he was ambulatory yet. It was several minutes before he responded, and judging from his terse answers, he was definitely feeling poorly. He said that Lander was at the hospital with William. And that was about all he had to say.

When Frances came back, she asked me how my evening had gone. I glossed over pretty much all of it. I said I'd hung out with Evan and a friend of his, but mostly it had been rather boring. All true. I'd wanted to spend more time with her, but I could tell she was tired and she seemed distracted, so I made my excuses and stood to go.

"Let me know if you have any trouble with my mother," I told her as we headed for the front door.

"I'm sure I can handle your mother," she said, leaning in to give me a hug. I could feel sharp bones under her shirt, and the hand she laid on my arm as she stepped back was pale and thin and reminded me of how William's had looked as Lander had held it so tenderly Friday night. Who would attack an elderly person? What kind of sick individual would lash out at someone so vulnerable? The thought of anyone ever hurting Frances twisted my guts, and I realized that I couldn't just let this go. I wasn't the one who'd hurt William, but I had left him alone.

Once home, I wandered around my house with an uneasy feeling that left me restless and tense. I didn't feel like making dog biscuits. I didn't feel like cleaning or doing any paperwork or anything else that might have been productive. But I couldn't think of anything I did want to do. I texted Evan again, hoping for a better update on William, but he said that it sounded like there was no change yet. I wasn't sure if that was good or bad. It was probably bad.

I finally settled on my patio with a bottle of sparkling water and a book. Addie roamed my small yard, sniffing her way around the edges before settling down next to me. I hadn't been out there five minutes when I heard my doorbell ring, followed by a pounding on the door that made me think it was Larry. I stayed where I was. I might not know what I wanted to do, but I did know what I didn't want to do—spend time with my next-door neighbor. I sat quietly, shushing Addie as she gave a low growl in her throat.

The ringing finally stopped and I breathed a small sigh of relief. Until I heard Larry's back door open.

"Hey, you over there?" he asked. I froze, not making a sound. Unfortunately, Addie didn't have that kind of self-restraint, and she let out a short sharp bark. "Oh good, you're there." I didn't say anything. "I know you're there. Your dog is never out unless you're there." I could hear him dragging something across his patio, and suddenly his head popped up over the top of the wall. "How come you didn't answer?" he asked.

I sighed. "Maybe I don't feel like talking," I said.

"Okay, whatever. Hey, let me ask you something," I didn't say anything. "Are you paying attention? This is important."

"What, Larry?"

"Do you think I'm attractive?" I thought about the vision in the Speedo yesterday. What could you honestly say to that?

"What's this about?" I picked up my phone, hoping it would ring and give me a reason to end this conversation before it went any farther.

"I'm looking for an honest opinion here." I glanced over, the expression on his face more circumspect than I would have ever expected.

"Yeah, I don't know. I mean, I guess you're fine." I punched a finger at my phone. *Ding, dang it.*

"Fine? Fine is what girls say when it's not fine," he persisted. "Unless you mean fine! Like, that boy is so fine!" I picked up my sparkling water, running a finger along the condensation beads. "So, which is it? Fine, like not fine? Or fine, like baby let's go?"

"Larry, I don't really know what we're talking about here."

He blew out a gust of breath. "I'm asking you, as a girl, as my neighbor, if you think I'm attractive. It's not a hard question." He stood peering over the fence, perspiration glistening on his baby-round face. Truth be told, if you could divorce his face and body from his personality, he might be okay, but since you couldn't do that, it was going to take a special woman to find him overall appealing.

"Larry, you're fine."

"Quit saying that. This is important to me."

"Why don't you give me a little more context as to where this is coming from?" I was moderately sure I was going to be sorry I asked, but I didn't want to have to actually address the question either.

"I had a date last night."

"Yes, you mentioned that yesterday while you were sunbathing."

"Right? I did everything I could to, you know, make myself hot for the lucky lady." He tapped a finger on the top of the wall.

"And your date didn't go well?"

"You could say that. She had this look on her face all evening, like, I don't know. Like, she smelled something bad or something, you know?" He took a minute to drop his head and sniff loudly in the direction of his armpits. He popped back up. "I showered. I wore deodorant. I wore a clean shirt. I'm pretty sure I smelled fine. But her face was like this—" He pulled his lips up above his top teeth, looking like a cross between a horse reaching for an apple and a villainous contestant on *The Bachelor*.

I couldn't help but laugh. "Maybe that's just how she was," I said. "Where'd you meet her anyway?"

He hesitated. "Online," he finally said. "On a dating app."

"Okay, so she wasn't the one. Pick someone else."

He sighed. "She wasn't the first one this has happened with. I was hoping you could help me fix whatever they think is wrong."

"Larry, I'm sure it's just a matter of finding someone you're compatible with."

"Is it my belly? Cuz you know, I can't really help this." The way his head bobbled made me think he was grabbing and jiggling his beer belly between his hands.

"You could maybe drink less beer," I suggested.

"That's not that helpful," he said.

"Don't you have any sisters who could help you with this? Or maybe some friends?"

"No. That's why I'm asking you. You think I want to be here debasing myself like this?"

I thought back to all the things that I found repellent. "Fine. Okay, don't burp. Don't scratch your butt. Sit up in your chair, not all slouched over. Actually pay attention to what your date is talking about."

He stared at me. "I don't do those things. Geez. You're making me sound like a slob or something." He stepped down from his perch and went inside, shutting the door with a bang.

Somehow I frittered away the rest of the day and was happy when Monday morning rolled around. Like a fussy toddler, I found comfort in my routine. I checked in with Evan midmorning for news of William. He said that he'd dropped

Lander off at the hospital on his way to work and hadn't heard from him. I guessed nothing had changed yet. I burned off some nervous energy by taking my dog-walking clients on super-charged walks and bestowing lots of extra belly rubs and head kisses. By the time I got home from my last dog, the magic of the routine was taking hold and I felt more relaxed.

At seven, my phone rang.

"Omigod, get this!" Evan said before I even said hello.

"What?" He sounded more giddy than distressed, so I pushed away the anxiety that had shot through me when I'd seen his name on my phone.

"There's a fan club meeting slash dinner Wednesday night!"

I took a moment to process this. "A fan club meeting for Lander?"

"Who else would be I be talking about? And there's a dinner! He got an email today, and we talked about whether he should attend," he said.

"Wait, so Lander is comfortable going out in public to this? I thought he was trying to stay in hiding."

"Well, yeah, but this is going to be a big group and he thinks it'll give us a chance to check out that crazy fan club lady."

"Where's it going to be?" I asked.

"There's an address on the invitation. It could be that Nell lady's house or maybe one of the other members. We're not sure." I wondered if Evan would sign up for membership while he was there. Maybe they had Lander Jones posters for sale. I could imagine his new decor now. "Do you want to come? It's gonna be great!"

Being that my social calendar was essentially empty, I said yes.

Tuesday was a repeat of Monday, baking biscuits in the morning, walking my dog buddies and spending quality time with my own four-legged furball. It was late afternoon, while I was trying to talk myself into contacting the insurance company to finally deal with my car situation but was instead having a wild game of tug-of-war with Addie, when my phone buzzed. The number wasn't in my contacts, but the texter identified himself as Lander.

He was at the hospital with William and wanted to know if I could pick him up. It was a real toss-up between talking to the insurance company and making a trip to the hospital, but in the end he won me over by telling me he'd wait outside for me.

I live pretty close to the medical center, so it was only a matter of minutes before I was driving slowly down the street, horns blaring at me as I crept along in the right lane. I finally spotted him breaking through a crowd of medical scrubs as he sprinted towards my yellow subcompact.

"Sorry and thanks," he said, knocking into my shoulder as he slid into the small space.

"No problem," I said. "How's William doing? Any improvement?"

He clicked his seat belt and leaned back. "Thankfully, yes. He seems to be having more brain activity. The doctors sound more hopeful than they have." His voice broke and I glanced over, a flood of relief washing over me.

"That's great news!"

"Yeah, for sure," he said, but now he sounded a little more guarded. "Don't get me wrong, this is great news, but they told me that he's not out of the woods yet." He leaned his head on the headrest. "It's just so hard to see him like that."

My heart gave a pinch. "It's great that you've been with him," I said.

"They've got him in a private room now, so I feel better about that." I wondered how he'd managed to keep the police at bay, but maybe they weren't as dogged as I'd always assumed. I mean, you watch any network police show and it seems like this would be the kind of case that warranted senior detectives, a fancy crime lab and a district attorney that had charges already drawn up and waiting for the perp. Whoever that might be. "But, hey, I was thinking. I feel like it's time to pay Seth a visit. I haven't talked to him in a while, and that call from Annalise was weird. I don't know. I need to figure this out, and I think he's somehow tied up in it. Would you be up for a ride?"

"Sure. Do you want to wait for Evan to get off work?"

"Actually, I think it might be better if it was just us. Or maybe you." Evan was not going to like this.

Hearing Lander's plan, I wasn't sure I liked this either. He thought if I showed up at Seth's door wearing something flouncy, I could pretend to be looking for someone else. He was pretty sure Seth would open the door and invite me in, and I could work my magic to see if he had any kind of alibi. This sounded highly unlikely to me—in fact, it sounded downright stupid, but I wasn't a guy, and Seth wasn't my friend, so maybe Lander's perspective was better. On the bright side, the insurance company would be closed by the time I got home, allowing me to postpone that misery for another day.

I turned around and headed to my house to get fixed up. Lander sat on the couch while Addie settled in two feet away from him, preparing to stare him down. It was one of her favorite things. I was glad I'd been able to bring her a new person to play with.

Upstairs, I really wasn't sure how slutty I needed to make myself. Lander had meant slutty, right? Being that it was only late afternoon, I felt a little weird putting on club clothes. In the end, I found a short ruffled baby-blue skirt in the jumbled and rarely viewed part of my closet that I paired with a cropped white top. I fished some dangly earrings from my jewelry box and teased my hair unnaturally high, tying my hot pink scarf around with a big bow on the side of my head. Checking myself out in the mirror, I groaned. I looked like the '80s. Were the '80s sexy? It didn't look like it to me, but I was still remembering how washed out I'd looked in my black clothes the other night. At least my scrapes were healing and fading, and I no longer looked like I'd been dragged down the road.

Lander stared at me as I came down the stairs. His face was inscrutable and I was getting ready to flee back the way I'd come and try again when he nodded slowly.

"Yes. Yes. That's perfect."

"Really? I feel ridiculous."

"No, seriously. He will love this sexy kitten vibe." I turned to go change. "No, wait, I'm not kidding, it's perfect." It took a couple more minutes before I was mollified and we headed out.

"So tell me about your friend," I said as I pointed the lemon drop north towards the Heights. Apparently, he lived pretty close to Lander, which made it seem odd that they hadn't seen each other in months.

"Seth and I have been friends since junior high. We're alike in a lot of ways—mostly we don't really conform well. Or at least we thought we were badass nonconformists back then. He's really into video games, game design, stuff like that. He's an IT guy, or I guess he was. I feel bad that I didn't know he was out of work."

"Sounds dumb, but could his being out of work give him any reason to kill you?"

"I don't see how that would help him at all."

"Maybe he thinks you're leaving him all your money?"

"I don't know why he'd think that."

"Is he married? Seeing anyone? Did you ever steal one of his girlfriends and he's just now getting around to killing you over it?"

Lander laughed lightly. "Not married. Not seeing anyone as far as I know. And no, I never stole any of his girlfriends. It wasn't like we had a ton of girls coming around. Maybe I haven't made this point strongly enough, but we were total dorks."

"Well, who wasn't a dork growing up?" I asked. I tried to push away the memories of my own coltish arms and legs that seemed to stick out at odd angles compared to my classmates, the braces, the unsuccessful attempts at makeup. Ugh.

We were nearing the Heights and Lander gave me directions, both of us reflexively checking for tails. I had the feeling I was going to be at least partially paranoid long after this ended. He pointed a finger towards a house on our right. "It's right there. He lives in the garage apartment just behind."

I drove slowly past, trying to get a look at where Seth lived. The front house was a battered bungalow, rattier than its neighbors, old siding well past the need for paint and moving quickly to replacement stage. The yard was overgrown and some kind of invasive vine seemed to be making its way up the front of the house and creeping along the side. Junk was scattered through the dark patches of yard, and I felt a desire to keep driving.

"Is this where you lived with Annalise?" I asked. I mean, honestly, if some guy brought me here to live, I don't think it would have gone well either.

"No," Lander snorted. "Oh, Lord no. Annalise would have never lived here. I mean, our apartment wasn't the greatest thing, but..." He trailed off. "Yeah, Seth *is* kind of roughing it these days." It sounded as if he was really looking at it for the first time. As I continued around the block, I noticed him get his notebook out of his bag. I'm not a writer, but if I was, I would surely situate a murder in this setting.

We went around the block two more times before I pulled to a stop one house up. The garage apartment was only partially visible from the street, but we'd established that Seth's truck was parked in a tight space between two thin metal poles underneath. We couldn't see the front of it to determine if there was any damage. I'd have to check that out when I got closer. The entire edifice seemed to lean to the right, and I wondered about structural integrity. It seemed like the additional weight of an extra person might bring the whole thing down.

"Okay," I said, trying to delay. "What exactly am I trying to find out? If he ran us off the road? If he's got a reason to kill you?"

Lander had put his window down and was slouched on his spine, his head barely level with the door. Between the way he hunched everywhere we went and the fact that he was sleeping on Evan's couch, he was going to be looking for a good chiropractor if he lived.

"Honestly, I'm not sure you'll get anything more than a look at his car, but just see what you can find out. Do you know what you're going to say?"

"No. Not really." Considering this had been his plan, I'd have thought he would have had some suggestions. For the first time in my life, I regretted never having taken an improv class. I dialed Lander's phone so that he could listen in on the open line. Originally he wanted me to record the conversation, but in the interest of safety, we decided the open line would be better. He connected and listened as I put my phone in my purse to test how well he could hear. He said it was a little muffled, so I opened the side pocket as wide as I could. Even being muffled, I would make sure he could hear my screams if I needed help. I'd also put my pepper spray in my purse. No telling how this might turn out.

Before I got out of the car, I popped a stick of gum in my mouth and gave Lander a toothy smile. "Wish me luck," I said.

I started cautiously down the narrow drive, feeling skittish. Taking a few deep breaths, I straightened up, fluffed my hair, and tried to get more into character. Whatever character that might be.

The garage apartment was up a rickety set of stairs. Before starting up, I glanced around as if unsure I was in the right place. Poking my head into the dim garage area, I could see front-end damage on the black pickup. My heart rate zoomed and I considered running back to the car and taking off. Then I thought of William and I grabbed hold of the wooden railing and bounced up the steps.

CHAPTER ELEVEN

After only three steps, I could feel the stairs shaking with my weight, so I slowed down and proceeded more slowly. I glanced towards the street but couldn't see the lemon drop or Lander. At the tiny landing, I paused before knocking gently on the peeling wooden door.

I didn't hear anything from inside and I wondered if maybe he wasn't home. Just as I was raising my hand to knock again, the door flew open. If this was Seth, he really wasn't what I'd been expecting. For some reason, I had pictured him as a giant teddy bear kind of guy, sitting around in old sweats, eating chips from a family-sized bag and playing video games. This guy was medium height but pin thin. His skin was pale as if he never went outside, and a shaggy head of hair hung over black-framed glasses. I nearly forgot myself and asked if he was Seth.

Catching myself just in time, I pasted a big smile on my face and tilted my head with a confused little twist. "Oh, hi!" I said, giving my hair a twirl on my finger. "I'm not sure, but..." I looked out over the railing. "I'm supposed to be meeting my friend Nicki?"

He stood and stared at me, and I feared he was about to shut the door in my face. "Uh, yeah. I think you're in the wrong place."

"Oh." I poked my lower lip out in what I hoped was an adorable pout but I feared might more closely resemble a koi looking for a fish pellet. "I was supposed to meet her, and I thought she said this was the address?" I scrambled for a way to carry this conversation. Damn that lack of improv training.

"Sorry, but yeah. I don't think you're in the right place." He leaned on the door and dropped his head like I was boring him.

I gave an inspired little cough and patted my chest. "Do you think I could get a drink of water? I have a little...tickle." His eyes followed my fingers to my chest, and I circled one finger around the top button of my shirt. His mouth opened and he made a small guttural sound as if he believed one of his porn fantasies was about to come true.

"Yeah, sure. Come on in." He stepped aside, ushering me into the small apartment. This, at least, was much as I'd imagined it would be. Essentially a studio apartment, it looked more like somewhere a college kid would crash than a place where a thirtysomething-year-old man would live. He kicked a white fast-food bag out of the way and ushered me in. I moved several feet into the small space while he raced around, gathering trash.

"Sorry for the mess," he said. "It normally doesn't look like this." He gave a nervous laugh as if waiting to be struck down. "Okay, maybe it does. I don't get a lot of visitors."

"Oh, don't worry about it!" I trilled. "It's fine. It's kind of cozy." I glanced around, hoping to see something that would be relevant, but honestly, this was tougher than those eye-spy puzzles. A double bed was pushed against the far wall, and this side of the room was set up as a living area. A stained sectional stretched in an L shape around an oversized coffee table where an expensive-looking laptop sat open. Scattered over the table were drawings and sketches, and I moseyed over to take a look.

Seth had cleared a swath to a kitchenette that stretched against the far wall and was trying to wrestle his armload of trash into a giant black garbage bag.

"Sorry, I'll get your water in just a second," he said.

"Oh, no hurry," I said, picking up a sketchbook. It was open to a pencil drawing, a roughed-out comic strip fight scene. A man in a dark overcoat was backed against a brick wall as a menacing figure brandishing a pistol advanced. I flipped a few pages, seeing the overcoat guy in multiple predicaments: a car nearly veering off the road, a chase scene across an open field. I'd just turned the page and spotted an owl, much like the owl Nell had on her poster, when Seth materialized next to me and snatched the book out of my hands.

"Sorry, I don't like people looking at that," he said, his voice harder than when he'd thought I was here for his fantasy.

"Oh, sure, sorry!" I said, reverting to button touching, my finger tracing a soothing circle. "I don't like people looking at my things either, but I couldn't help it. These are amazing! Are you an artist?"

His energy ticked down a notch and he swatted at a section of shaggy hair that had fallen over his glasses. "This is just something I'm working on. I don't know that it'll go anywhere."

"Like anime?" I asked. "My friend Nicki's been trying to get me into that. I just don't really know anything about it."

Seth headed back towards the kitchenette, the sketchbook tucked firmly under his arm. "Not really. It's more like a treatment for a video game I'm working on." He shoved the book into a drawer, then opened a cabinet and pulled down a water-spotted glass. "This okay? I don't have bottled."

"That'd be great," I said as he turned on the faucet with a creak. A burst of air gushed from the pipe and I jumped.

"It always does that," he said, filling the glass to the top with tepid water. I tried not to notice the visible particles floating around. He handed me the chunky water and stared at me expectantly. I tilted the glass to my mouth and let the water touch my upper lip.

"My little brother loves video games," I said, glancing around the room. "What's your game called? I'll buy it for him."

He stuck a finger in his ear and twisted it around. His nose wrinkled and he slumped over to the couch, plopping down in front of his computer. "Yeah. It's not even close to retail ready," he said.

I sidled over to the long side of the sectional and perched myself on the edge, trying not to crush anything that might be lurking under the clothes that were piled there. He hadn't kicked me out yet, and I was doing everything I could to think of something to say. I took another fake sip of water.

"Are you a graphic artist or something?" I asked. "I've always thought it would be so cool to be a freelancer of some kind. You know, like, be your own boss! How awesome is that?"

He leaned forward and poked a key on the keyboard. "I guess you could say I'm a freelance something. I'm actually between jobs right now."

"Aww, well, I'm sure a talented guy like you won't have any trouble finding something even better." I fluttered my eyelashes, but he wasn't even looking at me.

"I don't know about that," he said. "I had a little trouble with my last boss. It's not like I'm gonna get a good recommendation or anything."

I flashed back to my last boss that I'd worked for at Astor Oil. You could say I'd had a little trouble with my last boss too. "Omigod! That happened to me! You would not believe this woman I was working for!" I seemed to be channeling every stereotypical dumb blonde actress I'd ever seen.

"What happened with that?" he asked, reclining against the cushions. "You get fired?"

I cast my eyes down as if I was embarrassed to say. "It wasn't good," I hedged. "She was a nightmare." I looked at him, hoping I looked empathetically sad. "Did you?"

He chewed his lower lip, then picked up a beer can that I hadn't noticed buried in the papers on the table. He took a long swallow. "Yeah. They tried to say I was stealing from the company, but it was bullshit." He took another drink.

"How could you steal anything if you're a graphic artist?" I set my glass of water down and leaned back awkwardly, placing one hand behind me and pushing my chest out a little. It seemed as if he had no actual control over his eyes.

"I'm not a graphic artist," he said to my boobs. "I'm an IT guy."

"So, what? Did you take a power cord home?" I giggled at my own wit and twisted a lock of hair with my free hand. I could feel my bow starting to slip. I could also feel my skirt inching up, and I had to fight the urge to tug it down to a decent level.

"No, I had to buy some software for a project and they said it hadn't been authorized. Like I said, it was bullshit." In spite of his words, he looked away and took another drink.

"Well, that sounds crazy," I said. I ran a finger along the edge of my skirt, flicking at an imaginary lint ball. The edge fluttered up, catching his attention and he fixated now on my legs. "I mean, I don't know you at all or anything, but even I can see you wouldn't do anything like that." I leaned forward then and held my hand out. "By the way, I'm Janie. What's your name?"

His eyes moved from my legs to my face and I was afraid I'd ruined his fantasy. Should I have called myself something else? Honey? Sapphire? Sweet Rose?

"Hey, I'm Seth," he said, staring at my hand before taking it lightly in his sweaty one. He gave it one limp pump and then dropped it. Geez, someone needed to teach this guy how to shake properly before he went on his next job interview. I smiled anyway.

"It's really nice to meet you. I might have come to the wrong place, but sometimes we end up in the right place even if it's the wrong place. You know what I mean?" I crossed my legs, running a finger along my thigh. He was getting a glazed look on his face and I wondered how much he'd had to drink.

"Uh, what?" he asked as he realized he wasn't following me at all.

I giggled. "Oh, I'm just rambling. I just feel really comfortable with you. I'd love to hear more about your work."

This was clearly the wrong direction and he shook his head and used a finger to push his glasses up his nose in a practiced move.

"Yeah, there's nothing really to talk about. Anyway. So, sorry your friend doesn't live here."

"Oh, no! I'm just glad someone so nice was here." I realized Lander was listening to all this drivel and I felt a rush of heat race up my neck to my cheeks. "Um. Anyway." I fiddled with the bow in my hair again, looking down and trying to see if there was anything else on the table that could help determine if he was trying to kill Lander. "I'm sure you'll be fine with whatever you do," I said. There were a bunch of drawings and I wished I could snap a picture on my phone, but it didn't look like I would get that chance. "I'm sure your family and friends are supportive, right?"

He stood up, realizing this probably wasn't going to end up with me dropping my tiny top and flouncy skirt into the piles of litter on the floor. I stood too, fidgeting with my purse strap. I really hadn't learned anything. I started to move to the door.

"Is that your truck downstairs?" I asked.

"Yeah, why?"

"It looks like you got in a wreck or something?"

He reached the door and opened it, focusing on me as if he hadn't really been paying attention to me at all before. "How'd you notice that?"

"I just noticed. Like, I was looking for my friend's car 'cause I wasn't sure I was in the right place, and I saw, you know, the damage."

He stared at me now, not blinking behind his lenses. "Not that it's any of your business, but I got in a wreck the other night. It was stupid. I ran a stop sign. Now on top of everything else I'm trying to deal with some bitch's insurance company."

"Wow. I'm sorry to hear that. I guess when it rains it pours, right?" I slipped past him onto the rickety landing. I wanted him to close the door behind me, because all of a sudden I was afraid he was going to shove me down the stairs. "Well, thanks so much for the water! And good luck. I'm sure everything will work out."

I edged to the railing and grabbed the splintery board, holding on tightly as I made my way down the steps. I turned when I got to the bottom to give him a little pinkie wave, but he was already closing the door. Letting out a deep breath, I let the fake smile drop and trotted up the drive.

There was a soft click as Lander unlocked the car. I slipped into the driver's seat and threw my purse into the back seat. He swiped a finger across his phone, obviously disconnecting our call.

"You did great," he said as I turned to look at him. I could feel the red return to my cheeks. I felt similar to when you tried to recall a drunken message that you'd left for an ex on his machine. Rambling, embarrassing, incoherent. That's how I felt about this. And Lander had been online for the live performance.

"I feel ridiculous," I said, starting the engine.

"Why? You did great." Out of the corner of my eye, I could

see him looking at me closely. "You did. Seriously, that was perfect with Seth."

"Well, I guess the only thing we found out is that his truck is messed up." I shifted into drive and we moved down the street. "He said he was in an accident, but I don't know. He has a big vehicle and it has front-end damage. I mean, bam. I think we might have found who tried to kill us."

Lander sighed. "I know. I didn't want it to be Seth." He sounded defeated, and who could blame him?

"But why?" I asked. "I mean, he's your best friend. It's hard to imagine. And just playing the devil's advocate here, but maybe he *was* in a wreck that had nothing to do with what happened to us. He did say he ran a stop sign and is dealing with someone else's insurance. Maybe there's a way we could check that out?"

We'd stopped at a light and I glanced over. Lander was looking out the window away from me, but I could feel the misery wafting off of him. I felt helpless.

"Lander." I reached out and touched his arm. "It might not be him. Right?" I flashed to the sketches on Seth's coffee table. I wasn't familiar enough with Lander's books to know if those reflected his characters, but that owl looked remarkably like the one on Nell's big poster. I was going to have to tell him about that. I reached up and pulled the bow out of my hair, feeling as if I was wearing a clown suit to a funeral.

"Why don't we go back to Evan's? What time is it? He should be home soon. We'll get some dinner or something. Unless there's somewhere else you want to go?"

He mumbled assent and we rode in miserable silence to Evan's house. I'd been hoping Evan would be home from work already, but the driveway was empty. I pulled to the curb and we climbed out of the car. From across the street, I heard a door slam and Evan's neighbor, Kip, sailed towards us.

"Jessie! Honey, where have you been? I have not seen you in

the longest of ages." Lander ducked his head and moved towards the front porch. He was inside before Kip made it across the street, and I could hear Henry's excited yelps of greeting.

"Hey, Kip. How are you?"

"Who is your delightful friend? Someone has been holding out," he said, grabbing me by the upper arms and air-kissing both of my cheeks. He stepped back and looked me up and down. "Although before we get to that, my God, what has happened in your life that you have come to this?" He fluttered a perfectly manicured hand up and down. "If this isn't a cry for help, I don't know what is."

I'm not sure how the universe works, but somehow, somewhere, someone seems to get a kick out of me looking my absolute worst every time I run into this perfectly put-together man. I sighed. I mean, how could you ever really justify the outfit I had on?

"It's a long story," I said. He was still staring. His hand reached out and touched my teased hair.

"I think I saw this in *Pretty in Pink* during a throwback movie marathon. I just adored that movie, didn't you? The way she made her own clothes, although..." His lips stretched into a grimace. "That was the '80s and she was in high school. Not that you aren't adorable, but honey, this really is not your look."

I tugged at the bottom of my cropped top and sighed.

"I know," I said. "It's not my most shining moment. But enough about me. How's your business going?" Kip made decorative pillows, although I still wondered how it was possible to actually make enough money from decorative pillows to support yourself. I was having a hard enough time with my dog biscuit business, and dog biscuits are something you need to buy more often than every ten years.

"Amazing!" he said, clapping his hands together. "In fact, I only have a moment—you would not believe how busy I am. I don't even know how this happened, but I am a hit in Japan right now!"

"Really?"

"Yes! Apparently some pop star over there ordered some of my pillows and used them in a photo shoot and the next thing I know, everyone has to have them! It has been a whirlwind. I may even have to go over there to find a manufacturer."

"Wow, that is amazing. I'm really happy for you."

"But back to this man you've been hiding. I saw the way he skulked away there. Who is this and what is the mystery surrounding him?"

"Oh, he's just a friend of Evan's who's staying with him for a few days."

"Sister, you don't kid a kidder. I can tell this is not that." His hand swept in delicate circles towards Evan's house. "Your friend lives like he's a fish in a bowl. Then this little hottie shows up and now there's not a one-inch gap anywhere on those windows." He tilted his head, staring at me. "Tell your Uncle Kip the truth. Is your friend finally coming out of the closet?"

"Sorry, no. Evan is not gay. This really is just a friend who's staying with him for a few days." I looked away as I said it. It wasn't like I was lying, but it wasn't like I was telling the whole truth either.

"Well, you're probably right that he's not gay. His vibe is really just... not that. Although some of the most phobic are closet cases, you know."

We both turned at the sound of a car turning the corner. It was Evan. "Speak of the demon," he said, moving away. "It was wonderful to see you! Don't be a stranger. Come see me and we'll catch up properly. And please, don't do this outfit again." He was still clutching his chest as he ran across the street.

It was ironic in a way—I really liked Evan's neighbor, Kip. He was funny and creative and we'd really hit it off when we met.

And then there was my neighbor, Larry. He was none of that. I found him boorish, gross and annoying. But Evan had met him, and they seemed to get along fine. It was like we needed to do a neighbor swap.

Evan pulled into the driveway and got out of his Jeep, looking surprised to see me.

"Hey, Jess. What's going on? Is everything okay?" He pulled a black laptop bag from the car and glanced towards the house. "Is Lander okay?" He never even noticed my outfit, for which I was thankful.

I gave him a two-minute rundown of our trip to Seth's and how that had turned out. I thought he'd be more upset that we'd gone without him, but it seemed that his frantic fan energy was giving way to a more genuine concern for Lander.

"Oh, man. That's rough," he said.

"And there's more," I said. "I didn't mention it to Lander yet, although he did hear our conversation, so I'm sure he's wondering about it, but Seth had a bunch of drawings on his table that I'm guessing are from Lander's books. He said he was working on a video game, and I think it's a video game featuring Lander's books."

"But Lander said he couldn't. He said he wasn't letting anyone have any creative whatever, control or I don't remember exactly. But he said he couldn't." Evan frowned and banged a hand on his bag. "Oh hey, before I forget. I brought you a present." He reached into a side pocket and brought out a mashed plastic-wrapped square. "We went to that Cajun place for lunch today. I know how much you love their yellow brownies."

"A blondie! I love these." I hadn't had one of these in months. And probably a good thing considering they're mostly sugar and butter. "Thanks, Evan." I clutched the greasy square in my hand, hoping I could slip it into my purse rather than split it three ways.

We made our way up creaking steps to the house where Henry waited behind the door. He bounced around Evan, leaping and jumping as high as his little legs could launch him.

"Hey, buddy! Hey, Henry. Did you miss me? Who's a good boy? Who's a good boy?" Henry finally noticed I was there too and gave me a cursory greeting before rocketing back to Evan. I was glad to see how happy he was with Evan. The beginning of this dog relationship had been a little iffy, and I hadn't been entirely sure Evan was cut out to be a good pet parent, but it seemed like it was working out now.

I could hear the shower running. Evan dropped his bag on the floor and headed for the kitchen. I trailed along after him.

"You know, maybe I'll take off," I said as Evan poked his head into the refrigerator. He glanced at me over his shoulder before grabbing a beer.

"You sure? You don't want to stay and have a beer with us? Maybe have dinner?" He rummaged around a junk drawer, looking for a bottle opener.

"I don't know," I said, keeping my voice low. "I get the feeling maybe Lander wants to be alone. I think this is all catching up to him."

Evan turned to me and I noticed how tired he looked. His lips were tight with tension, and for the first time I realized this was harder for him than I'd thought. Here I'd been thinking he was having a blast, at least as much as he could while worrying about William.

"How are you doing?" I asked. "Is everything going okay with having Lander here?"

He took me by the elbow and steered me to the living room.

"I feel terrible," he whispered, leaning his head close to mine. For a moment I thought he meant he was ill. Then he pointed towards the couch. "I have Lander Jones staying on that."

There was no way I could tell him that his couch was okay. I'd spent a night on it once and it was probably the most uncomfortable night I'd ever had. Okay, maybe I'd slept on worse surfaces when I was a kid, but kids have soft bones and can sleep anywhere. I wasn't even sure a kid would make it through the whole night without slipping off at least once onto the floor.

"Well." I looked at the blanket folded neatly on one cushion, a pillow resting on top. "Well, he doesn't have to stay here, you know. I mean, he has enough money that he could go anywhere."

"He feels safe here. He feels safe with me!" He looked at the couch. "But I know he's not comfortable. I offered him my room, but he won't take it. Why haven't I fixed up my guest bedroom yet?" A muscle spasmed near his jaw.

"Because you have a million things you need to spend your money on first, that's why," I pointed out, contemplating how much work this money pit of a house was going to entail when all was said and done. "And you don't know how long he's going to be here. I mean, he could end up going home tomorrow."

Because if Seth was the one trying to kill him, and we could prove that, then there would be no more reason for him to be roughing it at Evan's.

CHAPTER TWELVE

I'd decided to leave Lander in Evan's caring hands for the evening and head home to Addie, when I remembered something that might help Lander in the short term. I trotted back up the porch steps and rapped on the door.

Considering that I'd literally just left, I would have thought that Evan would open right up, but it took a couple of minutes of knocking on the door, Henry barking at full volume and me texting Evan before the sheet at the front window cracked and he peered out to check that it was, indeed, me.

"Look, I got an idea. Let me check with Frances. I don't know if she still has it, but she used to keep a fold-out mattress over there for me when I would hide out at her house. I mean, it was a zillion years ago, so she might have gotten rid of it, but if she still has it, it was fairly comfortable."

Evan lit up. "That would be so great! I could set it up in the guest room. Anything would be better than the couch." He looked so relieved that I immediately regretted not checking with Frances first. "Can you call her now?"

He stepped out on the porch with me and drummed his fingers on the rail while I made the call. Frances sounded slightly winded when she picked up, but she assured me she still had the mattress and that I was welcome to pick it up whenever I wanted. Evan was ecstatic and asked if I could go now. I wasn't sure the mattress would fit in my rental, so he gave me the keys to his Jeep and began laying all the seats down.

"Be careful," he said. "My car is bigger than what you're used to, and some of those lanes are pretty skinny getting over to your grandmother's."

The thing about Houston is that the roads are often narrow and pitted with holes, and drivers see nothing wrong with veering sideways to miss a pothole, heedless of anyone around them. I was nervous wreck by the time I pulled into my parents' driveway. I wasn't sure if my parents had discovered the chicken project yet or not. I knew they had gotten back from Dallas yesterday and was hoping to just grab the mattress from Frances and be on my merry way without getting sucked into the drama.

"Jessie." Too late. My mother descended the stone steps behind the main house and headed down the path directly towards me. Judging from her tone, I had to guess she'd noticed the chickens.

"Hi, Mom." A slight breeze riffled past, lifting the hem of my skirt far enough to make me wish I'd taken the time to change before coming over here. I slapped it down onto my thigh and stood awkwardly trying to hold it in place like a high school girl before the head mistress. My mother paused midstride, taking in my outfit and the Jeep, and I could tell this was throwing her off whatever course she'd been on. She shook her head as if to clear her thoughts.

"Ah, where is your car?" She looked me up and down again as if maybe she'd had a vision glitch. "And don't you think this outfit is a little...let's say young for you?"

I sighed. I felt the same defensiveness I'd felt when I was sixteen and it seemed like everything was a criticism. "My car is having some work done, and I didn't know I'd be stopping over here or I would have changed. Believe me."

"But if you hadn't been stopping over here, this is what you were wearing?"

"Okay, Mom. I'm not here to get feedback on my clothes. Did you and Dad have a good trip?"

She glanced away from me and towards the guesthouse. She reached up a hand and fiddled with a heavy gold earring, clearly agitated. "It was very nice. We had a lovely dinner. The clients' wives were charming, and I got to hear all about their successful children."

"I'm sure that was very nice," I said.

She crossed her arms, shoving her balled-up fists against her chest. "Do you know what your grandmother is doing?"

"Right this minute? I hope she's finding the thing I came over to pick up." I twirled Evan's keys on my finger. "Anyway, glad you made it back safely. Say hi to Dad." I began to edge away, but I could tell it was no use. She intended to vent whether her audience was willing or not.

"Were you aware that she was getting livestock?"

"Mom, it's chickens. It's not like she bought a herd of cattle."

"What are the neighbors going to think? What was she thinking?" She twisted her earring again. If she didn't watch it, she was going to rip that thing right through her lobe.

"You said you were worried about her. Well, I don't think you need to. She's found a new hobby. Good for her."

We walked up the path to the guesthouse. I hoped she wasn't going to harass Frances any more than I had the feeling she already had been.

"I don't even know if the city allows this."

The front door flew open and Frances stood there in another pair of overalls, her hair tied loosely with a floral scarf and rubber boots on her feet. Hearing my mother's comment, she shook her head slightly and turned around to tug at a gray canvas tote. It was bigger than I remembered—then again, I'd never been the one to lug it around. My grandmother had always had it set up and ready for my sleepovers whenever I needed a break or the comfort of her company.

"Here, let me get that," I said. I grabbed a handle and slid it across the threshold. It was heavy and awkward and I was glad that I'd brought Evan's Jeep. No way this would have fit in the lemon drop.

"What are you doing?" my mother asked, trepidation that we'd cooked up some new hell for her to contend with ringing in her voice.

"I need to borrow this," I said, grunting as I tried to pick it up so it wouldn't drag on the stones. "Here, can you open the back of the Jeep?" I wiggled the fingers that held the keys, and she reached over and took them.

"Is that the old camping mattress?" my mother asked. "What do you need with that?" She stopped dead in her tracks and I nearly ran into her. She turned and looked at my outfit again. Unfortunately, my cropped top was riding up and showing a great deal of midsection at this point. "Jessica. What is this?" She looked at me and the mattress. "Are you...do you...I mean..." She trailed off into distressed silence.

"Mom, can you open the door, please?" I humped around her inert form, the mattress banging off my hip as I walked.

"Jessica, do you need anything else right now?" asked Frances.

"No, this should do it," I said. I set the thing down and snatched the keys back from my mother, hitting the unlock button myself. Frances took the opportunity to trot around the corner of the guesthouse, back to her flock. I swung the door up and grabbed the mattress. "Mom? A little help?"

My mother, still clearly flustered, nevertheless bent her

knees like a proper lady and lifted an edge, helping me hoist the bulky thing into the back of Evan's Jeep.

"I know you like to be independent," my mother said as she took a step away. "But you would let us know if you were in any trouble, right? Or if you needed a little cash to help you through a difficult time? I know starting a business is complicated."

Seriously, what did she think? That I was turning tricks on an ancient camping mattress with middle-aged clients who missed the Molly Ringwald era?

"Mom, I'm fine. Evan needed to borrow this because he has a friend staying with him and his couch is really uncomfortable." The gust of her exhale fluttered my hair.

"Oh, of course! I assumed it was something like that." Obviously, she hadn't assumed anything like that.

I slammed the tailgate and slid into the driver's seat. "Okay, it was nice to see you." As I pulled away, I could see her fluttering her hands and shaking her head. Between Frances and me, I think we were going to give her a breakdown.

Evan was overjoyed when he saw the mattress. I helped him carry it in and get it set up in the guest room. He'd pulled out his nicest sheets and a blanket, and by the time we got done, even I thought the room looked cozy. Henry hopped the five inches up onto the new bed and raced from one end to the other, spinning in circles, clearly thinking this whole setup was for him.

I declined their offer to stay for dinner, the thought of the blondie stashed in my purse starting to make my mouth water. I did, however, agree to go to the Lander Jones Fan Club event with them the next night. I could tell Evan was determined to blame everything on Nell, and truth be told, I couldn't wait to see the interplay between them. Evan could get feisty, as I'd seen firsthand when she'd tried to take his chair. No telling how this might go.

Wednesday morning, I pinged Evan to check on William,

and while the doctors were sounding more optimistic, his progress was negligible. But the fact that the doctors were optimistic somehow seemed to bring me some peace, and I was able to feel more normal.

The day flew by and the low-hanging dread that had weighted me down since last week lifted enough that I actually forgot the whole mess for stretches at a time. The only wrinkle had been trying to deal with my car. Everything had been so crazy that I wasn't even sure where my car had been taken. I'd spent a frustrating hour cycling between the insurance company and the police, trying to determine where it was and when an adjuster could get out and look at it.

The storm had wreaked havoc with a lot of motorists, and the adjusters were hustling to get to everyone. They hoped they could get to it this week, but since I had been so late in calling, I was sitting at the end of the line. I was sure mold was no doubt already growing in black swaths along the interior. No question it was totaled. It also turned out that the tiny rental I had was still more than my insurance company allowed.

Trying to put the insurance mess out of mind, I cruised to Evan's, sort of looking forward to the evening. I'd never been to a fan club meeting of any kind, but I assumed this would be like a regular book club meeting where the author just happened to be present. Then again, with Nell as the president of this particular club, there was no telling. Maybe it would be like a pep rally and we'd get pom-poms to shake. I could see us now, lining up in rows, screaming and doing high kicks while Lander burst through a homemade paper sign and ran to his chair.

Evan had changed after work and was in cargo shorts and a T-shirt. The pockets of his shorts bulged. He had his copy of Lander's latest book tucked under his arm.

"What do you have in there?" I asked, pointing at his shorts. "It looks like you're ready to bug out."

"I think we need to be prepared," he said. "This lady is crazy. You saw her at the bookstore. She might be the one trying to kill Lander. And you. You were nearly killed too. Didn't you bring anything to defend yourself with?" He looked aghast at my negligence.

"Wait, I think I still have my pepper spray," I said, remembering I'd picked it up before going to see Seth. "Yeah, here it is."

"Okay, that's good. But, Jess, if you have to go digging around for it like that, she could take you down way before you can get to it. Put it in your pocket or something."

I felt the pockets in my capris. If I put a pepper spray canister in one of those, it was going to poke an ovary when I sat down.

"I'll just leave the zipper partway open," I said. "It's on top now anyway. I think it'll be okay. Anyway, I thought we'd settled on Seth as the one that was after Lander."

"We don't know for sure. I still think it's more likely to be this nutjob, or maybe his wife."

I was going to ask what else Evan was squirreling away in his shorts, but Lander came around the corner.

"We ready?" he asked. He looked as excited as he had when the Q&A session had gotten underway at the book signing last week. He'd printed out the invitation and directions. We piled into Evan's car and headed out.

"Have you ever attended a fan club meeting before?" I asked, swiveling to look at Lander. He was a little more dressed up than Evan and me, in a pair of jeans and a nice shirt. Beads of sweat glistened on his upper lip.

"No. I can't say I have. I didn't even know there was such a thing. I did check with my agent, though, and he thought I should do it. Hometown author, all that. I don't know if there will be any press there or not, but he said this could be a good way to get more local exposure."

"You've sold millions of books, why would you need more press?" Evan asked.

"Never enough publicity, I guess. Of course, if I get murdered, just imagine what that could do for my sales."

It took almost half an hour to get to the house listed on the invitation. Personally, if I was hosting a big-name author, I'd have gone with a private room at a restaurant, or maybe a garden party. Then again, what did I know about running a fan club?

The house was southwest of the city off Highway 59 and Hillcroft, in an older development of 1950s ranch-style homes. The house we were looking for was at the corner of a quiet cul-de-sac strewn with plastic toys, abandoned balls and discarded bikes. Somehow, I'd expected to end up at a house that looked more like the one in *Psycho*, and the apprehension I'd felt began to melt away in this unassuming suburbia.

"Are we early?" I asked. "What time is this supposed to start?" There didn't seem to be a lot of cars other than ones parked in their respective driveways.

"It said seven o'clock, and it's a little after that now. Let's just drive around a minute," Lander said to Evan. "Make sure we remember how to get out of here."

We spent a few minutes driving around the neighborhood, but nothing seemed out of the ordinary, and the house we were going to looked exactly the same when we returned. It was still light out, although the sun had dropped, deepening the shadows between the houses. The yard was overgrown and two large trees dominated the front, the deep shade inhibiting anything colorful from growing. Evan slowed to a stop in front of the house and we all sat staring at it before cautiously getting out.

As we approached the door in a tight knot, I suddenly felt as if I should have brought a bottle of wine or a gift. Or something. Evan clutched his book to his chest while Lander arranged his ever-present messenger bag strap across his shoulder. I took a second to make sure my pepper spray was easily accessible, and when I looked up I realized they had both stepped back, leaving me closest to the doorbell.

Attached to a rickety storm door that had probably been original to the house was a puffy pink fabric heart with a big letter L embroidered across the middle. This must be the place. I glanced over at Lander, who was clearly having second thoughts.

"Maybe we should skip this," he said.

"Can't disappoint your fans," I said, sounding more confident than I felt. I tipped my head to listen before hitting the doorbell. I would have thought we'd be able to hear the chatter of the members, but I didn't hear anything other than Evan's shoes scuffing on the concrete behind me. Maybe they were going to jump out like this was a surprise party. I hit the button.

Behind a pane of glass that looked like it was made from old Coke bottle bottoms, a backlit figure approached. There was a pause and a hand reached up as if patting at a hairdo before the door flew open.

"Welcome!" Nell stood before me, transformed from frumpy prairie-wear to a va-va-voom evening dress that plunged uncomfortably between her breasts and encased her body in a tight shimmering sheath. Flyaway hair had been forcibly subdued, probably with a high-heat iron and a quart of product. She sported new bangs that I could only guess she'd cut herself, probably this afternoon. She was missing her glasses, and she squinted uncertainly at me before the smile on her face melted away and a fast-moving array of emotions flitted across instead: disappointment, irritation, dismay before spotting Lander behind me, at which point the smile reappeared in full wattage.

"Welcome, Lander!" She pushed open the storm door, nearly knocking me over, and reached out a hand for Lander. "I'm so glad you could make it." Her eyes flitted to Evan and me, and her smile dropped again. "I'm not sure I understand what this is, though."

Evan stepped forward, squared his shoulders and pushed his way past all of us and through the door. "We're here for the meeting and dinner," he said. "Where is everyone? And what's for dinner? I'm starving." He circled the small living room before raising his head to sniff the air. "It smells good. Back here?" He headed towards a dining area.

"Wait," she called after Evan, her tone sharp and irritated. Then she shook her head and affixed the smile again, working hard to moderate her tone. "Come in," she said to Lander. She shimmied one shoulder suggestively and he nearly bolted for the street.

Me, she was ignoring altogether. I followed Evan. The lack of chatter was due to the complete lack of people. There was not one person there for this so-called fan club meeting. I poked my finger into the top of my purse and felt the reassuring coolness of the pepper spray canister. Clearly, she had been intending to lure Lander over here alone. But to what end? To kill him? Seduce him?

We'd moved quickly through the living room, but a glance around showed lights dimmed almost to darkness, pink and red nylon scarves draped on top of the shades. If that wasn't a fire hazard, I didn't know what was. It also pointed more to seduction than murder. The dining room table directly ahead was set for two, also ablaze with candles whose flames flickered and danced with our movement.

"Oh," Evan said as he stared at the table. "I thought this was a meeting. A meeting about the Lander Jones books. With dinner." He held his own book up as if this might help clarify things.

Nell stood before us, a blotchy red flush working its way up her exposed chest and creeping up her neck. She grabbed the edge of the dress just above her breasts and tugged upwards, as if that might stretch the stiff fabric.

"Well, this is…" I trailed off. "You have a lovely home."

"You brought your wife?" Nell turned to Lander, confusion apparent on her face. "Your mother led me to believe you were divorced."

"Um, yeah. This isn't my ex, this is my friend, Jessie."

She turned and squinted at me. "She looks like your wife."

Now it was my turn to be surprised. "I do?"

Evan looked from Nell to Lander to me. "Really? You look like Lander's wife?" He moved towards Lander. "Let me see a picture."

"My ex-wife," Lander corrected. "And yeah, Jessie actually does look a little like her."

Evan pointed towards Lander's bag. "C'mon, don't you have one in there? Jess, don't you want to see?"

"Yeah, actually I do." I wasn't sure why, but it felt weird knowing I looked like his ex.

"I don't have one handy," Lander said. "I'll pull one up later."

Nell fumbled around a side table before finding her glasses and putting them on. "Oh, actually, her face is a little thinner. And her eyes are, I don't know, more catlike or something."

Now I really wanted to see a picture of Annalise, but Evan had lost interest. "Do we still get dinner?" he asked. "It smells good."

A sizzling sound jolted Nell into action as a pot of water boiled over onto the burner below. She shoved past Evan and grabbed two potholders, peeping out sounds of distress as she surveyed the damage. Evan made his way back to Lander and waved us in close like players to a huddle before the big game.

"Okay, clearly she's the one that's after Lander. It's just like I thought—that whole number one fan thing. One of us needs to run out and check her car. Maybe the other two split up and search the house. Lander, how do you want to proceed? Are you ready to call the cops in now?"

"I'm not sure she is the one who's been trying to kill him," I said. "I mean, why would she try to kill him and then set up something like this?" I glanced around, noticing a scattering of rose petals across the table and more on the floor. The red velvety path ran down a hall, presumably to her bedroom. I had an urge to go see what kind of seductive scene she had going on in there. Lander stood immobile, looking like a lamb tethered directly inside the lion's den.

"Do you want to leave?" I asked.

He looked on the verge of hyperventilating and his knuckles gleamed white against his bag. But he took a deep breath and straightened up.

"No." It came out sounding more like a question, and he took another deep breath. "No. I think we should stay and maybe we can get some information out of her. I mean, as weird as this is, I think you've got a point. Why would she go to all this trouble? And why would she be trying to kill me?" He gave a little shudder. "This seems like something else."

Nell steamed into the dining room and smacked a couple more plates onto the table before disappearing through the door again. She returned in seconds, slamming down additional silverware.

"I guess you're going to get to eat," I said to Evan.

"Good. I'm starving."

I poked my head into the kitchen. "Can I help you with anything?" I asked the back of Nell's head. She stood at the stove, stirring a large pot while a smaller pot of spaghetti sauce burbled on a front burner.

"No," she said, not turning around. A cookie sheet rested on the counter with rectangles of mozzarella sticks and chicken nuggets getting cold.

"Would you like me to take these out?" I reached for a platter that sat ready beside it.

"No," she said. Her voice wobbled and I could tell she was trying not to cry.

"Look, I'm sorry. Clearly there was a misunderstanding somewhere."

She whirled to face me. "Clearly." Her glasses were fogged over from the steam and sliding down her nose. "Here, could you stir for a minute?" She handed me a wooden spoon and began gathering up the appetizers. I took her place at the stove and stirred the murky pasta water.

Nell finished arranging the mozzarella sticks and chicken nuggets and headed to the dining area.

"Lander? Would you like some appetizers?" she asked. "I asked your mom what your favorite foods were and she said you liked chicken nuggets and fried cheese. She said you like macaroni and cheese too, but I wasn't sure that made for a good dinner, so we're having spaghetti. I hope that's okay." Lander's list of favorite foods sounded a lot like that of most toddlers.

"I love spaghetti," said Evan enthusiastically. "And cheese sticks and nuggets. This is great."

I stirred the pot again, feeling a burst of sympathy for Nell. The image of her chasing Lander through the pouring rain last week with her homemade sign, hair plastered to the sides of her head, was bad. But this—sending an invitation for a fake fan club meeting and actually answering the door in a formal gown while decking the house out like something from a low-budget romance flick—this was a whole other level.

CHAPTER THIRTEEN

To say dinner was a little bit awkward would be like saying sticking your finger in a light socket is mildly uncomfortable. Somehow in the chaos of seating ourselves, I found myself wedged between Evan and Lander, one of whom had dragged a chair around the far side so as not to have to sit next to Nell. So there we sat, the three of us lined up against Nell like an antagonistic hiring panel and a reluctant job candidate.

She'd opened a bottle of red wine and poured some for herself and Lander into two lovely wineglasses. Evan and I each got a half an inch poured into scuffed-up juice glasses.

In spite of his professed hunger, Evan suddenly became wary of his spaghetti.

"Did you see her put the sauce on this?" Evan asked me. "Like did it all come out of the same pot, or did she have a chance to do something to certain servings?"

I glanced across the table at Nell, who sat staring at him in disbelief. In spite of the warmth, she'd added a brown cardigan over her dress before sitting down, and she slumped under its bulk.

"I can hear you, you know," she said. "Why would you ask

that? I mean, I didn't ask you to come, so it's not like I'd have a bottle of arsenic waiting."

Evan stiffened. "See that? She knows about poisons." He shoved back, his chair knocking to the floor. "Let's go."

I reached over and righted his chair. "Evan, c'mon. I'm sure it's fine."

"Then you try it."

I had to admit, now that he'd put the thought out there, I was a little reluctant. Lander had his face close to his bowl as if examining it on a microscopic level, while at the same time sniffing suspiciously.

"Oh, for heaven's sake," Nell said. "There's nothing wrong with the spaghetti except it's too dry. I wasn't planning on having this many people"—her voice broke—"so I didn't have enough sauce, and now you're here, and you're being mean, and the whole evening is ruined." She pushed away from the table, throwing her napkin down, and disappeared around the corner, following the rose petal trail.

The three of us stared at each other. Evan reached across the table, swapped his pasta bowl with Nell's and began eating.

"Okay, someone needs to go talk to her," I said. Evan busied himself twirling spaghetti and Lander began buttering a roll. "Look, aren't we trying to get some information here? I mean, I know Seth is the one with the banged-up truck, but since we're here, don't we want to make sure that we can rule Nell out?"

"I think she needs a girl to talk to," said Evan.

I sighed. "Lander? Don't you want to go? You're the one she's got a thing for."

"I think Evan's right. This is female territory. I'm not comfortable going back there."

I sighed again. "Fine. But you guys owe me."

I extricated myself from between them and followed the rose petal path down a dark hallway to a back bedroom. The petals squished under my shoes, bruising and flattening against the hard wood floors. The door was partially ajar and I knocked softly before sticking my head around.

"Nell? Are you okay?" She lay facedown across the bed, a soft white faux fur blanket sticking out from under her prone form. One hand stroked the blanket as if trying to comfort herself, although judging from the muffled sobs, she wasn't having much luck.

I walked closer. The room was nearly dark. One small lamp in the corner was lit with no more than a twenty-watt bulb, also covered by a gauzy red scarf. I felt like I was in an amateur brothel.

"Look, Evan didn't mean anything by his comment. There's just a lot that's been going on, and I know we sort of sprang ourselves on you." Her sobs quieted a little, as if she was listening. "I know Lander really appreciates all the trouble you've gone to here. He would love the chance to have a nice dinner and talk about his work. I think that's what you want too, right?"

She sniffled and shifted to her side. "He appreciates it?"

"Oh, of course! I mean, you know he has a ton of fans, but none of them have ever gone to this much trouble to do something so special for him."

"They haven't?" She twisted around and lifted herself up. Her glasses had gone askew and her cheeks were red and puffy. Wet streaks of mucus pooled under her nose, and one breast popped out of its confinement. I looked away.

"Oh, yeah, no. This is way more than anyone's ever done for him. Why don't you, I don't know, maybe change into something more comfortable and we'll go enjoy the evening?"

She sniffed a plug of snot up her nose and tried to scoot across the bed. Her weight was on the cardigan and she grabbed it and tugged, the sudden movement ripping the side seam of her dress. A sudden view of black undies presented itself and I made a move for the door.

"We'll just wait for you, okay?"

I motored back to the dining room, where Evan was finishing his bowl of pasta. Lander was buttering another roll. The plate of appetizers was empty, except for a few bits of breading, and they'd poured themselves more wine, thoughtfully topping up my juice glass as well.

"Okay, she's going to come back out. She's really upset, so be nice."

I squished between them into my chair. Lander passed me a roll and we waited.

"What's taking her so long?" Evan finally whispered. I knew from experience that it took a lot longer to repair the damage from a crying jag than it did to cause it. One sudden outburst could cause puffiness that lasts for days.

"I'm sure she's just freshening up," I said. When she finally did reappear, she'd changed into stretchy pants and a tunic. Most of her makeup was gone, whether washed away in the torrent of tears or removed voluntarily, I wasn't sure, but she actually looked better. Well, except for the redness. And the puffiness. And the continued sniffing.

She slid into her chair and smiled across the table at Lander. "You were waiting for me?" she asked, gesturing towards his still full spaghetti bowl.

He didn't say anything, and glancing over, I could see how freaked out he still looked.

"We were just saying how nice this is," I said. "It's delicious." I twirled my fork in the cold spaghetti and took a bite, Lander watching intently. I chewed slowly, ready to spit the mess out if I felt any signs of burning or numbness or if my throat started to close off. I chewed it till it was mush and finally swallowed. "So good," I said, jabbing Lander with my elbow. "I'm sure you're hungry."

Evan had finished eating and was performing a visual survey of the room from his chair. He'd focused on a bookcase against the wall, his head tilting sideways as he scanned the titles. "I can't help but notice," he said, "you have a lot of books, but they're all romance. How is it that you're such a fan of Lander's when he writes, well, real books? Not this mushy stuff."

Nell fiddled with her fork before glancing over at Lander. I thought she was just going to ignore Evan's question.

"It's true that I've always loved the romance genre," she said. "I'm sure you wouldn't understand that." Evan ignored the barb. "But when I started working with Lander's mother and I found out her son was a famous writer, I thought I would at least try one of his books. I thought maybe it would give me something to talk to Cecilia about." I guess Nell had not been invited to call her CiCi. "She can be a little intimidating."

"Don't I know it," said Lander, looking at Nell directly for the first time. "I could also tell you, it probably didn't help at all."

She smiled. "Not very much," she said. "I guess she's not one of your fans?"

"No one in my family is really into reading fiction," he said.

"I can't imagine that," Nell said, her face lighting up. "Fiction is a wonderful escape. I mean, when everything else is going wrong, you can fly away into these wonderful worlds. I am so amazed that you're able to create something so fantastic. I didn't think I would like thrillers, but your books are so much more than that. They're everything! Action, romance—"

"There's no romance in Lander's books," Evan said, wrinkling his face.

"Of course there is," said Nell. "If you had any sense, you would see how romantic Magnus is. Strong, brooding, just waiting to find the right woman." Evan stared at her as if she'd just declared that the Dalai Lama was even now building a nuclear bomb to unleash on the earth. "Lander, Magnus is really based on you, right? A man who's involved in the dark side of the world, all the while searching for his love."

Evan stood up, clearly appalled. He made a noise of disgust and walked away from the table, pacing the small living room. "Magnus is about finding justice in any way he has to. Right, Lander? There's no romance."

"These books are so much more than what you think," said Nell.

I looked to Lander. He was sitting Zen-like, chewing yet another dinner roll. Maybe he had some tranquilizers in that bag of his. "These rolls are really good," he said. "And the wine is nice."

Evan went outside and the tension at the table dropped somewhat. Nell tried to get Lander to admit that he layered romance into all his books, but he sidestepped neatly by telling her that he wrote what he wrote and he trusted his readers to take from it what they needed. She nearly swooned with delight at this bit of insider information.

Evan wasn't gone long, but by the time he came back in, we'd all finished eating as much as we were going to. I helped Nell clear the dishes, carrying them into the kitchen and trying to find room on the cluttered counters.

"So, how do you like working for Lander's mom?" I asked, trying to make conversation while we worked. "It must be interesting working for a chemist." I balanced two more plates on an already teetering stack.

She didn't say anything for a minute, clearly still irritated by my presence. "Can I ask you something?"

"Sure."

"Are you and Lander, you know, together?" I could see her muscles tense as if expecting a gut punch.

"No, no," I said. "I just met him recently. He seems like a really nice guy, but we're not seeing each other."

She exhaled so hard I could feel the force of her breath from four feet away. "Okay, good. It's just that you really do look so much like his wife, ex-wife, that I thought maybe he has a certain type, and I'm"—she glanced down at herself—"not like either of you."

"I've never seen what she looks like. Now I'm really curious," I said.

Neither one of us had noticed Evan and Lander standing in the door.

"How do you know what my ex looks like?" Lander asked. "I don't think there's too many pictures of us out there together." Nell's face erupted into red blotches. "I doubt highly that my mother has any in her office. She never really cared for my ex."

Nell stood frozen, her mouth moving as if forming words and discarding them before they came out. She finally turned towards the sink, unable to look at Lander.

"I asked her once if you were married," she mumbled. "She told me you were divorced. She said you'd had a starter marriage. Then she said it was really a nonstarter marriage. She told me her name, and I looked her up online." She finally looked at Lander. "I was just curious."

"Kind of stalker-like, don't you think?" asked Evan.

"No, I was just curious!" Nell glared at Evan. "Like you're not hanging all over Lander, kind of stalker-like."

"I'm not hanging all over Lander!" Evan said. "And where were you Friday night?"

"What?" asked Nell, nearly shouting. "You're interrogating me now? None of your business where I was."

Lander touched Evan's shoulder. "C'mon, man. Let's go wait in here."

"Why do you want to know where I was Friday night? What? You think I'm following him or something?"

I tried to picture Nell bashing William over the head. It seemed unlikely, but not impossible. If he'd caught her red-handed going through Lander's study, maybe she'd have lashed out. I took a step back.

"Why is he asking me these questions?" Nell asked me, her voice still several octaves too high. "He shows up at my house, crashes a private gathering, and he has the nerve to ask me intrusive questions?" She flung a soapy sponge into the sink, muttering to herself. "What is that guy's name again?"

I flashed back to William's inert form on the floor. "Uh, Evan."

"Evan what?"

"Evan," I hesitated, wanting to give a fake name but my mind went completely blank. I glanced around the kitchen. "Evan Ragu." She turned away from me and I glanced over to make sure she wasn't pulling a butcher knife from the murky dishwater, but she'd just returned to rinsing dishes. I considered hanging around and trying to get some information from her, but she was clearly in no mood to talk. I wandered into the living room, where Lander was sitting close to the door, holding his bag on his lap.

"Where's Evan?" I whispered. Lander nodded his head towards the bedroom. I poked my head around the corner and could see him in Nell's room, his back to me. What was he thinking? I took a couple steps down the hall. "Evan," I whispered. "What are you doing?"

"Give me a minute," he said.

"You can't just go through someone's drawers." I headed back to sit next to Lander. I wanted no part of that.

I heard the water in the kitchen shut off at the same time that Evan slid into the room clutching a small flowered journal.

"Here! Here, put it in your bag," he said, shoving it at Lander. Lander stiffened as Evan dropped it on him.

"You can't steal someone's diary," I hissed.

"What are y'all doing?" asked Nell, striding through the dining room from the kitchen. "What's going on?"

I wanted desperately to look at where the journal had ended up but didn't want to draw attention to it. Instead I bounded to my feet and launched myself towards Nell, trying to a break her line of vision. She leaned left, then right, as if trying to see past me, but I reached her side and grasped her arm, trying to turn her around.

"Lander had a little tickle in his throat. He was hoping for a glass of water." Who knew this line could be used in so many situations? It was like the all-purpose tool of distraction.

I followed Nell as she hurried into the kitchen. She pulled a glass from the cupboard, filling it with chilled bottled water from the refrigerator. On the counter rested two individual chocolate cakes on white plates, a fancy swirl of raspberry sauce culminating in a heart at the bottom of one plate.

"I only have enough for two," she said. Obviously she had no plans to split those babies up, which was a shame, really, because they looked incredible. I was pretty sure Lander would share his with me, although that really might be the tipping point for Nell. It took all the willpower I had not to run my finger through the raspberry heart.

Nell picked up the plate, clearly concerned I might swipe it, and carried it out with the water, presenting them to Lander with a flourish.

"Here's your water, and I brought your dessert. I had hoped we could linger over dessert and coffee, but..." She looked pointedly at Evan and me. "Anyway. I hope you enjoy it."

Evan stood a couple of feet away, his expression smug, so I guessed they'd successfully squirreled the journal away in

Lander's bag. In spite of feeling appalled that he'd stolen some-thing so personal, I couldn't wait to actually read through it. There's something fascinating about other people's innermost thoughts. Then again, for all we knew, it was just filled with poufy hand-drawn hearts and endless rows of *Nell loves Lander.*

"Oh, good, dessert," said Evan. "That looks great."

"I only have enough for two," snapped Nell.

"Here, have some of mine," said Lander. "I can't eat all this."

Evan headed for the kitchen and returned with another fork. I followed his lead and retrieved one for myself. Nell looked on with resigned dismay, the last vestiges of her fantasy dissolving away. At least she'd have the other cake to cheer her up.

Before we left, she asked if I could take a picture of her and Lander together. She handed me her phone and plopped down on the sofa, patting the cushion next to her. Evan and Lander exchanged a look before Lander reluctantly sat down against the far arm, shoving his bag between them.

"Maybe you could move your bag? It's in the way," she said. He inched it halfway onto his lap before she reached over and snatched it, plunking it on her other side. Her hand caressed the leather and her fingers moved slowly towards the clasp as if she couldn't control the urge to peek inside.

"Hey, no," Lander said. "Don't open that."

"Why not?" she purred. "Is this where you keep your secrets?" She ran her tongue over her upper lip and scooted closer, pressing her hip against his and seizing his hand, holding it firmly against her bosom. I snapped the picture. The look on his face made me wish I could get a copy.

Lander grabbed his bag and headed out the door while Nell bustled around behind us, trying to fit in all the things she'd obviously planned to say but hadn't gotten around to. Such as her phone number, in case he wanted to reach her. A list of people she'd been keeping track of who'd left negative reviews on his books. An offer to help with any typing needs he might have, free of charge, of course.

Lander raced across the street and zipped into Evan's back seat, hitting the lock button on his door.

"Wait! I forgot to give you the gift I made for you!" Nell shouted. "I was trying to give it to you at the book signing, but you left too fast then too. Can you wait?" She rocked sideways as if half of her wanted to race inside while the other half was afraid he would take off.

Evan and I got in the car. "Let's go," said Lander.

"What? You don't want your gift?" I asked, watching Nell disappear into the house at a dead run.

Evan started up the engine and had shifted into drive when Nell came flying out of the house. She ran directly in front of Evan's car, forcing him to stop.

"Here! This is for you!" she said, gesturing to Lander's window. I glanced back where he stared straight ahead, window still in the full upright position. I lowered my window and Nell handed me what looked like a handmade crocheted owl. "That's for Lander," she said, as if I had plans to keep it for myself. I handed it over the back seat. "I made it myself!"

Evan revved the engine and she stepped onto the curb. She was still waving as we pulled away, one hand clasped to her chest like a bride sending her soldier off to war. Unrequited love is hard, but I wasn't convinced she was the one who was trying to kill Lander, or the one who'd attacked William.

Apparently Evan wasn't as convinced as I was, because as soon as we got back to his house, he took a pair of scissors and started eviscerating the owl.

"There could be a listening device in here," he said as he pulled the poor thing apart. "Or a micro-camera. Or a tracking mechanism." Henry, never one to miss out on ripping something to shreds, grabbed one of the wings that had already been amputated. With a joyful growl, he held it between his front paws like a rawhide bone, turning his head sideways and cutting through the yarn with his sharp little molars.

While they worked on that, I turned to Lander. "So let's see the journal, or whatever it was that Evan stole."

"I didn't *steal* it," said Evan.

"What would you call it, then?" He huffed and cut the owl's beak up the center.

Lander unzipped a rear pocket on his bag and extracted the flowery book. I plopped down on the couch beside him and he dropped it on my lap.

"I'm not sure I want to see this," he said. He looked much more relaxed than he'd been all evening. Leaning his head back, he smiled. "You look. Seriously, I'm not sure I want to know."

"You should have seen the bedroom she had waiting for you," said Evan, picking through the stuffing he'd pulled from the owl. "I mean, dude. She was gonna have her way with you. Jess, did you see that place?"

"I did," I said. "It was a bit over the top." I cracked open the journal. A puff of scent wafted up, a mix of rose and bergamot with maybe a little vanilla thrown in.

"It smells girly," Lander said.

It wasn't so much a journal as a small scrapbook. Or maybe a combination scrapbook and journal. Whatever you called it, it was dedicated to Nell's love of Lander. I closed the cover.

"I don't know, guys. This seems pretty invasive."

Evan looked up from the shredded pile of yarn he was gathering. "No, come on. You have to look. Give me a minute and I'll look at it."

I opened it up again. Maybe it was better having another woman look through this. If there was nothing pertinent, then we could trash it. Or return it somehow. I could only imagine CiCi handing it to Nell at a staff meeting.

The first page was hand-lettered, *Lander Jones*, surrounded by hearts and flowers in alternating pinks and reds. The next page had a printout of all Lander's books in order. Three blank pages followed, indicating that Nell had high hopes for additional titles.

But it was the pages following that were most disturbing. Okay, everything about this was disturbing, but the following pages had pictures of Lander, mostly looking like they'd been taken from web images or interviews, which would have been fine, I guess. Except Nell had photoshopped herself into the pictures with Lander. I had to hope she didn't use Photoshop as part of her job, because she was terrible at it.

"What's it say?" Evan asked. "I opened it for a minute when I grabbed it. It looked like she had a lot of creepy pictures." He wrestled the owl wing away from Henry, tossed the whole mess in the trash and joined us in the living room, plopping down on the other side of me.

"She's photoshopped herself into these pictures with Lander."

Lander sat up and leaned forward. "What?" He peered at the open page on my lap. "Well, that's creepy."

We leaned over the book, our heads nearly touching as I leafed through the pages.

"Look at that!" Evan shouted in my ear. "You can tell she's not really in this picture. She's pasted herself halfway across Lander."

"They're all like that," I said.

"That was on *Late Night*," Lander said. "My agent likes me to go on those shows sometimes." He leaned closer. "It looks like she took a picture of the TV with her phone, then printed it out and put herself in. That's a lot of trouble for something so..."

"Weird?" supplied Evan. It was indeed weird. A smiling Nell, proportionally too large for the photo, hovered on the love seat beside Lander, looking out at an imaginary audience.

"This must have taken so much time," I said as we passed page after page. I began to flip ahead. We'd pretty much figured out she was obsessed, no need to dwell. As we reached the end, I saw she'd included multiple pictures from the book signing. These she'd clearly taken herself, and I recognized the crowded bookstore. It started with a photo of an empty table and the brown door from which Lander had emerged. Then there were some blurred shots, random heads and one of the carpet before she'd captured a half dozen of Lander signing books. The last picture was of Lander's backside as he fled towards the back door of the bookstore.

"Is that the end?" asked Lander. I flipped ahead.

Luckily for us, it was.

CHAPTER FOURTEEN

The next day I spent a good portion of my dog walks thinking about William and sending up good thoughts for his recovery. I wondered if he even knew who'd attacked him. If, or hopefully when, he woke up, he might not have any recollection of the attack.

I'd just arrived home after my last dog walk when I got a text from Lander. I hadn't even finished typing in my password when the phone rang in my hand. At first I barely recognized Lander's voice, he was talking so fast. William had woken up. The relief that washed over me nearly knocked me off my feet.

"When? What did the doctors say? Is he going to be okay? Oh, thank heavens, this is wonderful," I babbled.

Lander took a shaky breath, his voice unsteady. "I was sitting with him. I've been working here a lot this week, and I started talking about a scene I'm struggling with, and when I looked over I realized he was looking at me."

"That's so great!"

"I know, right! I just stopped talking and he said 'Hi.' Just like that. Hi. Like nothing was going on."

"Does he remember anything? Have you talked to the doctors?" I noticed I was bouncing, and I made an effort to still myself.

"He doesn't really remember anything. He wasn't sure why he was there. The doctors said not to push it, he still needs to rest. But—" He gave a small shaky laugh. "He sounds like William. You just don't know. I have been so worried."

"I do know," I said softly. "I have been too."

"He asked about you," he said. "He at least remembers that much. He felt like he was worried about you, but that's as close as he's getting to what happened. He said he'd like to see you, if you can come down. The doctors don't want him overexcited—they keep stressing how much he needs to rest. But now that's he up, he seems concerned about you, and I think if he could see you, it would make him feel better."

I ran a quick brush through my hair, put a few biscuits down for Addie and raced out the door. Lander had said if I was going to come, I needed to come as soon as possible. William's doctor wasn't keen on visitors at this point, and he wanted to be available to ensure I didn't upset him or cause any setbacks. Believe me, that was the last thing I wanted too.

Traffic was at its peak and by the time I found the right parking garage, my blood pressure had escalated into a new zone. I rushed along the wide corridors that ran between buildings, filled with sandwich shops and gift stores. I should take up some flowers or a get-well card or a gift of some kind. I raced into a small store and pinwheeled around the racks, trying to find something that seemed right. I could feel the clock ticking away as I surveyed the meager offerings. I finally grabbed a nutbar just because the cashier was giving me the eye like I was a serial gift shop shoplifter. In the elevator, I shoved the bar in my purse. A nutbar. Why can't I be normal in hospital settings?

By the time I reached William's floor, my classic hospital-phobia was kicking into high gear. The smells, the beepings and visions of dangling tubes converged as I raced past opened doors, looking for the right room. I reminded myself to breathe. Up ahead, a man in dark pants and a black windbreaker sat in a plastic chair, watching everyone who went up or down the hall. Built like a bull, he stood up as I slowed down. This must be Lander's private security.

"Can I help you?" he asked in a low rumble.

"Yes, I'm looking for William Wagner's room."

A nurse walked quickly past, trying to catch up to another one. "Could you come help me suction my patient in room 18?"

Oh Lord. I took a deep breath, trying not to notice the small black dots that were emerging in my far peripheral vision.

"Ma'am? Are you okay? You don't look well."

I closed my eyes. "Yeah. Yeah, I'm okay." I was not okay. In fact, I was pretty sure that I was going to faint, but if I fainted, the suction-y nurse might come back and that was just going to exacerbate the problem. Small beads of sweat broke out on my forehead and a flush of heat exploded across my armpits.

"Here, why don't you have a seat?" The bull-sized man sounded nearly as panicked as I felt. I got the sense that any second he was going to race up the hall, screaming for a doctor. I reminded myself to tell Lander he needed to find a less compassionate guard and let him steer me into his chair.

"Sorry," I said as I leaned over my knees. "I hate hospitals."

His bulky frame vibrated anxiously in front of me, and I could see his hands fluttering in my side vision. "Can I get something for you? Water?"

Smelling salts, I thought.

"Jessie?" At Lander's voice, I opened my eyes, trying to stop thinking of the suctioning going on nearby. "Are you okay?"

"Boss, do you want to get her some water or something? I could go, but you said to never leave my post."

"Thanks, Fred," said Lander. He came to my side and knelt down beside me. "Are you okay?"

"Yeah," I said, feeling stupid. Not stupid enough to stand up right away, I knew better than that. "I'm not really good in hospital settings."

"You should have told me," he said. "Let me go get you some water. I'll be right back."

I listened to his rubber-soled shoes make soft sucking sounds on the overglossed linoleum floor. I could feel Fred hovering nearby, his breathing quick and anxious. I guessed Fred was better suited for a shoot-out than he was for dealing with fainting females.

It didn't take Lander long to return with a cold bottle of Dasani water. I took a few sips, then held the bottle to my temple and looked up. Lander and Fred had matching expressions of helpless concern. I took another sip and tried to smile.

"Sorry about that," I said. "I'm a total baby in medical settings."

They both fussed around, looking uncomfortable until I said I was okay to go in and see William now.

"Are you sure?" asked Lander. "He's up and he'd love to see you, but if this is too much, then you really don't need to go in."

I sent up a prayer that he didn't have tubes sticking out anywhere visible and told Lander I'd be fine. He took my arm as I stood and led me gently into the darkened hospital room.

William had a private room, probably a VIP private room judging by the looks of it. A wood-paneled accent wall behind the bed attempted to soften the hospital look, and a long couch stretched along under the window. Next to the bed was a low-slung visitor's chair, and on the other side was a small work desk, on which Lander's laptop sat. Folders were stacked beside the computer and a notebook lay open, indicating that Lander had indeed been hard at work while he was here.

I worked up the courage to look at the bed and its occupant. William lay propped on pillows, raised to a half-sitting position. A rolling tray with a carafe of water and a small vase of daisies was within arm's length. To the side, an array of monitors that rivaled the screens at the Johnson Space Center had been erected. And lying wanly against the white sheets was William.

I focused on his eyes, which looked tired but still held remnants of the twinkly blue kindness I'd first noticed last week. I tried to ignore the tubes, bandages and IV needles that threatened to reignite the dancing black dots in my vision.

"Hi," he said. His voice sounded weak, and I moved closer. He raised a hand and I reached out and took it in mine. His skin felt cool and dry, the bones light and delicate. The thought that someone could attack this gentle man with such ferocity that he'd nearly died touched on an ugliness in humanity that I didn't want to acknowledge.

"William. I am so sorry," I said. His head settled on the pillow and he seemed to drift off. My heart leapt and I looked frantically to Lander. He nodded reassuringly and gestured to the monitors that were all showing rhythmic lines and bars.

"He's been fading in and out," Lander said in a voice so quiet I could barely hear him. I set William's hand back onto his blanket and slipped my hand away. "The doctor said it's okay. His body is doing what it needs to to heal." We stepped away from the bed and he leaned close to me. "I'm sorry to bring you down just to have him drift away so fast. I knew he was tired, but he seemed agitated and worried about you."

"Me? He's the one we're all worried about."

"I know," he said. "But even though he has no memory about what happened to him, he seems to remember that you were there, or you were in danger of some kind. So sorry to drag you down here for just that one second." He smiled. "Particularly when you have such an aversion to hospitals. But I can tell that just seeing you has relaxed his mind. I think that's why he fell asleep so fast."

"I guess," I said. "So, does this mean he's going to be okay?"

"He still has a long way to go," said Lander. "I mean, this is a great sign. But they're not sure if he's had any damage. The doctor said he's cautiously optimistic, though." We stared at each other, relief nearly palpable. "The police had wanted to talk to him when he woke up," he went on. "But I asked the doctor not to notify them. I don't want anyone to know he's awake."

The relief faded at the thought of the attacker realizing that William had awoken and could potentially identify him or her. We really needed to figure out what was going on.

"You're going to keep your security guy, right?"

"Oh yeah," he said.

Lander said he was going to stay because he wanted to be there when William woke up again. I took that as my cue to go. I waved to Fred as I dashed down the hall looking straight ahead, trying to block out the sights and sounds. And the smells. I didn't know how anyone could work in one of these places. Give me the smell of raw liver waiting to be turned into biscuits or a dog poop waiting to be picked up any day over those hospital smells.

I spent the evening soothing myself by baking biscuits. I talked to Addie as I worked, discussing who could have attacked William. I tried and tried to think of anything I might have seen that night. But other than my flight into the bush to keep myself safe, I hadn't seen anything helpful.

If I had to pick one culprit, I'd say Seth probably shoved us into the bayou. His truck was the right size and he had all that front-end damage. Okay, it did seem like more damage than what he would have had from shoving into my car, but maybe he'd deliberately crashed into something else to disguise it. But if he *had* pushed us into the bayou, I would assume he was the one who'd bashed William over the head as well. As far as we knew, he didn't have an alibi for either night. But why? Why would he want to kill his best friend?

It sounded lame, but his vibe didn't strike me as that of a killer. On the other hand, when I'd asked about his truck, he'd tensed up rather aggressively. But really, he'd seemed more lost than angry. And wouldn't you have to be really angry with someone to want to kill them? Particularly your best friend? I hadn't talked to Lander about the drawings I'd seen. He'd overheard the conversation, but we hadn't talked specifically about what Seth was working on. Maybe this was it. Maybe if Lander was dead, Seth could put out his video game. Lander had said that there was a copyright that went seventy years or something, but maybe Seth didn't know that. It was possible he thought all his problems would be solved by his video game.

I washed the biscuit batter off my hands and texted Evan. He called me back and put me on speaker while I ran my theory past them. As much as Lander didn't want to admit it, I could tell he had Seth in his sights. For some reason, Evan seemed to be giving Seth a pass. He was vacillating between CiCi, Nell and Annalise. When pressed, he couldn't really articulate why he thought it might be Nell, other than he thought she was crazy. CiCi, he was convinced, had tried to poison him. And he suspected Annalise because he said it was always the spouse. They said they planned to check Annalise out, but they didn't indicate how, and since they didn't say they needed my help, I assumed they had this one covered.

I assumed wrong. Thursday evening, my phone rang. Once again, Evan put me on speaker. Judging from the noises around them, I assumed they were outside, maybe on a patio somewhere.

"Where are you?" I asked.

"We're at Limitless Learning," said Lander. "Do you know it?"

"I've heard of it," I said. "I get their catalogs in the mail all the time. It's like classes for adults on a range of random things."

"Exactly," he said.

"What? You guys taking a class? Creative Writing? Detection 101?"

"No, we followed Annalise over here," he said.

"She's taking a class," said Evan.

"What's she taking?"

"We don't know."

"Do you think you could meet us here? Obviously, I can't go in," said Lander. "And frankly, she's more likely to strike up a conversation with you than Evan." I heard a car door slam nearby.

"Wait, you want me to just show up at her class?" I asked. "That's awkward. I haven't paid for it, and I'm pretty sure the teacher will notice."

"No," Evan said in his overly patient voice. "We thought you could go into the building and see if you could figure out what class she's in. Then just maybe strike up a conversation when her class gets out."

I sat in silence for a minute. This wasn't a very good plan. Look how well we'd done so far.

"I don't get the sense that Annalise is the kind of person to strike up a conversation with a strange woman," I finally said. "Y'all need to find a cute guy. Evan? Maybe you need to handle this." Even as I said it, I knew that Evan wasn't the kind of guy Annalise would stop and chat with. He was normal and rumpled. Not powerful and sexy.

There was a minute of silence, cross talk, and finally Evan said, "Please, Jess? Please come over? You're going to have a better shot at talking to her than I am."

I sighed. If it would help figure out who'd attacked William, of course I would go. But I wasn't getting all dolled up this time.

CHAPTER FIFTEEN

L imitless Learning resided in an old '60s era office complex off Richmond Avenue. Five stories high with vertical windows, its exterior sported what looked like a pebble coating, probably laced with the original asbestos. Maybe Annalise was here rounding up recruits for a class action suit for her husband. It had only taken me about fifteen minutes to get there, but then it took another five to find Evan and Lander in the overstuffed parking lot. The spaces were tight and I'd finally given up driving around and wedged the little lemon drop between two giant SUVs in the very last row.

I grabbed my purse and started walking towards the building, my head pivoting side to side, trying to find Evan's Jeep. I finally spotted them, tucked into a prime space that gave them a good view of the doors. The door locks clicked as I walked up beside the car and I slipped into the back seat, swatting an empty fast-food bag out of my way. It fluttered to the floor, where it joined a host of kindred bags. It looked like they'd been on a three-day stakeout.

"So, I'm hoping you've come up with something better than me wandering around trying to find her," I said. "I don't even know what she looks like, other than she kind of looks like me."

"Okay, we found the schedule online, and based on when she got here, we've narrowed it down to three possibilities," said Lander.

"Unless she was running either really late or she got here really early," said Evan.

"Let's assume she was on time," said Lander. "So she's either in Dandy Doodles Drawing Class, Getting Better Results from Camera Traps, or Next Steps for Expanding your Business."

"What?" I asked. "Read those slower. What's a camera trap?"

"You know, it's like those wildlife photographers that set up cameras in obscure places and get those really cool photos of animals," said Evan, sounding like he'd had enough time to think about this and decide it was something he'd like to do.

"Is Annalise into wildlife photography?" I asked Lander.

"Oh, no way. She doesn't like anything to do with the outdoors."

"Maybe she's not thinking of camera traps for the outdoors," said Evan. "Maybe she's setting up cameras for something else. Like to trap you. Or Dick. Or something like that."

"That seems like a stretch," I said. "I mean, maybe. But why take a class that's really geared to the outdoors and wildlife? Why not take a private-eye class or something more useful?"

"It's always possible," said Lander. "I doubt if she's in Dandy Doodles. That doesn't seem like anything she would like."

Too bad. I thought that sounded fun.

"She's got to be in Next Steps for Expanding your Business," Lander said. "I've been searching online since we've been here, and I think she's actually started a little online business. Some sort of accessories thing?" He sounded perplexed.

"Let me see," I said, leaning over the console. He handed me an iPad with a website pulled up. *Annalise Style and Accessory*

Transformations. I studied the screen. In spite of the clunky name, the website itself was lovely. I skimmed through a brief welcome message that was written in soothing tones about how we are all beautiful in our own way, but often we can shine more brightly with just a few well-chosen accessories or tweaks to our outfits. A lovely array of accessories popped up when I hit the shopping button.

I was getting sidetracked by some cool chunky turquoise bracelets she had for sale when Lander said, "You wanted to see what she looks like—that's her under the Tips section, modeling the scarves or whatever it is she's doing."

I immediately backed out of Shopping and clicked into Tips. There was a photo array of a woman showing how to tie a scarf properly in multiple ways. I made a mental note to come back here later and learn the techniques, but right now I was too interested in seeing what Annalise looked like. I stared for a long time, realizing that I'd had a mental image of her that was close, but somehow not right.

She was pretty with silky blond hair, elegantly braided in a loose swoop. I instinctively brushed at my own blondish hair that I could feel escaping from my ponytail holder. I really should have taken a little more time to get ready. Her makeup was flawless, if a little heavy on the foundation, and dusky colors enhanced her hazel-gray eyes. What seemed lacking, however, was any kind of... what? She seemed flat. I couldn't discern any personality in these pictures. She wasn't smiling—it was more of a neutral look. Maybe that's what she was going for since this was a tutorial about scarves, but still.

I clicked forward to more photos. She was pairing earrings and necklaces with different looks—business casual, formal, beachy. Still no smile. No spark.

"She's very pretty," I said evenly.

"She is," agreed Lander.

"She looks cold," said Evan, who'd obviously seen these before I got there.

"Evan," I said.

"No, it's okay," said Lander. "He's right. She basically is."

"Well, she does look rather serious," I said.

"Oh, she's always serious," said Lander. "I think the woman literally has no sense of humor at all."

"I still think it's her," said Evan. "Especially now that I've seen her face. I know I wouldn't want to cross her."

"I can't think of a reason why she would want me dead," said Lander. "Believe me, I've tried."

"It's probably something you did when you were married and she's still pissed," said Evan. "You know how women can be."

"Geez, Evan."

"Not you," he said. "But like her. You can tell she's a mean girl."

"Great, and I'm supposed to go strike up a conversation with her?" Now that I'd seen her face, I was pretty sure a spontaneous chat session seemed unlikely. "What exactly am I trying to find out anyway? If she's taking this class and it didn't just start today, then we know she was in class last Thursday night. It couldn't have been her who pushed us off the road."

Evan and Lander looked at each other.

"What?" I asked. "You didn't think of that?"

Lander turned and looked at me. "I feel like when my editor catches something stupid. I can't believe I didn't think of that." He looked embarrassed.

"It doesn't mean she didn't get someone else to do it," said Evan. "Like Seth. He's the one with the busted-up truck. Maybe they're both in on it."

"I thought you said it was all the women in his life," I reminded him. "His mom, Annalise, Nell."

"Or it's Annalise and Seth. I mean, you don't know either!"

I handed the iPad back to Lander. "I know, but I'm also not sure what I'm supposed to be trying to find out tonight."

I looked out the window at the now-quiet parking lot. It appeared everyone was already where they should be. A couple stood leaning against a concrete planter, smoking and flicking ashes into the littered jasmine behind them.

"Anybody?" I asked. "Any ideas?"

We spent the next fifteen minutes kicking thoughts around. Sure, there was a ton of stuff we wanted to know. Was she trying to kill Lander? If yes, then why? Did she attack William? If so, then why? Was Dick involved in this? All these were great questions that we'd like answers to, but none of them seemed likely to come up in a casual chat with a stranger.

Ten minutes before her class was due to be over, I headed out to find a good place to wait and accost her. Evan and Lander had pointed out three cars that might be hers; unfortunately, they were in different parts of the lot, so I'd need to snag her closer to the door. The smokers had departed, so I perched against the raised concrete planter, feeling enveloped by the residual tobacco smell. Whoever was in charge of keeping this place clean was certainly shirking their duties. In addition to the piles of dead butts, there were cans and coffee cups buried in the jasmine. And as I stood there in the warm, humid evening air, the smell of poo wafted up as well. This was a bit high for a dog to have gotten up there to do their business. I shuddered and moved to find another place to wait.

A handful of people began drifting out the glass doors, so I headed up the steps and made my way into the building. A wide hallway stretched the length of the building, wooden doors bisected by narrow vertical windows spread along at even intervals. Dead ahead, a bank of elevators squatted, cloudy yellow tiles overhead indicating the location of each car. One was approaching the first floor, and with a flat ding announcing its arrival, the doors groaned open, discharging a middle-aged woman toting a box and wearing a scowl.

I wasn't sure if the Limitless Learning classes were on this floor or one of the upper ones. Or maybe both. I spotted a directory near the elevators and had taken a couple steps towards it when one of the doors down the hall opened and a few people began trickling out of one of the rooms. It was an odd mix, people ranging in age from teens to seniors. The only thing they had in common was the large drawing pads they all carried. Using my ever-sharp deduction skills, I decided that this must be the Dandy Doodles class.

In a matter of seconds, three more doors opened and more people began spilling out. They'd told me there were only three classes, but even as I stood there, another door opened. Suddenly the hall was filled with people and I felt as if I'd landed in a high school hallway between classes. How was I ever going to find Annalise in this crush?

I hugged the wall as the river of bodies flowed past me, holding my phone as if distracted by an important message, all the while scanning faces as they went by. If Annalise was in this crowd, it was going to be well nigh impossible to cut her from the stampede without being obvious. In a matter of minutes, most of the people had made it out the doors to the parking lot, where there was about to be a sudden traffic jam. I had missed her.

Now I powered up my phone for real and shot Evan a text that I hadn't seen her. Just as I hit send, she strolled out of a door farther down. She was talking to an older man who looked like he might be the teacher. They drifted to a stop while Annalise held up a yellow legal pad for his inspection. He slipped a pair of readers off the top of his head and bent over the paper. Running his index finger in a quick side-to-side motion, he finally stopped and poked at something on the paper.

"This is where you need to put your energy now," he said. Two guys walked past talking about going out for a beer and I couldn't hear the rest of what the teacher was saying. I quick-walked towards the exit, then turned around as if I was just coming into the building. Annalise was alone now, carefully writing out notes on her legal pad. She finished writing, read over what she'd written and then dropped the pad into an over-sized canvas tote. I was about six feet away now, staring openly at her. Feeling my gaze, she glanced over.

"Sorry," I said, smiling at her. "I didn't mean to stare, but oh my gosh I love your earrings. And that necklace. And, like, your whole outfit." I waved a hand to encompass the entire ensemble, right down to her gladiator sandals that coordinated with the leather-banded necklace that circled her slim neck.

She smiled at me, although I could see her coolly checking out my own outfit.

"Thank you," she said, clearly unable to find anything positive to reciprocate with.

"I wish I could do that," I said. "But, I'm usually in a rush out the door and I just end up, well..." She looked at me as if afraid I might be contagious. "Where'd you get your necklace? I'd love to get one like that." Truth be told, it reminded me a lot of Addie's collar. I could probably get something cheaper at Petco.

"Actually, I sell these," she said. "I have an accessories business."

"Really? That's so cool! I have a business I'm trying to start too. Hey, are you taking that Expanding Your Business class? I was thinking of taking it, but I wasn't sure if it would be worth the money or not."

She began walking towards the exit. I trotted along beside her. "Yeah, I am. Actually it's pretty good. I mean, I know a lot of it already, but he's been really helping me fine-tune parts of my business that I had some questions about." She glanced sideways at me. "What kind of business do you have?"

"Gourmet dog biscuits," I said. "I mean, I started it a few months ago, but I'm not really making much money yet. Maybe I should take that class. I'm having trouble figuring out how to expand and still keep up with demand."

She pondered that. "Yeah, I can see how it might be hard with that kind of business model. Mine is maybe a little easier to manage. I sell accessories and I do consultations." She looked me up and down again, clearly hearing the sound of money clink as she considered how many consultations I might need. "And I have inventory that isn't perishable."

I sighed. "Yeah, maybe I should have done something different. I love the idea of the consultations. So, you help people look..." I glanced down at myself. "Good?"

She smiled, and this time it almost looked genuine. "I love helping people look good. Everyone gets it wrong. You don't need a ton of money. You just need some quality pieces and you need to know how to pair things. And once you know you look good, you get more confidence."

We'd reached the door to the parking lot, and we walked out and down the steps. I frantically searched for things to say that would not just keep the conversation rolling but maybe net me a little information, but I was coming up blank. Fortunately, she was talking about something she was passionate about, and it seemed that I just needed to show some genuine interest. I had to guess Dick wasn't that interested in an accessories business.

"Actually, this is how I met my husband." So, I guessed wrong.

"Your husband's into accessories?" I asked. I stopped walking, not wanting to reach the parking lot too fast and give her a reason to bolt.

"No, he's a lawyer."

"Lucky you. Free counsel for your business," I said. "I've just been piecemealing my stuff together. I don't even have a bookkeeper."

She laughed lightly, showing perfectly aligned teeth.

"It's funny you say that. I was actually working as a book-keeper for my father when I met my husband."

"Really? You looking for a side gig? My files are a mess."

"Sorry," she said. "I was just doing it for my father for a while to help out. He's got an auto repair business. I would imagine your stuff is a little simpler. You probably don't need a book-keeper, just better software."

I thought of my spreadsheets that I hadn't updated in way too long and sighed.

"I guess so. Supplies in, biscuits out. It shouldn't be as hard as I make it." I wracked my brain, feeling like I had while trying to carry the conversation with Lander's mother. Maybe spending most of my time with dogs was causing me to lose all my social skills. "So how'd you meet a lawyer at your father's auto busi-ness? Was he in for a little car work?"

"No, actually my father serves as an expert witness some-times. You know, when you need to explain how an accident did or didn't happen?" Maybe he could help match the paint on my car to whoever had run Lander and me off the road. "Anyway, Dick walked in one day to discuss a case with Daddy, and I pointed out that his tie was all wrong. He was due in court and the tie, ugh. It made him look, I don't know, shady or something. For whatever reason, he took me seriously, changed the tie and won his case. After that, he would come by the shop whenever he had a big case." She glanced around the parking lot, not seeming to focus on anything. "He would bring in two or three ties for me to pick from. He started calling me his lucky charm."

"Aww, that's sweet," I said.

"Yeah, I thought so. And then he started bringing me in when he was doing jury selection. You know, just to look at the potential jurors. You wouldn't believe how much you can tell about a person from the way they dress." She glanced over at me again, and I wondered what she was gleaning about me. "Anyway, that's way more than I'm sure you wanted to know."

"No, actually that's a great story," I said.

The parking lot had cleared remarkably fast, and she began moving towards a giant black SUV a couple of rows over from my lemon drop.

"Are you parked this way?" she asked.

"Yeah, just over there." I tipped my head, indicating no particular direction. She looked from me to the remaining cars and seemed to stiffen when she saw the yellow Kia. Or maybe it was my imagination. "Anyway, thanks for the info. I'll probably look into taking this class. I really appreciate the insight."

Annalise stood motionless, staring across the parking lot before turning slowly to look back at me.

"What class were you taking tonight?" Her face was completely emotionless in the yellow-tinted glow of the parking lot lights.

"Dandy Doodles," I said brightly. "Oh my gosh." I smacked my forehead. "In fact, I forgot my drawing pad. That's where I was headed when I got distracted by your necklace." I smiled, showing all my teeth, which probably looked ghastly in this light.

"You weren't sure about spending money on a class that could help you make money, but you thought it was worth doodling?"

"Kinda dumb when you say it like that," I said. Something between us had changed. Could it be my yellow rental? She didn't even know who I was—how could she have any idea what kind of car I drove? Could she have spotted Lander in the parking lot? I took a surreptitious glance sideways towards where Evan was parked. As far as I could tell, it was too dark to make anything out. Could she know what Evan drove? A feeling of unease crept over me. "Anyway, I do appreciate the information on the class. Good luck with your business. It sounds fascinating."

"Yeah, you too," she said, studying my face as if she planned to draw me later. The unease grew and a prickle of sweat popped up on my chest. I'd have to ask Lander if she could draw. Maybe she was memorizing my features to commit me to a poster later. You know, for the hit man or something.

"By the way, I'm Annalise," she said, shifting her bag and holding out her hand. "And you are?"

I took her smooth hand in mine and gave it a brief pump.

"I'm Lacey." I'd never had to make up names on the fly like I had this week. I really needed to put a list together. Or maybe I should just create an alias so that I'd be ready and wouldn't have to think about it. Maybe Lander had a name generator he used for his books. I'd check on that.

"Lacey. What's your business's name? I'd like to look it up."

My heart pitter-pattered and I fought the urge to run away. I was horribly unprepared for this.

"Lacey's Famous Dog Biscuits," I said. She wrinkled her nose a little. As if someone who named their business *Annalise Style and Accessory Transformations* had any creative high ground to stand on.

"You might want to jazz that up a bit," she offered.

"Yeah, you're probably right," I said. "What's the name of your business, if you don't mind me asking?"

"Annalise Style and Accessory Transformations," she said, lifting her chin as if daring me to say anything negative.

"Oh. Well, I guess that covers it," I said flatly. "Anyway, good luck."

"You too," she murmured. I turned and went up the steps into the building to retrieve my imaginary doodle pad.

The building had cleared and I rounded the corner out of sight, thinking I should wait a couple of minutes before reemerging. I leaned against the wall, fighting the paranoia that was creeping through my head. That entire encounter was harmless. It seemed like a seminatural conversation two strangers would have outside of an adult learning class. Right? So why was I suddenly feeling so unsettled?

My phone pinged and I pulled it from my purse. I had a message from Evan telling me not to come back to his car. Apparently, Annalise had gotten into her car and had moved a couple of rows over and was idling in her car, as if watching the door. My heart quickened. Was she going to shoot me as I exited the building? Okay, this was dumb. Maybe she'd started to leave and had to make a call. I suddenly understood Lander's paranoia. That was probably it. He'd just made me feel like everyone was out to get me. Or him. I wasn't even sure who was the target anymore. I hadn't done anything to anyone. I was fine.

I squared my shoulders and headed out the door doing an awkward half-run half-skip towards my car. There were still a handful of cars in the lot, but I wasn't sure where Annalise was. I veered from parked car to parked car until I made it to the last row, where I fumbled with my keys, inadvertently hitting the panic button and nearly wetting my pants as the alarm blasted to life. Finally managing to turn the alarm off, I threw myself into the driver's seat and locked the door behind me. A thought drifted up that had I locked my doors at the book signing event, I wouldn't be in this position. I would still have my Honda. I would probably be home with Addie, sitting on the couch and watching something dumb on TV. I would most definitely not be sitting in a lemon-drop Kia in a Limitless Learning parking lot, wondering if my window was going to be blown out by a bullet flying towards my head.

Ping. *Nice job not drawing attention to yourself.*

Whatever, I replied. *What now?*

Just start driving. We'll follow her. Don't go home. And don't go to my house!

I threw my purse on the passenger seat and started the engine. Great. Where exactly was I supposed to go? I headed for the exit, following a small sedan. The driver paused at the street, and I could see the driver's head tip forward and the glow from a phone light up. In spite of the fact that I wasn't sure where I was going or what I was supposed to do next, I tapped the horn. Honestly, have some consideration. Three cars were lined up behind me; I assumed one of them was Annalise. Should I make a break for it? Drive like a crazy person in and out of traffic trying to lose her? Or just meander around until she lost interest and went home?

The Kia didn't have a ton of horsepower. I mean, I could barely merge safely onto a highway access road much less try to outzip Annalise in whatever torqued-up monstrosity she was driving. I made a decorous turn right and cruised along, heading in the general direction of the Galleria. I didn't want to go to the Galleria, but I wasn't sure where to go. They say if you're being followed you should go to a police station, but to be honest, I wasn't even sure where a police station was around here. Not to mention, I didn't think that was what Lander had in mind. Or go to a well-lit, highly populated area. I flitted through and discarded ideas. Grocery store, pet store, restaurant, coffee shop. All no. It seemed like if Annalise was intent on following me home, all of those places would just postpone the inevitable.

I glanced in the mirror, trying to spot Annalise and Evan, but I couldn't tell one set of headlights from another. I wanted to go home, but there was no way I was going to risk someone following me to what should be my safe zone. There was only one thing to do. Get on a highway and drive until she wasn't willing to follow me anymore. God knows you could go a long ways on Houston highways without ever actually getting very far.

I hooked a left at the next light and made my way to the Southwest Freeway. A trail of cars followed me onto the entrance ramp and we all merged into medium flow traffic heading east towards downtown. Paranoia was creeping up again, filling my car like a toxic mist. Was that her to the left of me? My neck muscles tensed and I had flashbacks to the car hitting my left rear quarter panel before shoving me off the road into the bayou. If she hit me here, going sixty-five miles an hour, I wasn't sure I would be able to control this little can on wheels.

My breathing was shallow and I began to feel slightly dizzy. I gripped the wheel tightly and tried to relax. I counted my breaths, one, two, three, four. In, out. I stopped checking my mirrors and focused on the road in front of me. Drive. Breathe. Drive. Breathe.

When we got close to downtown, I made my way to the left lane and took the I-45 North exit, slowing down for the heavier traffic. Drive. Breathe. The downtown buildings were brightly lit in spite of the fact the workers had left hours ago. But hey, energy capital right here. Might as well burn it. We made our way north, passing the Aquarium, the 610 Loop, the giant Gallery Furniture showroom and still I kept going. I was starting to loosen up a little. Traffic moved steadily and I stole a look in my mirror, trying to see who was behind me. I caught sight of a beat-up panel van, doubted that was Annalise and kept driving. She was back there somewhere, I could feel it.

I passed the exit for the airport and began wondering when I should turn around. If she was behind me, it would look really strange for me to come all this way out just to turn around and head back downtown. Settling myself deeper into the compact seat, I relaxed my grip on the wheel and just started to go with the flow. Twenty minutes later, I approached the Woodlands. I really didn't want to go any farther. As it was, it was going to take me at least thirty-five or forty minutes to get home. I couldn't believe some people did this commute every day.

The panel van had veered off a few exits ago, and I surveyed the vehicles behind me again. I still couldn't tell anything. Moving into the right lane, I took the next exit and cruised down the access road, looking for somewhere to pull off. Up ahead I spotted a bowling alley, the lot slightly more than half-full. I signaled and pulled in, watching for anyone following me. A pickup truck pulled in behind me but then wheeled past impatiently as I came to a stop. He found a space the next row over, and I watched as a couple of teens swung out of the cab, grabbed hands and headed for the door. The young guy checked me out as they passed my car, decided I was old and reached over to nuzzle his date.

No one else pulled in, so I reached over and picked up my phone. There was a message from Evan's phone, time-stamped thirty-five minutes earlier: *She wasn't following you. She went home. We're headed to my house. Come over if you want.*

You mean I was all the way out here in the Woodlands for no reason? I sighed, put the Kia in gear and hit the highway headed south. At least traffic was moving steadily. Evan hadn't indicated what the next steps were going to be, but I was tired and ready to go home to Addie. I'd been so worried about William, but besides that, this whole mess of Lander's had been just that— Lander's mess. But the way Annalise had looked at me tonight, the way she'd studied my face as if memorizing it, had left me unsettled and I really just wanted to step away from this whole thing and go back to my regular, albeit excitement-free, life.

CHAPTER SIXTEEN

E ven though I visited my distributors on Fridays, making for a busy morning, my dog walking workload tended to be lighter in the afternoons. One of my clients was off every other Friday, and I'd noticed a tendency amongst my other pup parents to engage in long weekends or work-from-home days. Which was all very fortunate for me this Friday because Lander had sent me a text indicating that he intended to rectify my car situation today. As it stood, I was able to finish my rounds by two o'clock, and to my surprise, Lander pulled up to my house at two fifteen. I hadn't realized that he'd retrieved his car from wherever it had been, probably an impound lot somewhere, but it was an indication to me that he also wanted to get his life back to normal too.

Okay, maybe he wasn't totally back to normal because he asked if he could put his car in my garage to hide it away. Nevertheless, considering he was taking me car shopping, who was I to quibble?

There was a moment of awkwardness as we settled into my rental and I started the engine. He had said he was going to rectify my car situation, but what exactly did that mean? I assumed he was buying me a new car, but was that presumptuous? Was this like insurance, where you hoped you'd taken the replacement value option rather than cash value? My car hadn't been new, so should I suggest we try to find a used equivalent? I didn't want a used equivalent. And I was still waiting for the insurance to come through with the valuation of what they were going to pay me. Even if they weren't going to pay me the full value of a new car, they would pay me something. Should I offer to contribute that to the purchase? Then again, he was the reason my car was in the bayou, and he had sold a gazillion books. He could afford this. Nevertheless, I felt weird.

"You've got all your insurance information, right?" he asked, looking at me from behind dark sunglasses. "I mean, we're getting something today and you want to be ready to drive it off the lot."

"Yeah, of course. Right here." I glanced towards my purse on the floor behind me. "So, where should we start?"

Turned out, he had actually done quite a lot of research and had multiple options ready for me. If I wanted to replace my car, same make and model but new, he had mapped out which Honda dealer had the biggest inventory to choose from. Or, if I wanted something entirely new and different, he had options for that as well. I hadn't actually thought through this nearly as well as he had. I never even considered getting something entirely different, but he had reviews, safety data and reliability history by year. I could hardly take it all in.

"This is entirely up to you," he said as I riffled through the sheets of paper he'd handed me. "I will get you whatever you want, but I was thinking, with all this dog stuff you do, a Subaru might be more on brand. You know, they're like the dog car company. And the reviews are good. And there are different models depending what size you want." He trailed off, waiting for my response. I have to admit, I hadn't really thought that much about this.

"That sounds cool," I said. Who was I to argue branding with someone this successful?

I've always hated buying cars. First you have to get past the predatory salespeople who stalk you around the lot while ascertaining how much money you have and how much of a pushover you might be. If you have a trade-in, it's even worse as you haggle over what that might be worth. Then on to the swift-talking finance guys who tie you into terrible deals by throwing numbers at you faster than a pitching machine set to left-handed fastballs. You never feel like you're coming out ahead. Or at least I usually didn't.

Shopping with Lander was not like that at all. We cruised into the Subaru dealer, where I slid into a front parking space. I could see a trio of salesmen elbowing each other behind the plate-glass front of the building, but instead of charging out the door, they looked unimpressed. Finally, a fairly young, florid-faced guy with a crew cut and a tight pale blue suit strode out the door towards us. He pasted on his widest smile as he approached.

"Help you folks?" he asked, beads of sweat already popping out on his forehead.

"Thanks," said Lander. "But we're just going to take a look around if that's okay with you. What's your name? We'll find you if we need you."

"Everyone calls me Boomer," he said, handing a card to Lander. "Take your time. Let me know if I can help you."

We waited until he retreated before heading out into the lot. Lander and I made our way to the SUVs, where we compared sizes, specifications and looks. I still felt slightly odd about the whole thing, and I found myself comparing prices like I was on a first date with a guy who probably couldn't afford the restaurant.

"Why don't you just tell me which model you like the best, and what color you want? I'll take it from there," he said. He lifted his sunglasses so he could look me directly in the eye. "Seriously, I want to do this. And I can afford to replace what I am responsible for ruining."

For the first time, a small beat of excitement ran through me. It's fun getting a new car. I opted for the smallest model, then debated the color choices. After spending the past week in something so noticeable, I decided to go with silver. Or white if they didn't have the silver.

We headed to the showroom in search of Boomer. I told him I didn't want the most expensive model. I didn't want the nav system, didn't need a moonroof. Leather seats would just cause Addie to slide all over the back seat. Lander listened to me, then headed across the floor to where Boomer was throwing back a Mountain Dew.

Boomer nearly choked when Lander said we would like to buy a silver Crosstrek. "Great," he sputtered. "Do you want to take it for a test drive?"

Among the many other reasons I hate buying cars, I've always hated the test drives too. In spite of being an excellent driver, trip into the bayou notwithstanding, I'm always afraid I'll crash the car on the test drive. Not to mention the whiplash you give the salesperson while adjusting to different brakes. And the uncertainty of the horsepower, leading to sitting for long stretches in the driveway, estimating the speed of the cars careening down the access road. Why are car dealerships always on a highway? My palms started to sweat.

"I guess," I said. I handed over my license for Boomer to make a copy. Lander followed him down a short hallway, then reappeared seconds later with my license and the keys. Boomer waved us off.

"He's not coming?" I asked, hopefully.

"Nope. Just us," Lander said, holding open the heavy glass door for me.

The test drive was the most relaxed test drive I'd ever taken. The car we were in was nicely appointed with a moonroof, although no extensive navigation system. It did have leather seats, which Lander said I would love because they were heated. Although really, how many days does one need a heated seat in Houston? He also found a lovely seat cover for dogs while scrolling through his phone, which he ordered before we even made it around the block. He was making it hard for me to object to anything.

It wasn't long before we were back in Boomer's cubicle.

"So do you have a trade-in?" he asked.

I thought about my poor Honda, sitting in a car graveyard somewhere. The bayou muck would be solidified by now. The stench of the fetid water was probably still marinating.

"No," I said, shoving away the feeling of abandoning a friend. It's dumb to have attachments to inanimate objects. They're inanimate. They don't know you're abandoning them.

"Okay, so let's talk financing, then."

"I'm just going to write a check," Lander said before Boomer could even get started. He looked startled in the way you would if your underdog team just scored in the first minute of the game.

"Awesome," he said. "Then I'll just take you over to the finance manager."

"Okay, one thing," said Lander. Boomer's face fell as if he knew this sale couldn't possibly be so easy. "I understand it's his job to try to upsell this. He's required to read his little checklist of extras. So, he can do that. Once. I am going to say no, and then he needs to move on to taking payment and processing the paperwork. Understand? If he tries to push the extended warranty, or a coupon package for ten percent off future oil changes, or any bullshit like that, we're leaving." He smiled. "Understood?"

Boomer started to sweat again. "Of course! Understood!" He stood up and yanked at his tie, which was too tight for his neck. "Let me talk to him first. He can be kind of—" He mumbled something I couldn't understand. His face was a mix of hope and tension as he walked out of his small space.

Whatever he said must have worked because a sour-faced finance manager flicked a finger at the chairs in front of his desk. He read through a lengthy list of things that Lander declined and then started work on the paperwork. Within minutes we stood and headed towards the showroom. Boomer was standing near a tall café table, talking to the other two sales guys we had seen when we pulled in. His face fell when he saw us approaching.

"That was fast," he said.

"Yeah, it was," said Lander. He turned to me. "You want to call your insurance company? Make sure you're covered while they're getting it ready."

"Wait, you're done? Like you bought it?" asked Boomer. His face lit up like he'd just won a year's pass to an all-you-can-eat BBQ buffet.

"Yeah. Thanks for smoothing that out for us," said Lander. "I hate dealing with those guys." The other two salesmen stared at each other in disbelief. I'd known they'd be sorry.

After I called my insurance company, I called the rental car company and arranged for them to send someone over to collect their car. Fortunately they had an office fairly close to the car dealer and their representative was there before my new car was done being shined up for its release into the world. Lander whipped out his credit card and took care of that invoice as well, and I watched as the lemon drop rolled towards the freeway. Finally, things were getting back to normal.

On the way to my house, I was effusive in my thanks to Lander, but he gently brushed it off and busied himself paging through the new owner's manual.

"Well, at least I won't feel so visible anymore," I said, pulling unobtrusively into a lane of traffic full of other black, white and silver cars. Nothing like blending in with the herd.

"Definitely," he said. "I don't know what was going on with Annalise last night, but even from where we were, it seemed like she was staring at your car. It made me uncomfortable."

"No kidding," I said, wishing traffic was lighter. I wasn't worried about anyone following us right now, but I was feeling paranoid about keeping my new car ding-free. "Anyway, I know you don't really want to talk about it, but what are you going to do now? I hate to point out the fact that Seth seems to be the most likely person to have run us off the road last week. He's the only one we've seen with car damage."

Lander tucked the manual into the glove compartment and clicked it shut.

"I know," he said. "But I'm still trying to figure out what the point would be. We've been friends forever."

"I think you should call him," I said. "At least hear what he has to say. It sounds like he's got a mess going on. Right? Maybe you can help him or something, and then all this will go away and you can get your life back." Maybe help him to prison for attempted murder, vehicular assault on us, and physical assault on William.

He stared silently out the window.

"You don't still think your mother is doing this, do you?" I tried to keep the skepticism out of my question, but I wasn't fully successful.

"No, you're right. Everything points to Seth. Frankly, if he has been trying to kill me or he attacked William, I don't think we can just work that out."

"Yeah, I get that," I said. I tried to imagine how I'd feel if Evan tried to kill me. I couldn't even process the thought.

"You're right, though," he said. "I've been saying I want to get to the bottom of this, and yet I can't bring myself to call my best friend." He sighed. "I'll call him."

I was hoping he meant he would call now, but after a couple of minutes I realized he didn't. I guess calling from the confined space of the car wouldn't offer much in the way of privacy. Don't get me wrong, I was dying to hear what Seth had to say about all this, but I also understood that this conversation would likely be difficult for Lander.

When we got to my house, Lander declined my invitation to come in, saying that he wanted to get back to Evan's and put the call through to Seth. I gave him a big hug and thanked him again for the car.

"It was the least I could do," he said. "Why don't you come over to Evan's in a little bit, and I'll take you both out to dinner? You guys have done so much for me, I can't even begin to make up for all this."

I told him I'd be there after I walked Addie. It seemed like buying the car had been the catalyst Lander needed to start taking charge of this situation.

I got to Evan's house before he got home from work, which was a little surprising since it was Friday and I'd have thought he'd want to skip out a little early to get a head start on his weekend with Lander. Lander's car was pulled up Evan's driveway as far as it could go, the back end barely visible from the street. I was surprised he hadn't put a tarp over it or maybe a stack of tree branches to camouflage it. I should have left the extra space in the driveway for Evan, but I didn't want to leave my new car at the curb. I'd seen too many cars take a fast turn off Montrose, and I wasn't willing to risk losing a bumper this early.

The front windows were still fully covered and I heard

Henry begin to bark as I clomped up the sagging porch steps. This house needed so much work that I wasn't sure how Evan was ever going to get it all done. Judging from the last couple of months, maybe he wasn't.

"Hey, it's me," I called out as I rapped on the door. Henry's barks morphed from ferocious to an excited whine. Lander cracked the door open a few inches and I pushed past him, slipping inside and shutting it hard behind me. I wondered when he'd ever get to the point where he could open the door like a normal person.

The living room looked nothing like the last time I was here. A large brown sectional spread across the space in front of the windows, traversing the length of the room and hugging the far wall. The inside wall was taken up by an oversized TV, which rested on a long black stand, complete with more cubbyholes underneath than an average kindergarten class. A series of complicated-looking boxes filled most of the holes, and Lander had dropped onto the floor, where he picked up a knot of wires.

"Wow, what's all this?" I asked.

Lander glowered at one of the wires before grabbing a crumpled instruction page from the floor, turning it first one way, then another.

"I thought I should get Evan a little something as thanks for his hospitality. Here, can you look at this? Can you tell what this means?" He handed me the instruction sheet, although I could have saved him the time. I've never been able to make sense of diagram instructions.

"This is amazing. I'm sure Evan is super excited."

"He doesn't know about it yet. I was hoping to get it all set up before he gets home." He leaned closer to the box and jammed a yellow-tipped connector into a hole. "I'm not sure about that." He slid the whole mess into one of the cubbies and lurched to his feet. "I guess I can finish it later."

Chunks of Styrofoam packing littered the floor, alongside more instruction sheets, plastic sleeves and little twisty wire holders. I was surprised that Henry wasn't in the middle of it, ripping and tearing like he's been known to do. But he had found himself a soft perch, nestled into the crook of the sectional, clearly hoping no one would notice and kick him off. Lander and I began gathering the debris and piling it into an empty cardboard box. We'd barely finished clearing the mess when Evan pushed through the front door.

"Whose car is that in the driveway?" he asked, just before noticing the new additions. With a thump that didn't bode well for his laptop, he dropped his bag and stood staring open-mouthed at the new setup. "What..." His eyes swept from the big screen to the sectional. "What..." Henry gave a woof, still reluctant to move from his spot in case he wasn't allowed back. "What is all this?" One hand reached up over his heart as if he might be having palpitations.

Lander watched him like a parent watches their four-year-old on Christmas morning.

"It's no big deal," Lander said. "I just wanted to get you a little something to thank you for all your hospitality."

Evan noticed one of the vertical boxes tucked underneath. "Is that the latest PlayStation?" he yelled. I was getting the feeling that all future interactions with Evan would be with the side of his head while he stared at the screen on his wall.

"Yeah, I haven't tried it out yet. The setup took longer than I thought it would, and I think I need to do a few more things."

Evan rummaged around and unearthed a wireless controller. "Let's do it!" he screamed.

"Actually," said Lander, taking the controller gently from his grasp, "I thought we could have dinner first. And then we need to stop by Seth's."

"Did you get a hold of him?" I asked.

"Yeah. He sounded kind of rough and said he was glad I called because he needed to talk to me."

Evan was still wandering his living room, reaching out and touching things one by one as if afraid the mirage would evaporate on contact.

"What did he say? What'd he want to talk to you about?" I couldn't imagine he was going to confess to trying to kill Lander just all of a sudden like that. Then again, if he had any kind of conscience whatsoever, maybe he was bursting to come clean.

"He said he's going to be watching the game tonight and said I should come by. And actually, I think it would be better if I could see him in person for this. I've known him forever. I've always been able to tell when he's lying." He watched as Evan lightly stroked the corner of the TV. "I thought we could go get something to eat and then go over."

"Do you think it's safe?" I asked. "I mean, no offense, but what if this is just another ruse to get you alone where he can finish this?"

The stress lines reappeared on his face. "I thought maybe Evan could go in with me, and you could wait outside. It might be hard to explain your visit the other day. And also, if you wait outside, you can get help if we never come out."

A small tremor of apprehension snaked its way up my neck, and I shivered in spite of the warmth.

CHAPTER SEVENTEEN

I t took a little effort, but we were finally able to get Evan's attention. I fed Henry while Evan changed, although I thought we might lose him again when he came out of his bedroom and saw the living room anew. Lander finally prodded him from behind all the way out the front door.

I opted to drive, and Evan switched his attention from his new living room to my new car, although he complained that the back seat was smaller than in my last car. We headed towards the Heights, the mood lighter than it had been since we'd first met Lander. It seemed like we'd known him longer than the short week we had. I guess the pressure of the past week had bonded us in a way that normal interactions wouldn't.

We'd decided on a barbeque restaurant that Evan liked, and as I scoured the parking lot for a space, Lander's phone pinged. I glanced over and saw him scowling at the screen.

"Problem?" I asked, spotting a space up ahead.

He raked a hand through his hair. "My mom. She wants me to return her admin's property that"—he raised one hand to mimic air quotes—"'one of my cohorts appropriated from her house.'"

"Nell told your mother that we took her *diary*?" Evan asked from the back seat.

"I don't think Nell specified what it was exactly." Lander checked his screen again. "She mentions some important documents. Was there anything in there that could be considered important documents?"

"She's loopy enough to think those faked-up pictures are important documents, I guess," said Evan with a snort.

"Maybe we *should* return it," I said. I'd been uncomfortable with Evan having taken something so private, and I could imagine how mortified Nell must feel knowing that Lander had seen such a personal, albeit crazy montage.

I passed the parking space I'd spotted. It was small, and one of the cars on either side could easily ding one of my doors.

"Hey, you missed that spot right there," Evan said.

"Yeah, it's too tight. I don't want my car to get dinged."

"I'm starving," Evan groused. "And this car is small. It'll fit just fine."

I exited the lot and headed down the street towards an organic restaurant nearby. They had more parking, and in spite of the meltdown I knew Evan would have, their food was wonderful. The meltdown didn't happen, probably because Lander declared that he loved this place, so consequently Evan was all for it. In a way, Evan actually had a lot in common with Nell.

We ordered our food and found a table in the corner. Evan prattled on about his new big-screen television and gaming system, peppering Lander with questions that I neither understood nor cared about. My mind wandered to Nell. She was a bit over the top, but I felt sorry for her. She'd obviously read too many romance novels and had created her own fantasy where she and Lander would get together and he would fall madly in love with her. Of course, then she'd be stuck with CiCi as her mother-in-law. That should give anyone pause. But my gut said she wasn't the one trying to hurt Lander. Evan had probably been right the first time—if anything, she might be thinking about kidnapping Lander and hiding him away until he married her. But trying to kill him? It didn't make sense.

When our food came, the conversation shifted to the upcoming visit with Seth.

"I doubt that he's going to say he's been trying to kill you," I said. "Maybe he really does just want to catch up. You said it's been a while. Even though I *do* think he's the one who shoved us into the bayou."

Lander set his grass-fed burger down and wiped his fingers. "He sounded weird enough that I think he might just spill what's going on." I couldn't imagine how it would feel to know your best friend was trying to kill you. His shoulders drooped as if his bones had gone soft, and he picked at a tomato wedge that had skidded off the bun.

"What if he just wants to talk about losing his job or something? I mean, he could sound weird because he feels awkward with you being so successful and him being not," Evan said. "Or maybe he's going to ask you for money. I'm sure he'd feel weird about that. Or what if we go in and he intends to kill you right there?" For the first time I could see his attention shift off his new toys at home and onto our current discussion.

"Maybe you guys should take a weapon," I said. "I think I have my pepper spray still in my purse." I reached over and began rummaging through my bag. "Here. Take this with you." Lander and Evan looked at the bright pink cylinder. "Oh, come on," I said. "Would you rather be dead or carry a pink pepper spray?"

I shoved it towards Evan until he finally took it and tucked it into his front pocket. Judging from the expression on his face, the vision he had of saving Lander from a killer didn't involve popsicle-pink pepper spray. But hey, at least they had a weapon now.

On the way to Seth's, I could feel Lander pressurizing beside me like a carbonated bottle being shaken in the heat. By the time we got there, I had to check to make sure he was still breathing since he was so completely silent.

"You going to be okay?" I asked. I pulled to the curb across the street from Seth's, trying to find a spot where I could see past the vegetation to the garage apartment. May twilight descended slowly, heralding a chorus of chirping frogs and crickets. I fumbled for the unfamiliar window button, lowering my window before turning off the engine.

Lander stared past me down the driveway, then rolled his shoulders twice and lifted his chin. Seth's truck was tucked into the same space it had been when we'd been here earlier in the week. I didn't see any lights in the windows, but Seth seemed like the kind of guy who would sit in front of his computer, oblivious to the fading light. I hoped Evan didn't become like that. Sudden visions of him in stained sweats, slumped on his sectional while Henry danced at the door to go out, filled my head. I shook the image away and looked at Evan.

"Your best friend lives here?" Evan asked, appalled. "It's a dump." While he was right, I felt like he should be careful about passing judgment when his house was one strong wind away from blowing over itself.

Lander looked like he'd never really noticed the disrepair. "Yeah. He moved here a few years ago. I thought he'd find someplace nicer, but I don't know. He's never really cared about where he lived. Now that he's not working, I guess money's tight."

"It's kind of weird you bringing me along," said Evan doubtfully. "Don't you think?"

"Yeah. Of course it is," said Lander. "If you don't want to go in, I get that."

Evan shifted, feeling his front pocket where the pepper spray cylinder was probably poking him. "You can't go in there alone. I mean, what if he *is* trying to kill you? I'll go. Even if it is weird." He reached for the door and stepped out of the car.

Lander looked at me. "Okay, I'm not sure how long we'll be. Hopefully, I can get to the bottom of whatever's going on. Sorry to make you sit here."

"Oh, it's no problem," I said, glancing again at the garage apartment. I halfway expected someone to start shooting out of one of the windows, although likely they'd been painted shut and were incapable of opening. "Do you want to call me on your cell and leave the line open like we did when I went in?"

"No. It's okay. I'm pretty sure he's ready to tell me whatever's going on. I thought he was going to on the phone, but someone was at the door." Something about those words filled me with a sense of dread strong enough to make my stomach clench. Lander was still talking. "I really don't see Seth doing anything we need to worry about. And I'll have Evan with me. We'll be fine."

"I don't know. Maybe this is a bad idea. All of a sudden I have a bad feeling. Come on. Get Evan. You can call Seth from Evan's house."

Evan was already moving up the driveway towards the apartment. He turned towards us and held up his hands in a question. Lander ducked his head and gave me a half smile. "Jessie, it's fine. I have Evan with me. But maybe be ready to leave in a hurry." That did not make me feel any better.

I watched the two of them make their way up the overgrown drive. They paused at the bottom of the rickety stairs, heads together as if finalizing their plan. My heart rate had ticked up, an uneasy anxiety rising in my chest. This was a terrible idea. Who had been at Seth's door earlier? Was this a setup?

They started up the stairs, Lander in the lead. Evan shook out his hands as if trying to fix a circulatory issue, then pulled out the pink pepper spray and held it up before putting it back in his pocket. Hopefully he was checking which way to depress the plunger so as not to spray himself. At the top of the stairs, Lander paused. Evan stood a few steps down, leaning forward, arms curled in a gorilla stance. I could only imagine what Seth was going to think of this. I looked away, belatedly scanning the street for anything suspicious. It must have been trash day here, and more than half of houses still had empty black cans dumped haphazardly near the curb. As I watched, an older man from the main house in front of Seth's wandered towards the street in a tatty plaid robe and flip-flops. He squinted directly at me, and I hurriedly ducked my head, acting like I was texting on my phone. A breeze caught his robe and I got a quick peek of some old man parts before looking away for real. Seriously, people should wear underpants. The man wrestled the can onto its wheels and lumbered up the drive towards the garage. Lander and Evan had already disappeared inside.

The trash can made a loud rumbling noise as it trundled up the drive. The hard plastic wheels cracked and popped as they hit loose stones in the driveway, several times coming to a hard stop. With some muttering that I could hear from my car and a bit of effort, the man finally managed to shove it into its resting spot just below Seth's apartment. His robe was too lightweight for this kind of activity, and by the time he'd reached the top of the drive, the sash around his waist had come undone. I looked away again before he could turn fully around. By the time I looked back, he'd just finished arranging the can to his liking and was securing his robe when I saw Seth's door swing open and Evan's head pop out. He caught sight of the old man and disappeared back inside.

Okay, at least they were still alive. The man puttered around a little before making his way towards the back of the house, where, I assumed, he went inside. About two minutes later, Seth's door opened and Evan's head popped out again. He looked around, then slipped out the door and raced down the stairs, causing them to shake alarmingly. He ran towards me, his mouth open and his hands flapping as if loose at the wrists. I opened my door and got out of the car, rooted with dread.

Evan reached me, his normally flushed cheeks drained to the color of chalk. He bobbed incoherently in front of me and I wondered if you were still supposed to slap hysterical people across the face to calm them. I grabbed him by the upper arms instead and shook him hard.

"What? Evan, what happened? Where's Lander?"

His hands fluttered and I shook him again.

"He's dead." His eyes darted wildly around and panic flooded my body.

"Lander? Lander's dead?" I shoved Evan towards the front of my car, waving a hand for him to go around and get in. "Get in! Are you sure? Evan!" I was shouting now and he suddenly lunged at me, clamping a hand over my mouth.

He leaned close. "Shh. Shh. Be quiet." His head touched mine, my own panic seeming to calm his. "No. Lander's fine. Seth is dead."

Relief washed over me too late to stop the adrenaline rush that had already flooded my bloodstream. That was quickly overtaken by guilt and then I cycled all the way back to fear in a matter of seconds.

"Where's Lander? We need to call the police." Guilt came back around. I was relieved that Lander was alive, but Seth was dead. I thought of his floppy hair, dark-framed glasses and funky despair.

"No. He doesn't want to call the cops. We need to get out of here. He was trying to clean up..." He paused, a sudden sheen of sweat popping out on his upper lip. "Jess." He ran a hand over his forehead and I realized that this must be how I look when I'm in hospital settings. Evan was about to pass out. Or throw up.

"Evan, sit down." I opened the back door and shoved him towards the seat. He sank down, and I hoped he wasn't going to get sick in my new car. "What happened in there?" I moved around and squatted down in front of Evan. "Did Lander kill Seth?"

Evan's eyes had been darting side to side, watching over my shoulder, but as my words sank in, he turned and focused on me. "Why would you ask that?"

"What's he cleaning up? And why can't we call 911?" The adrenaline was eliciting a cranky agitation and I stood suddenly, pushing away from Evan. "I'm so sick of this guy not wanting to call the police. If he'd called the police last week, maybe Seth would still be alive!"

Evan was on his feet now too. This time he grabbed me by my upper arms. "Shh, Jessie. Look, he's going to be right out."

"What happened?" I hissed at Evan.

"His friend didn't answer when we knocked. So Lander tried the door and it was open. It's dark in there and the place was a mess." He looked towards the apartment. "There's beer cans all over everywhere and some pills or something. And he was—" He closed his eyes. I know what it's like to find a dead body, and it's not a good thing. Closing your eyes is not recommended for a while. I poked him to get him back on track. "He was behind the couch. He had this white, I don't know, crusty white stuff around his mouth." He let go of my arms and raced around to the other side of the car, where he barfed up his dinner in the bushes.

I stood at the open car door. Seth was dead and Lander was inside "cleaning up." What did we really know about Lander Jones? He was a famous thriller writer. That was all we really knew about him. What if he was actually a psychotic killer who was doing some kind of twisted research for his next book? What if there wasn't someone trying to kill him, but instead he was running around killing other people and taking notes so as to impress his readers with the accuracy of details in his next book?

Evan slouched towards me, looking only somewhat recovered.

"Evan, what if Lander's behind all this?" I spoke quietly, keeping an eye on Seth's apartment door.

"What? What are you *talking* about?" He wiped his knuckles across his mouth and I felt a wave of sympathetic nausea roll through me. I swallowed hard.

"What do we really know about him? I mean, what if he's doing this all as research for a book or something?"

"Jess, Lander isn't doing this. I've spent the last week with him—he's scared to death. He would never hurt anyone. He would definitely not hurt William. And now"—he pointed toward Seth's rickety apartment—"now he's lost his best friend. I think he was right from the beginning. I think his mom is doing this!" He was getting worked up again.

"But I'm pretty sure that Seth was the one that ran us off the road," I pointed out, my arguments all over the map at this point.

"So maybe they were in on it together and now she's done with him. He looked like he'd been poisoned, and she's the crazy chemist." The small bit of color he'd regained faded away again. "I told you that tea she gave me was tainted. That could have been me." He looked as if he might faint.

I swatted a mosquito away and thought of William. Evan

was right. I couldn't see Lander hurting William for any reason. All the more reason to hand this over to the police. Evan's head jerked up and I followed his gaze. Lander was making his way down the stairs rubbing a cloth along the rough wooden handrails before making his way quickly down the drive. Seeing us watching, he motioned for us to get in the car, sliding in just seconds later. He pulled the door softly closed behind him.

"Let's go," he said, dropping his rag on the floor. I hesitated, looking over at him. I'd been ready to demand we call the police this time. Refuse to move until we heard the sirens approaching. Turn this whole mess over to the authorities like we should have the first night. But looking at him, I was overwhelmed by a sense of defeat and hopelessness radiating off of him. He looked like a child whose puppy had just been run over. Any thought that he'd killed Seth, attacked William or somehow set it up so that he and I had been driven off the road flew out of my head. He looked broken.

I started the engine and pulled slowly away from the curb. The seat belt alarm began to bleat and he reached listlessly over for the strap, securing it without looking. He slumped in his seat, his face turned away, staring blankly out the window.

Evan leaned over the seat and patted his shoulder awkwardly. "Man, I'm sorry," he said.

"Yeah, me too," I echoed. I wasn't sure where to go, and I hated to be a pain, but we couldn't just leave Seth there like that. I got the sense that he didn't get many visitors, and since he wasn't working and no one would think to worry... well, I didn't even want to think about it. "Lander? We need to call someone. We can't just leave him like that. Whatever happened, someone needs to know."

I heard a small sniff and I knew he was trying not to cry in front of us. "I know," he said, his voice breaking. I looked in the rearview mirror at Evan. He looked as uncertain about what to do as I felt.

"Do you want me to call the police?" Evan finally asked. "There's no reason you have to be involved." I could only imagine how well Evan would hold up under police questioning, explaining how he'd found a complete stranger dead in an apartment he'd never been to before.

Lander shifted in his seat, pushing himself a little more upright. "No. Let me think. I don't want them to have a record of you calling."

"What about the guy in the front house?" I asked. "He was out earlier. It's probably the landlord. If we knew his name, we could call him and ask him to check on..." I hesitated, reluctant to say Seth's name. Lander ran a hand through his hair, looking almost exactly the same as Evan did with that mannerism. They'd been together too long.

"Yeah," he said, leaning over his cell phone. "Yeah. We could call him. But I still don't want any of our numbers traced to this."

"That's easy," said Evan. "If we can get his number, we can just call from a pay phone."

In the end, getting the phone number was the easy part. Evan did a quick reverse address search on his phone and came up with the number for a Harce Padgett. The harder part was finding a pay phone. It turned out that pay phones had become extinct without me even noticing. I drove around the parking lot of every convenience store and gas station we saw. Where had they gone? I know almost everyone had a cell phone, but what about the people who didn't? What about the people who wanted to make anonymous calls? What were the cranks supposed to do?

"Okay, what if I just call from my phone and hit star sixty-seven?" asked Evan after about a dozen failures. "Doesn't that block your number?"

"It does to a point," said Lander. "It'll block it so Harce Padgett can't see it on his caller ID, but the carrier still has access, meaning the police could still track it." He'd really thought through this whole keep away from the police business. I sighed and turned east.

We finally spotted a pay phone on the wall outside a convenience mart in a rather sketchy neighborhood. Two beefy gentlemen stood nearby as if expecting a call.

"Do you want me to keep driving?" I asked. The guys had noticed us staring and one puffed up, squaring his shoulders and giving his chin a quick jerk in our direction. Lander pulled his wallet out of his back pocket, extracted something and stuck it in his pocket, leaving the wallet on the floor.

"This might be dumb," said Lander. "But no. Evan? Come with me?"

I put my window down, left the engine running and watched as Lander and Evan approached the men.

"Yo," said the bigger one. If I had to guess, it seemed like that one weighed more by himself than Evan and Lander combined. His biceps were the size of rotisserie chickens, and his neck bulged under a heavy rope of gold chains.

"Hi," said Lander evenly. "I was wondering if we could get your help with something. I'd obviously pay you for your time."

The second guy made a derisive grunt and knocked his shoulder into the first one. "Dawg."

The first one ignored him and stared at Lander.

"I'll give you a hundred bucks if you'll call this number and ask the man who answers if he could go check on the guy in the garage apartment." He reached into his pocket and held up a bill along with a slip of paper with a phone number on it.

"What is this? Some kind of setup?"

"No," said Lander. "Easy money for you. A favor for me."

Evan was bobbing up and down like he might tinkle on the sidewalk.

The muscle man reached out and took the paper. "That's it? Check on the guy in the garage apartment."

"Yep," said Lander. "That's it. But could you ask it more like a question?"

"Ya got fifty cents?"

Lander turned to Evan, who shook his head. They both looked to me. I had change in the console of my old car, but it was in the bayou now. Maybe there was something in the bottom of my purse. I reached into the back seat, snagged my purse and shook it, listening for change. Hearing nothing, I reached in and began digging through.

I heard a snort. "Jayz, give me some change. We ain't got all day for this." Second guy dug a couple quarters out of his low-slung pants and handed them over.

The quarters clinked into the machine and the muscle held the receiver in a beefy hand up against his head. We waited. What if Harce Padgett didn't pick up?

"Hey yo. Could you go check on the guy in the garage?" Lander touched his arm, miming a word. "Garage apartment," he amended. He paused. "Hey! I don't give a rat's ass that your show is on, I'm asking you a favor. Go check. Yeah! Well, same to you." He slammed the phone down. Lander handed him the hundred-dollar bill.

"Thanks," he said. "Appreciate it if you forgot you ever saw us."

Both guys laughed. "Heard that. Pleasure doing business with you."

"Do you think Harce Padgett will actually go check?" I asked as they both slid into the car.

Lander rubbed his face. "I hope so, but I don't know." He'd

rallied for a bit while we had a mission, but now that we'd accomplished it, he looked like he was fading again.

"You ready to go back to Evan's?" I asked, trying to get my bearings. We'd ended up wandering pretty far from where we started, and I was unfamiliar with this part of town. I noticed the bright red direction indicator on my rearview mirror and figured if I got that pointing west, we'd eventually end up somewhere that I recognized.

"No, I don't think it would be safe to go back there," said Lander.

I drove a few blocks and turned right at the next major street in order to get a W on my mirror. I was getting a bad feeling about Lander's state of mind. What did he want us to do? Did he think the three of us were going to go on the lam? Drive until the bad guys couldn't find us? Well, if that's what he and Evan wanted to do, they were welcome to it, but I had a Border collie waiting at home for me, and I wasn't leaving her for anything.

"It was your mom, wasn't it?" asked Evan. "I mean, if anyone knows about poisons, she does, right?"

"*Evan*," I said.

"It's a fair question," Lander said. "She is a pharmaceutical chemist."

"You were right this whole time," Evan said supportively. "We should have listened to you."

I looked for street signs as I drove through an intersection, but the names meant nothing to me. I kept going.

"So, where do you want me to drop you guys?" I asked.

"I don't think you can go home either," Lander said, turning towards me. Streetlights reflected in yellowed flashes against his face, making him look even more strained. I didn't want to argue with him, but there was no way I was abandoning Addie.

"Evan, if you're not going home, you need to make arrangements for Henry. I can drop you guys somewhere and pick him up if you want."

"*No!*" said Lander loud enough to make me veer out of my lane. "Sorry, but there's no way you should be at Evan's house alone. None of us should be alone. We'll all go and get Henry."

I finally found a street I recognized and headed into more familiar territory. Evan and Lander were throwing around ideas of where to go and what to do next. None of their ideas involved contacting the police, and I'd settled into a contradictory silence. When I was about a mile from Evan's, I finally chimed in again.

"Okay, explain to me why you think it's not safe to go to Evan's? I mean, I get not wanting to go to your house, Lander, but no one knows you're staying with Evan. No one related to you even knows who Evan is. So what's changed?"

"Seth is dead is what's changed," said Evan, leaning forward and nearly screaming in my right ear.

"Yeah, but now at least you know Seth can't come after you. So, if it is Lander's mom, just don't answer the door if she knocks."

Evan drew in a breath as if preparing a torrent of arguments for me. Lander held up a hand. "Okay, okay, you're right to an extent. Seth is no longer a threat, but I'm not positive my mom is behind this."

"I thought you said she was," Evan said, sounding personally injured.

Lander rubbed his hands over his face and seemed to shrink into the seat. "I think she is," he said. "I think she is, but I'm not positive. I need some time to think."

"So can I drop you guys at Evan's?"

CHAPTER EIGHTEEN

Not to be selfish, but I wasn't particularly thrilled when I found myself with two unexpected houseguests later that night. Evan knew my spare bedroom was now a home office. I barely had room for one guest on my couch. I literally had nowhere for a second person to sleep unless Addie was willing to give up her spare bed. And why he thought they would be safer at my house than his, I still wasn't grasping from his convoluted arguments.

Nevertheless, they had appeared at my door within thirty minutes of my arriving home, after I truly thought I'd convinced them that they would be fine at Evan's. At least they had the sense to bring Frances's old foldup mattress with them. Addie and Henry were delighted at the situation. Way more than I was. Also, the amount of stuff they unloaded from Evan's Jeep had me concerned that they were planning a lengthy stay. Admittedly, I have some personal space issues and value my alone time, and as I watched my living room turn into an overstuffed rec room, I could feel my mood turning snippety.

Lander brought in enough beer that if I hadn't known he was trying to hide, I'd have feared they were getting ready to throw a frat party in my living room. More likely he was about to go on a bender. Evan held out a flimsy cardboard box that clanked as I took it. "I know you like this kind," he said as I lifted a bottle and looked at the label. Inside were several bottles of New Zealand sauvignon blanc, which happened to be my favorite type of wine. I felt the band of bad mood lessen a little.

We made room in the refrigerator, then bustled around trying to figure out where they were going to sleep. Lander still looked shell-shocked and I pushed aside my own annoyance at the intrusion and remembered that he'd lost his best friend today. I offered to let him stay upstairs in my study. He lugged the mattress upstairs, dodging the dogs, who were racing around like kids at their first sleepover. Evan watched us go up, looking forlornly after us, and I halfway expected him to follow along with the couch cushions.

"You can stay in here," I said, bustling around throwing papers into my desk drawers. I snatched my laptop off the desk and looked frantically around for anything embarrassing that might be sitting out in plain sight. I certainly hadn't been expecting anyone to come in here, much less come in and spend the night. Then again, it wasn't like I had a collection of cleavage shots, or any other indelicate items. I tried to think what I had in my desk drawers in case Lander was a consummate snooper. I fought the urge to pack up everything and move it down the hall to my bedroom. Surely he wouldn't poke through my things. Then again, he was a writer—weren't they always nosy? I grabbed the books that were piled on my desk, not wanting him to judge my reading tastes, and ran my armload of things to my room.

When I returned, Lander was wrestling with the mattress. It was stuck between the wall and my reading chair. There really wasn't a lot of extra room in here.

"If you grab an end, we can move my desk over a little," I

said. "Then we can move the chair over and you'll have more room."

"It's okay. This is fine," he said as he managed to get it open. There wasn't enough room to lay it flat, and it curled like a taco shell with just enough room for Lander to wedge himself in as the filling.

"Are you sure? It'll just take a minute."

"Jessie, thanks. But this is perfect. Really." I guess if someone was trying to kill me and had just succeeded in killing my best friend, I might prefer to cocoon myself into a taco shell too.

"Okay, well, there's a bathroom right next door. You and Evan can share the shower. He has a powder room downstairs. Um, let me get you some towels and sheets. Do you have a pillow? Can I bring you something to eat? Let me get a new bar of soap." I had suddenly turned into my mother.

He looked up, making an effort to smile. It didn't work. "I'm fine. I brought stuff from Evan's, I just need to put it all together."

I edged out of the room, calling the dogs to come with me, but Addie and Henry had put aside their differences and claimed their spaces at either end of Lander's bed. Their mouths hung open in identical smiles and he stepped in between them and sank down, his hands reaching for their soft fur.

"I'll be downstairs for a while if you need anything," I said, leaving him alone with the best therapists I know.

Evan had converted the couch with gray sheets, two bed pillows and a dog blanket. Henry's bed was on the floor by the coffee table, and the table was covered with a stack of Lander's books. Seriously, Evan had dragged his Lander Jones collection over? Maybe he was afraid someone would break into his house and steal them.

"So, you set here?" I asked. "I'll bring you some towels in a few minutes. Do you need anything else?"

"No, we brought everything we need," he said. "We didn't want to make any work for you." He wandered towards the kitchen. "Want a drink?"

"Sure," I said. He twisted the top off the wine bottle, found a glass for me, and doled out an oversized pour before getting his own bottle of beer and settling down at the kitchen table.

"Lander okay?" he asked, his blue eyes somber with concern.

"I don't know," I said. "He doesn't look great."

He twirled his beer in a circle, not looking at me. "Yeah. That whole thing was awful," he said. "When Seth didn't answer the door, we just thought maybe he was in the bathroom or something. And Lander said half the time he's got his earbuds in, so then we thought maybe he couldn't hear us. So Lander tried the door, and it was unlocked, so we went in." He twirled his beer again until it sloshed up the sides of the bottle. "The place was a mess. I figured it always looks like that, you know? But Lander knew right off that something was wrong. He saw—" He broke off and took a swallow of beer. "I didn't see at first."

I turned as I heard the dogs racing down the stairs. Lander followed more slowly, holding the handrail like he needed support. Evan popped up and headed for the refrigerator. "Beer?" he asked.

Lander plunked into an empty chair at the table and nodded.

"Evan was just filling me in on what happened," I said. I took a sip of my wine. It was cool and crisp and I felt a pleasant tingle as it went down.

Evan handed Lander a beer and sat down. "Yeah, I was just telling her that you knew something was wrong right off. I was so busy looking at all the junk everywhere."

Henry bounded over to Lander's side and put his front paws up. His short little legs hopped in place as if trying to get enough bounce to catapult himself into Lander's lap. "Is it okay if I hold him?" Lander asked.

"Of course," I said. He bent down and carefully lifted Henry by the rump, depositing him squarely in his lap. Henry immediately twisted around and began covering Lander's chin with kisses. A small smile curled the edges Lander's lips, stress creases on his forehead lessening ever so slightly.

"I saw you look out," I said to Evan. "When the guy was taking the trash can back."

"Oh, yeah," he said. "We'd already found Seth and we were afraid he was going to come in and it would look like we'd done it."

"I'm pretty sure the medical examiner, or whatever, would know you didn't," I said. Didn't Evan watch crime shows?

"Well, not if he'd been killed right before we got there." True enough.

I glanced at Lander and tried to think of a sensitive way to ask my question. "So, you said you thought he'd been poisoned?"

"Ugh, it was awful," said Evan, clearly unencumbered by emotional attachment to the victim. "He'd thrown up and he had this nasty, I don't know, gunk all around his mouth." He paused, his mouth pulling back like Addie's does before she barfs, and I worried we were about to have a replay of what happened by the car.

"What kind of poison do you think it was? Or could it have been a drug overdose?" I touched Lander's arm. "Sorry, I'm not trying to judge your friend."

"I know," said Lander, stroking Henry's side. Henry had settled against Lander's chest, half-asleep, his breaths slow and steady. Lander's breathing had slowed and seemed to be syncing up. "It could have been a drug overdose. Seth was never into anything more than an occasional joint before, but I don't know about lately. There were a lot of beer cans, and there was a pill bottle on the floor."

"What was in it?" I asked.

"It was empty and there wasn't a label." Well, that saved us hours of trying to identify a random pill by matching it up with something on the internet.

I reached down and rubbed Addie's neck. She sat by my side, her gaze drifting reproachfully from Henry to me. "Might he have killed himself? I mean, what if he was the one that pushed us into the bayou, and the one that attacked William? Maybe he couldn't handle what he'd done."

"Oh, no, he looked awful!" Evan chimed in. "No one would do that to themselves." As if someone contemplating killing themselves cared about how they would look. I felt a little queasy thinking about it myself, and I hadn't even seen it in person.

"There was something else," Lander said. "There was a letter on the table from his employer. They were coming after him for having stolen something. It said he had to pay back the cost of the assets he'd stolen, and if he did that they wouldn't press charges."

"Oh yeah," I said. "Remember? He'd mentioned to me that he'd been fired because they said he'd ordered some software that wasn't authorized." I thought about the expensive laptop I'd seen on his coffee table. Maybe there was more than just some software. "That's even more reason for him to kill himself. If he couldn't come up with the money, he was looking at being charged."

"It also means he was desperate for money," said Lander. "Someone could have taken advantage of that desperation and promised to pay him for doing all that—" He broke off, dropping his chin forward onto the top of Henry's head.

"I think your mom hired him to kill you and then she killed

him when he didn't get the job done," said Evan matter-of-factly. "Out of everyone you know, she's the only one who would know how to make a poisoning look like an overdose." He shuddered. "I'll never forget that tea she tried to get me to drink." He was never going to let that go.

"Did you see his sketchbook?" I asked Lander.

"Yeah, it was there. It definitely looked like a mock-up of my characters. I didn't have a chance to look closely, but it seemed like he was putting something together that he couldn't actually do anything with."

"So even if he killed you, he couldn't capitalize on using your characters in this video game?" I asked. Lander had explained this before, but I hadn't fully grasped the nuances of the copyright laws.

"That's right," he said. "Unless my estate granted him the rights, which it won't." I was dying to ask who his beneficiaries were, but that seemed out of bounds.

Evan got up from the table and retrieved his duffle bag. He unzipped it and rummaged around before pulling out a beat-up notebook and Nell's journal. "Hey, look. I still have our original list. Remember the one we made that night?" He trailed off and looked carefully at Lander, seeming to suddenly remember it was the night William had been attacked. He handed me the notebook. "Here, you made the list."

I took the notebook and tried to straighten out the curved spiral wire that ran along the spine. The first page was covered with scribbled phone numbers and pizza doodles. The second page was where I had made notes the night we'd had dinner with William. It seemed like so long ago.

"So, here's our list of suspects," I said brightly. "Let's see where we are." I glanced at the short register of names: CiCi, Annalise, Dick DeLuca, Nell and Seth. And at the bottom I'd written: Stranger / Stalker / Fan. I sighed. "Okay, well I guess we can take Seth off the list."

"No," said Lander. "It still may have been him."

"What if it's all of them?" asked Evan. "I think I saw a movie like that once, where everyone was in on it."

"Or it could have been Seth and my mom working together."

This was going as well as the first time we'd tried to figure this out. Not to judge, but you'd think a guy who made a living plotting murders would be better at unraveling this.

"Let me see Nell's diary again," I said to Evan, shoving the worthless list towards him. We swapped books, Evan taking the list of names and studying them like he was cramming for a test. I picked up Nell's journal and began leafing through it again, moving quickly through the pages. "I can't believe Nell told your mom about us taking this." I was using "us" loosely. "I'm sure it means a lot to her, not to mention how embarrassing it is. But as for this being an important document, I think that's a stretch."

"Did your mom say anything else?" Evan asked. "Like, I'm going over to kill your best friend now."

I reached the last page of photos, still not seeing anything important here. Creepy, yes. Important, no. There were still a lot of empty pages awaiting new fake family photos, and I began turning them one by one. Lander lifted his phone and pulled up the text from his mother.

"She just said that bit about returning Nell's documents, and she said she and my dad were going out of town this weekend."

Evan and I looked up. "Your mom's out of town?" Evan asked. "Are you sure she is, or is she just saying that?"

I'd reached the end of the journal, having found nothing in the empty pages. At the back, however, was an expandable pocket that I'd not noticed the first time. The opening was near the spine, ensuring that anything tucked inside would not inadvertently fall out. I gently pulled the edge open and peered inside. Sure enough, there were a couple papers nestled in the folds. I slipped a finger in and coaxed them out.

"Oh no," I said, unfolding the first document. It was Nell's birth certificate. The second document was short, but equally distressing to have in our possession. It was a health care power of attorney granting Nell the right to make all medical decisions for someone named Eunice Rey. "Oh no," I said again. I handed the documents over to Lander, who glanced at them before raising one hand and running it so roughly through his hair I could see strands raining down on Henry's head. He set the documents on the table.

Evan picked them up and stared at them in disbelief. "Well, who would put something like this in a *diary*? I mean, you put important documents somewhere safe!"

"We have to return these," I said. "Do you want to let your mom know we found them and we'll return them to Nell as soon as we can?" I asked Lander.

"Did you tell her we took them?" asked Evan. "Can we get in trouble for this?" His voice rose to a warbly tenor.

"I never responded," said Lander.

"Okay, whatever. We have to get them back," I said. No wonder Nell was freaking out. I mean, in addition to missing the fantasy photos. "You could give all this to your mom to give to her," I suggested. The two of them looked at me like I'd lost my mind. "What? Okay, we could mail it."

"She can't know we took it," said Evan. "She's crazy. She might press charges or something."

"She knows you took it," I said, no longer willing to be so generous with the "we." "You could mail it."

"We could burn it. All of it. Do you have any matches?"

"Evan! We can't burn these documents!"

"Okay, then we have to get it back to her without her seeing us. Let's go now."

Lander looked like he could barely make it up the stairs, much less go on an ill-advised trip to Nell's, where I presumed Evan was planning a reverse break-in. I suggested we call it a night and reconvene in the morning, when, hopefully, we would be better rested and could actually come up with a plan that wasn't half-baked.

CHAPTER NINETEEN

Surprisingly, I slept pretty well. I've had issues before when I have houseguests, where just the energy of another person in my space is enough to induce insomnia. But for whatever reason, I slept like a rock. Maybe it was because deep down I had the sense that Seth's death meant the end of the attacks on Lander. William could go through rehab and come home to recover in a safe place. Obviously, Seth's death was a terrible thing, but whether he'd killed himself deliberately or accidentally, whether out of remorse over what he had done to Lander or fear of being arrested for stealing from his company, it would end the reign of terror on Lander and those close to him. And we could all get back to normal.

In spite of all that, I felt bad about Seth. I'd only met him once, but I could kind of relate to his goofy sadness. He'd been close to my age and struggling to find his way. Without family money, I might be struggling like that too. Okay, I'd never steal anything, and I certainly wouldn't try to kill anyone, but I'd never been cornered like he was. No, no, no. I had to let that go. Seth had made his own decisions, that was all there was to it.

The door to my study was still closed as Addie and I made

our way downstairs. I'd meant to go quietly in case Evan was still sleeping, but Addie had other ideas. She loped down the stairs in graceful leaps. Henry heard her coming and set up a high-pitched yodel as he raced around the living room, vaulting off of Evan's prone form on the couch, around the coffee table and up onto Evan again. Oops. So much for quiet.

By the time I got down the stairs, Addie had jumped onto Evan and was trying to dig his head out from under the pillow. "Addie, no!" I hissed at her. The last thing we needed was to spend the day at the emergency room having Evan's eye put back in. She popped her black-and-white head up and gave me a wide grin. Evan shifted under his sheet, holding the pillow in front of his face as he struggled to a sitting position. He grunted sharply as Addie dug a paw under his rib cage, repositioning herself, and Henry bounced near his groin, the excitement of my arrival fueling his joy.

"How'd you sleep?" I asked, heading for the door to let the dogs out. Evan oofed as they pushed off and raced towards the door. I filled the coffeepot, taking a surreptitious look over the counter at Evan. His hair stuck out in dark clumps, lines from the pillow cut furrows along one cheek and his whole face looked puffy. The neckline of the T-shirt he was wearing stretched out in a saggy oval, exposing a bony collarbone. I looked away before he stood, afraid of how the bottom half would appear. He staggered towards one of the barstools at the counter and slumped onto the seat. "That good, huh?"

He rubbed his hands up and down over his face as the coffeemaker burbled to life. "I couldn't stop thinking about how Seth looked," he mumbled. "I didn't know the guy, but man. It was awful." He trailed off, looking queasy. I was thankful I'd stayed in the car. "Jess, I really think Lander's mom poisoned him. He had to have been poisoned. Do you think the cops will be able to trace what she used? I mean, she's a top-flight chemist. What if she used something untraceable? She's gonna be leading that government task force. What if she feels like she has to poison all of us to make sure we can't rat her out?" He looked so wrinkled and small this morning, it was like he'd been shrunk in the dryer.

"He could have died of an overdose, Evan. He could have done that to himself."

"No. No way. I just don't think so."

"Evan, people kill themselves all the time. Or overdose accidentally." I heard a muffled woof and opened the door. "I don't think they put that much thought into how they're going to end up looking." I poured him a cup of coffee and slid it over. The dogs raced past and up the stairs in search of Lander. Amid a chorus of Henry yaps, several thuds, and thundering paws, Lander appeared looked as good as Evan. I poured him a cup of coffee too, dribbled the rest into my own cup and started another pot.

"Hey, man," said Evan. "How'd you sleep?"

Whereas Evan's hair stuck out in crazy angles, Lander's had gone oddly flat. And here I'd thought that guys just fell out of bed looking good.

"Oh, you know," said Lander, rubbing his face much like Evan had.

"What are we going to do about your mom?" Evan asked.

Lander sighed and wrapped his fingers around the coffee mug. "I don't know."

"We don't know that your mom did this," I said. "I mean, you've said yourself she has a lot riding on this task force she's trying to get onto. I'd hate to ruin that for her if she had nothing to do with any of this."

Evan looked astounded at me. "Jessie! How can you say that?"

"Well, we don't know. Lander, you said your mom was going

out of town. If she was out of town, she couldn't have killed Seth."

"She could have been emailing from Seth's apartment as she watched him die. Email is not an alibi. When did they leave?" Evan asked. "She could have poisoned Seth and then left town with your father for an alibi."

Lander flicked the screen on his phone, scrolling until he found her email. She'd sent it while we were at dinner last night, most likely after Seth was already dead. He read it to us twice, but other than telling him to return Nell's property and letting him know that she and his father were in San Antonio for a conference this weekend, it didn't reveal much. The consensus was that if Seth hadn't killed himself, which I still thought he had, then the killer was the one who'd knocked while Lander was on the phone with him. We went in circles all the way through breakfast.

"Okay, look," Evan said as he pushed his plate away. "There's a way to know if it was your mom knocking on Seth's door while you were talking to him. Ask Nell. She's your mom's admin, right? She would know what your mother's schedule was. I'm willing to bet your mom didn't leave till last night. And while you're talking to her, you can somehow slip her diary back in her dresser."

Since we had no better ideas and I was adamant that we return Nell's documents, we decided to give this a try. Evan refused to drive because he didn't want Nell to get his license plate number and track him down to prosecute him over the diary theft. Lander tossed out close to a dozen options he could give Nell as to why he was there, giving us some insight into how adept he was at plotting. If he could control his expressions better, he'd be a tremendous liar.

I really thought this was going to be a straightforward endeavor. Lander would check his mom's schedule with Nell, tell her whatever lie he came up with, drop the diary somewhere in the house and we would move on. Evan and I would wait in the car. The one issue we couldn't get around was how he was going to sneak Nell's diary into her bedroom without her noticing. I suggested he shove it between the couch cushions, but Evan insisted that it be returned to the original hiding place. That way, one could argue that it had never been taken from the premises.

Somehow, don't ask me how, they came up with a plan they both thought was great. Me? I did not think it was great. Here's how it went: Lander would tell Nell that he wanted to see her backyard. He'd say he had looked out the window while we were there and was taken by how it would be perfect for a scene he was working on. Nell, of course, would eagerly show him around. While they were outside, I would sneak the diary into her bedroom, slip it in her dresser and run out the front. On the face of it, it seemed simple enough. The part I didn't understand was why Evan couldn't be the one to sneak in and return the diary. After all, he was the one who'd taken it.

"Jess, please," he said, dragging the word out. "If she saw me in her house, she'd call the police for sure. She has it in for me. You know that. You saw how she attacked me at the book signing. And then how she was at dinner. She doesn't hate you like she does me."

"Evan, she doesn't hate you," I said. But honestly, it seemed like she did. Although, I wasn't exactly one of her favorites either. At any rate, I had more confidence in my ability to get in and out without freaking out or becoming distracted than I did in Evan's. "Fine. But so help me, if this goes south, you better come up with a way to fix it."

"Great!" he said, cheering up immediately. "Tell you what I was thinking. You know how her house is on a corner? I could go around on the street side, hide behind a tree or something and then signal you when Lander gets her outside. Then you just run in, straight to her room and put that thing in her dresser. I think it was in the top drawer." He paused as if considering. "Yeah, just look for something lacy." He shuddered. "It was under some lacy things."

"What if she locks the front door after she lets Lander in?"

"Lander, you make sure the front door is unlocked." Evan certainly sounded like he was on top of this plan now that he had the easy lookout role.

Nell's street looked much as it had Wednesday night, although the collection of balls and bikes seemed to have propagated in the intervening days. I parked across the street, my car partially hidden by an older-model pickup truck. I couldn't see Nell's door without twisting my neck at an impossible angle, but it would keep her from looking right at me when she opened the door.

We huddled together, finalizing our plan. Evan spotted a dense grove of red-tipped photinias on the side street that would allow him to see into the backyard without being noticed. He called my cell and we connected, planning to keep the line open. He would then keep watch for Lander and Nell as they headed outside. Lander had his notebook with him and planned on poking around the backyard, asking extensive questions and eliciting Nell's input on whatever came to mind. This would thrill her to no end. As soon as Evan gave me the go-ahead, I would zip up the walkway into the house, head down the hall and return the diary and documents. Then I would beat a hasty retreat to the car, where Evan would join me, and we'd just wait for Lander to finish up. It was that easy.

Lander and Evan exited the car, closing the doors softly. Evan trotted off, looking as suspicious as he possibly could. If I was looking out my window, I would be dialing the police right now. We probably looked like we were getting ready to kick off a home invasion. Well, in a way, I guess we were.

Lander went slowly up the walk, glancing around as if regretting this plan. I ducked as low as I could while still maintaining a clear view. It was only a matter of seconds before my neck muscles began seizing and I had to sit up in order to stop the pulsating cramp that threatened. Hopefully Nell would be so excited to see Lander that she wouldn't notice anything else. I guess we'd abandoned the thought that she might be dangerous. Or else Lander assumed he could hold her off until Evan and I heard his screams should it come to that. He stood at the door for nearly a minute before finally stepping inside. I hadn't been able to see Nell clearly—I'd just caught a glimpse of something pink and floaty.

"He's in," I said into my phone.

"Copy that," said Evan. "I have a good view of the back door. I'll let you know when they're out." With great restraint, I resisted the urge to repeat his "copy that." I shifted in my seat, clutching Nell's diary. I'd checked at least five times to ensure the documents were tucked safely inside. Hopefully she wasn't crazy enough to have this thing dusted for prints. I started rubbing it roughly against my shorts, knowing full well that wasn't really going to help, but maybe it could smudge my prints enough to confuse things. Not that it would come to that.

"Okay, go!" said Evan loud enough that I was afraid Lander and Nell would hear him across the yard. I slipped out of the car, not even bothering to fully close the door. Race-walking up the walk, I wondered belatedly what kind of charges I could face if we were caught. Technically I wasn't breaking and entering. Okay, I was entering. Uninvited. But I wasn't stealing anything, I was just returning her property. From next door, an older woman popped her head out and began yoo-hooing at me. I was nearly to the door, just about to grasp the handle and go in. I tried to ignore her, but she was having none of that.

"Miss! Miss, hello! Over here." She turned up the volume, clearly not going to let me get away.

"Yes?" I asked, my face flushing and my heart pounding.

"Are you here to see Nell?"

I hesitated. What could I say? No? Then she'd want to know why I was going in. "Um," I waffled.

"Could you please take these?" She was waving a Tupperware container at me. "I've made some cookies for her to thank her for her help, and I've been meaning to bring them over, but" —she stuck out a bare foot from under her housedress, showing me her pressure wrap—"I hurt my foot and I haven't been able to get up. Well, I actually feel just fine, but my daughter, oh, she's an overprotective one, she is. She insists I just sit around all day. 'Ice, rest and elevate, Mom.' That's all she says. But she ran to the store, and I saw you heading in, so could you please take these to her? She'll know who they're from."

I felt the seconds ticking away. Lander could be running out of things to talk to Nell about in the backyard. Maybe we *were* just going to have to mail this thing. Suddenly I heard Evan squawking through my phone. "Jess! Jessie, what's going on? Are you in?"

I raced across the yard, jammed the journal under my arm and snatched the container from the woman. "Thanks, I'll give them to her," I said.

"Who's the young man that went in a few minutes ago? He looks so familiar to me." The woman propped herself against the doorway as if preparing for a long neighborly gossip session.

I smiled distractedly at her and trotted to Nell's door. I needed another hand to juggle the cookies, the journal and my phone. "Evan?" I whispered into my phone. "Are they still out there?"

"Yes, are you done?"

"No, I'm just going in now."

"What have you been doing? I told you to go!"

"Shh." I grabbed hold of the storm door and peeked a look at the neighbor. She was still leaning against the door frame, watching me with interest. This was a disaster. She could clearly identify me. I had an unbidden thought that we might have to take out all the witnesses, before I took a calming breath and shoved into Nell's front room. I dropped the Tupperware container just inside the door and eased the rickety storm door closed. I pushed the main door closed, but not all the way. I'd pick the cookies up on my way out and leave them on the step as if the neighbor had just dropped them off.

The living room lacked the nylon scarves on the lamps, and the candles had been put away. The coffee table was covered with bags of cookies and dirty glasses, and strewn across the sofa was a cluster of hardback books. A quick glance showed they were all Lander's. She'd draped a napkin across one of them as if trying to hide them before letting Lander in.

I veered right towards the hall to the bedroom. The rose petals had been cleared away and I raced the short distance. Clearly Nell wasn't quite the housekeeper that it had seemed the other night. The bed was unmade, clothes lying in wrinkled heaps near the bottom, the covers spilling every which way. Several romance novels lay on the floor beside the bed as if dropped upon completion.

There were two dressers in the room. Rather than paw through each, I raised the phone to my ear. "Evan, which dresser?"

"Jessie! She's coming in!" I heard his words at the same time I heard the back door squeak. My heart raced into overdrive and I scanned frantically for a hiding spot. I disconnected the call with Evan, afraid he would start yelling into the phone and give me away. Footsteps sounded in the living room, clearly making their way towards the bedroom. I threw myself down on the far side of the bed, wedged as far under as I could fit, and burrowed under the discarded bedclothes.

Nell was muttering to herself as she made her way into the bedroom. "He's here. He's here! I can't believe he's here. Lander Jones is at my house. Alone!" Here she gave a little squeal. "Oh, gosh, but look at me." Words gave way to a high-pitched keening as she thumped quickly around the bedroom. Fully aware that one of the two dressers was on my side of the bed, I held my breath and prayed she wouldn't come this way. I was pretty sure at least one of my legs was exposed. My heart was thumping so loud, I feared she would hear it, but the muttering and keening had morphed into a nonstop loop as she moved into her closet. My phone vibrated in my hand and I panicked as I pulled it towards my face. I didn't want to accidentally answer it and have Evan whisper-yelling through the speaker. I swiped my thumb across the red dot and shoved it under my body to muffle it in case he was dense enough to call again.

I lay perfectly still, listening. I didn't hear anything. Had she heard it? Was she even now creeping around the side of the bed, raising a baseball bat high over her head? All my muscles tensed in preparation for the blow, and my bladder tweaked nervously. I was afraid I might tinkle. Just as I was about to pop up to defend myself, I heard her rustling in the closet. She was humming softly now, something familiar but hard to place. She didn't seem to know all the words, but by the time she reached the chorus, I realized it was "Unchained Melody." A couple of grunts and puffs of breath later, I assumed she had worked her way into whatever fancy outfit she was changing into for Lander. A moment later, four spurts of a perfume dispenser sounded, followed quickly by a flowery scent raining down on the room.

As soon as I heard the clicking of her heels against the floor,

I inched to my feet, ready to dive down if she turned around. The squeal of the back door reassured me, and I jumped up, pausing as I had a semi-blackout from the blood rushing away from my head. I held on to the bed and reached out for the dresser closest to me. I'd stopped caring about getting this diary back in the exact spot Evan had taken it from. Returned was returned. I opened the top drawer and jammed the thing down along one side, throwing a handful of panties on top. Lacy things. Perfect. I quick-stepped down the hall, pausing at the door to the living room. Voices sounded closer as if they were coming in.

"Are you sure you can't stay?" Nell was asking. She sounded close to tears. I realized we hadn't set up a system to let Lander know when my part of the plan was complete. I waffled. If they were in the kitchen, it would just be seconds before they came around the corner into the dining room with its clear view of the living room and front door. I could run back to Nell's bedroom, but then how would I get out of here?

"Yeah, I need to go. I really appreciate your help with this." Lander sounded faint, as if he was still outside. I raced for the front door, ripping it open, pushing the screen door forward and pulling the main door shut behind me. I'd forgotten to pick up the container of cookies. Oh well. No time for that now. I raced sideways across the yard, toward the side street where Evan was stationed. Another mistake—we should have parked the car completely out of sight. How were we going to get in and pick up Lander if Nell walked out with him?

Evan was crouched down behind the bushes and I threw myself down on the grass beside him. He leaned forward and grasped my shoulders.

"Are you okay?" he asked. "I thought she was going to find you for sure! I just kept thinking about that Kathy Bates character and what she was going to do to you if she found you in her bedroom." He sank back, looking shaken. "Did you put it back?"

"Yeah," I said. "It's back. Now how do we get Lander?"

Evan settled into a cross-legged position and plucked at a strand of grass. "We should have probably parked over here," he said. We sat for a few minutes in silence, wondering what Lander was doing. I was sorry I hadn't snagged the neighbor's cookies because the stress of this was triggering a sugar craving. Eventually Evan began popping his head up and peering through the bushes to look out at Nell's backyard, but neither she nor Lander appeared.

Finally Evan's phone chirped and I started, reaching out a hand to stifle it and shushing him simultaneously. He muted it and peered at the screen, holding one hand over to block out the glare.

"It's Lander," he said, whipping his head around to look towards the street. "He said he's walking down towards the main street and we should wait a few more minutes, then pick him up when we leave." He must have crossed the street behind us. Clearly he was better at being stealthy than we were.

Two minutes later, Evan and I did our version of stealth, which consisted of hunched jogging on my part and a zigzag run on Evan's part. I tried to look at Nell's house without looking like I was looking, to see if she was watching, but I only ended up making my eyes hurt from the sideways stretch. We threw ourselves into the car and I started the engine, risking a peek at Nell's now that we were behind tinted glass. The door was closed and I didn't see her pressed against any windows. Maybe she was gathering up sacred Lander relics for her Shrine of Things that Lander Jones Touched, which was no doubt being erected right now somewhere in her house.

At least Lander had managed to get out.

CHAPTER TWENTY

Back at my house, we collapsed with cold soft drinks while we rehashed the morning.

"What was that she was wearing?" Evan wanted to know. "She looked like a big pink chicken or something."

"I think it was a nightgown," said Lander. "Although it had feathers all along the edges. Do ladies' nightgowns have feathers on the edges?" he asked, turning to me. I shrugged. Considering I slept in an old T-shirt, I probably wasn't the right person to ask.

"And the slippers!" Evan snorted and collapsed on the carpet laughing. I regretted not lifting my head to take a peek when she came into the bedroom to change.

"Okay, wardrobe aside," I said, "did you find out where your mom was yesterday afternoon?"

Evan pulled himself to an upright position on the floor and dragged Henry halfway across his lap. Addie jumped up on the couch, leaning against me while batting a paw out at Lander to entice a pet. He obliged, running a hand absently along her neck.

"Yes," he said, sounding mildly disappointed. "Nell insisted my mom left for San Antonio at lunchtime."

"Well, she *said* she left at lunchtime, but maybe she lied."

"I don't think so. Nell said my mom made her stay at the office until she arrived at the conference in case she forgot anything. She's doing some kind of presentation and she's really paranoid about making sure it's perfect. Nell said she called her from the hotel around five, so there's no way she could have been knocking on Seth's door when I was on the phone with him and also be in San Antonio by five."

"So, then it probably wasn't Nell at Seth's door either."

"Yeah, I don't think Nell would risk missing my mom's call to the office."

"We're assuming whoever knocked on his door killed him," I said slowly. "But what if he really did kill himself, and someone just happened to be knocking on his door? For all we know it could have been the guy in the front house, or another friend of his. And when no one answered, they left."

They silently absorbed this theory and I couldn't tell if they were in agreement or not. Both looked as if they could use a good nap.

"Anyway," I continued. "The good news is if you really think your mom is involved, at least you know you don't have anything to worry about this weekend. And maybe it was just Seth by himself, in which case, you don't have anything to worry about that way either." Addie had settled in against the cushions, nestling her head between snowy paws. "I'm not sure what you guys want to do, but I'm going to go see Frances. I want to see how she's getting on with her chickens."

I realized I hadn't had a chance to mention Frances's new hobby to Evan, and I was surprised when he perked up and declared he wanted to go too. Lander, in spite of looking like a bobblehead doll, said he would love to go meet the chickens as well. I doubted the sincerity of this, but he assured me that he never knew where inspiration would strike and it could even come from a small flock of backyard hens.

I let the dogs out for a break before leaving. Hopefully at some point Addie would get used to the chickens, because I did spend a lot of time with Frances, and Addie loved to visit with me. I couldn't imagine having to leave her home all the time. Today I didn't feel so bad leaving her since she had Henry to keep her company. It was nice that the two of them had become, if not exactly friends, friendlier. I no longer worried that Addie would kill or maim Henry if we left them alone. On the other hand, I didn't fully trust that Henry wouldn't eat my furniture since he had a history of shredding things, but Evan assured me that he'd outgrown that phase. I could only hope.

We headed towards my parents' house, the route so familiar to me I could probably do it in my sleep. As we approached the wide treelined lots of River Oaks, my sugar craving from earlier reemerged as my inner radar realized how close we were to my favorite cupcake store. The sugar high might also rejuvenate Evan and Lander enough to pack up their stuff when we got back to my house.

"Hey, do you guys mind if I pick up some cupcakes?" I turned right on San Felipe instead of left, not even waiting for an answer. The detour would only take us about a half mile out of our way.

"You know, I think Dick's offices are around here," Lander said.

Evan perked up like Addie did when you mentioned biscuits. "Where? Near the cupcake place?" I was sorry Lander had mentioned it, because as obsessed as Evan seemed to be with this guy, I feared he would insist we find it and take some selfies. "Whoa, you know how some big law firms have art out front that's like their brand? Like that one lawyer who calls himself The Rattler and he had that giant bronze rattlesnake in front of their building. Do you think Dick has a giant—"

"Evan! Please. I don't think they would allow something like that," I interrupted.

"You don't know what I was going to say," he said.

"I think I do," I said, turning onto West Gray.

He pulled his phone out, tapping at the screen. "It's right around here somewhere," he said. "It's on the right." He looked out the window, trying to find a street number.

I continued on towards the cupcake place, hoping we'd find a parking place. The open-air center had first opened in the 1930s, and traces of its art deco lineage still graced some of the buildings. There were seventy retailers and restaurants, and Saturdays were probably the worst time to come if you wanted to avoid the crowds. Sure enough, the parking lot looked like Kroger's the Wednesday before Thanksgiving.

"Tell me if you see a space," I said, rising slightly in my seat, trying to see over to the next aisle. A lady with a turquoise-blue shopping bag was making her way up our row and the taillights of a giant SUV lit up as she chirped her way into her vehicle. I put on my signal, claiming the space as mine.

"I think it should be right around here," said Evan, squinting at the storefronts. "I don't see a sign, though."

"Kind of weird to have a law office in a retail space," I said doubtfully. "I don't think I've ever seen it. Maybe it's farther down, or on the other side. There're some second-floor offices over there."

The car behind me honked as I waited for the lady to reverse out of the spot. I waved to show that I'd be turning in just as soon as this lady moved. Argh. Why wasn't she moving? Another horn sounded from two cars back.

"It says it's right around here," said Evan. He hit a button on his phone. *You have arrived at your destination*, it said. "See? I'm gonna hop out and see if I can find it."

"You're not going to do anything, are you?" asked Lander.

"Nah, man. I just want to see it. I mean, it's probably really ritzy." Evan gave an abashed shrug and climbed out. The car behind honked again, longer this time. What is wrong with people?

Abandoning hope that the SUV was actually going to exit, I pulled forward, hoping to snag another spot. Glancing in my mirror, I saw the lady ease backwards as soon as I passed, allowing the honker behind me to slip in. Lander and I made two more turns around the lot before I was lucky enough to find my own spot.

"You coming in with me?" I asked as I turned off the engine.

"No, I'll just wait here," he said. It was already creeping towards the upper eighties, so I turned the engine back on and put the windows down for him. I would never leave Addie in the car, but Lander was certainly capable of getting out if he started having heatstroke.

The cupcake store was a madhouse. Half of the tables were taken up by a birthday party in progress. A dozen six-year-olds, jacked up on sugar, were racing around two tables, chasing each other with fairy wands and screaming at a pitch that made me rethink ever having children. Three women, who looked like they should be chaperoning these monsters, were instead drinking a bottle of wine and shrieking at each other over the din. It was like they didn't even notice the irritated glares being sent their way. I fought the urge to smack the closest one in the back of the head and instead made my way towards the line at the counter.

The handwritten menu board on the wall listed at least two dozen varieties, each sounding better than the last. I wasn't sure how I was going to narrow my choices. Two teenage girls behind the counter worked at a leisurely pace, having to lean forward to hear the orders over the ruckus. Like the chaperones, they seemed oblivious to the chaos. A pimply boy was running cupcakes from the kitchen in response to the orders. He looked like he was on the verge of grabbing a broom and sweeping all the partiers out of the store. I put a finger in the ear closest to the screamers and tried again to focus on my selections.

"Pretty awful, huh?" The man in front of me turned around and grimaced.

"Kind of." There was no way I was going to be able to narrow this down to four selections. Maybe I should get eight—then we could each have two. But should I get eight different kinds or two of four?

"Don't I know you from somewhere?" I lowered my chin and shifted my gaze to the man. Middle-aged with a wispy combover and a belly that strained against his shirt, he looked like he enjoyed his cupcakes on a regular basis. I'd never seen him before.

"I don't think so," I said, scooting away as he moved closer to me.

He wagged a finger at me. "I know I know you from somewhere." He studied me with unblinking assessment. "Yes, I've got it. I see you going in and out of that nail salon down the street." He puffed out his chest with pride. "I've never understood why anyone would pay good money to have someone fuss over their nails when you can just buy a pair of clippers."

I've never been to whatever nail salon he was referring to, but I didn't want to engage. The man was still staring at me, his pale eyes smug behind his metal-framed glasses. One of the teenaged girls stood waiting for his order. "Next," she said lethargically.

I pointed towards the counter. "Are you going to order or

not? I'm in a bit of a hurry," I said. He turned away from me and faced the menu board.

"Let's see. What do we feel like today?" He rocked on his heels and rubbed his belly. "What would you suggest?" he asked me over his shoulder. I had some suggestions, but none of them would be appropriate in a room full of children. The second cashier called for the next customer, and I raced over and ordered a dozen cupcakes, literally just reading off the first twelve items from the menu. Classic impulse buy fueled by irritation.

"You must be hungry. Heh heh heh," said the man, stepping close to me as we waited for our orders. I looked away from him and sighed loudly. A little princess in a blue cape flew towards us, pushing her way between us and throwing a small arm out, hitting him squarely in the crotch. I nearly tipped her a five. When he got his cupcake, he winked at me and made his way towards the door.

The box the pimply kid handed me was large and heavy and seemed too flimsy for the weight of the contents. I balanced it carefully as I made my way through the birthday party. I felt slightly more charitable towards the little girls, although I was pretty sure my long-term hearing had been impacted. Holding the box with both hands, I pushed backwards through the door and nearly fell on my rear when someone pulled it quickly out from behind me.

"Need some help? Heh heh heh." Oh joy. I grasped my box, feeling the cupcakes shift. If these things got mashed I was going to hurt this man. I righted myself and stepped off the curb between two parked cars. "Honey, where you going? I thought we were having a nice conversation."

I glanced back to see if he was following me and bumped into someone else. Hands reached out to steady the box as the cupcakes shifted yet again. "Creep," said a woman. She stepped around me, between me and the guy. It took me a few beats to register that it was Annalise and I froze, uncertain of how to play this. The man stood staring at her with his mouth open until she shot a look at him that nearly made my hair stand on end. He turned around and headed the other way down the sidewalk.

"Thank you," I said. "I was afraid he was going to follow me all the way to my car." I could see why he'd been staring at her, though. She was wearing a tiny sapphire-blue dress, loose enough that an errant breeze might slip it right off her shoulders. It was nicely accessorized, though, with a necklace dangling provocatively between her breasts and a blue ribbon tied loosely around her hair. She would look perfect on the cover of one of Nell's romance novels. I had to make an effort to look up. "Oh hey!" I said, acting as if I just recognized her. "Wait, aren't you the one with the accessories business? I saw you outside your class?" I found myself speaking as if I'd suddenly lost a few dozen IQ points.

She'd been looking past my shoulder but turned her attention and looked me over. Sadly, I wasn't much better put together than I had been the other night. "Oh, right. The Dandy Doodle girl with the dog biscuits," she said, placing me after a long moment.

"Yes, exactly! Oh my gosh, well, thank you for helping with that guy. Creep is right." She was staring past me again, barely paying attention to what I was saying. A small breeze kicked up just enough to show me the ruffle of a black bustier under her dress. "Anyway..." I trailed off, suddenly remembering I had given her a fake name and I couldn't remember what I'd said. Hopefully she wouldn't ask. "Thanks."

I edged away, but her attention was still focused over my shoulder. As I turned towards the parking lot, I glanced in the direction she was looking. Evan stood on a sidewalk across the way outside a door I'd never noticed before. It must lead to the second story over the eyeglass store, which, I admit, I'd never even realized existed until now. He was holding his phone aloft and posing for a selfie with Dick. Ah. Annalise was here to surprise her husband. Just as Evan lowered his phone, a young blond moved forward and attached herself to Dick's side like a suction cup on wet glass. He turned to her, lifting a strand of hair away from her neck and rubbing his thumb in a line towards her collarbone in a move that was both possessive and erotic. I heard a sharp intake of breath beside me and I froze, an unwitting witness to Annalise's distress. The good news was, she couldn't possibly have a handgun concealed anywhere on her person or it would be completely visible.

I hustled across the parking lot, dodging the slow-moving cars that were circling for spots. Evan and I reached the car at roughly the same time. I handed him the box of cupcakes as he slid into the passenger seat.

"Did you see that?" he asked. "I found Dick's office. He doesn't have a statue or anything. In fact, it took me a while to find the door. It just has a little sign on the brick next to it. I really would have thought someone like him would have a statue. Or a neon sign or something more pronounced. But he was just coming out when I found it and he let me take a selfie with him!"

"Let's get out of here," Lander said from his nearly prone position across the back seat. "I don't want Annalise to see me."

"Annalise is here?" asked Evan, twisting to look towards Dick's door. "But I just saw Dick. He was with—" He trailed off. "Uh-oh."

I put the windows up, cranked the air conditioner and focused on getting us out of there. I pondered how the tiniest shifts in timing can alter the course of events. If Annalise hadn't stopped to help me ditch the weirdo, she would have run straight into Dick and girlfriend—if that's what she was, and it certainly appeared she was more than just a colleague. Or maybe they would have been gone already if Evan hadn't stopped and asked for a picture.

"Lander, did you see where Annalise went? Did she confront them?" I'd been too busy trying to keep my new car safe in the overfull parking lot to watch what had happened.

"Nope. She just watched them leave. I don't think he saw her."

"I'd hate to be him coming home tonight," said Evan, looking at the screen of his phone. "Oh cool, I got a picture of the other woman. Maybe I can sell it to one of them for the divorce." As soon as we stopped at a light, I made him show me the picture. I'd never seen her before, nor had Lander. Probably just one in a line, although actually looking at Dick in this photo, he was much better looking than I'd thought. I guess those commercials didn't do him justice.

I pulled into my parents' long drive and drove past the main house to Frances's little guest cottage. Piling out of the car, we went first to the door, but when no one answered we made our way around the side to the newly fenced chicken yard. Frances stood in the shade of the live oak, wearing a loose pair of overalls, blue clogs and the same straw hat she'd had on the last time I was here. She stood at an easel, dabbing paint from a palette clutched in her left hand. Beside her, a small table held an assortment of acrylic paint tubes in various stages of depletion.

"Hey, Frances," I said as we approached the gate. She turned quickly, looking embarrassed.

"Jessica." She glanced at her canvas as if regretting not having a cloth nearby to throw over it. "I wasn't expecting you."

"I know. I'm sorry. I've got to stop doing that." She set her palette on the table and walked towards us.

"Hello, Evan," she said.

"This is Lander," I said. "He's staying with Evan for a few

days. I was telling them about your chickens and we wanted to come see how they're doing. We brought some cupcakes." I gestured towards the box that Evan was holding at an alarming angle. She smiled and made her way through the gate, closing it carefully behind her.

"How lovely. Nice to meet you," she said, glancing quickly at her hands before giving Lander an informal pat on the arm. "Why don't you come inside and we can have some refreshments. I needed a break anyway. Your timing is perfect."

Frances kicked off her clogs at the door, and we followed her to the kitchen, where Evan and Lander plunked down at the table. I pulled down four tall glasses and filled them with tea and ice while Frances cut up a lemon into neat wedges. She set a sugar bowl on the table and distributed four pretty little dessert plates next to the box of cupcakes. Frances and I chatted about inconsequential things while everyone tried to select a cupcake. Fortunately, they were only a little mashed, and the tantalizing aroma made up for the lopsided aesthetics.

After Frances and I finished, she asked if I would help her cut up some treats for the chickens. She began cubing a chunk of watermelon while I hacked at a head of lettuce. Evan and Lander rooted through the cupcake box for seconds.

"So how is it going with the chickens?" I asked Frances.

She smiled and pushed the watermelon cubes into a plastic bucket. "My girls are doing wonderfully," she said. "They are characters. Harriet is the smartest. She's also the most curious. Hannah is my act-first-think-second girl. She also mistakes toes for bugs, so you have to watch out. And Helen is a hoot." Frances had clearly bonded with her flock, and I felt a surge of gratitude. I'd noticed a creeping discontentment lately, and it was refreshing to see the change.

We gathered our chicken treats and headed out to observe the girls. As soon as they saw the snack buckets they ran towards us, jostling side to side like avian Roller Derby participants in an overtime jam.

"Okay, girls, we have guests! Manners, please," called out Frances as they squabbled for space at her feet. The three of us crowded through the gate behind her, and I closed and latched it. Evan and Lander skirted the fence as if afraid of being mauled, and even I had to suppress a small shriek as one of them ran over and began pecking at my shoes. Frances tossed a chunk of watermelon and the hen veered away from me.

It didn't take long to see why Frances was so enamored. Lander and I settled down on a bale of hay while Evan perched on an overturned bucket. Frances pointed out who was who, and it wasn't long before I could tell them apart, from appearance as well as mannerisms. Harriet was more enamored by the buckle on Lander's bag than the treats Frances had brought out. She stared at it, studied it, then gave it a tentative peck. Then she tilted her head to the other side and studied it some more before pecking with renewed energy. Lander had his notebook out and appeared to be taking notes and doing chicken sketches.

"I believe she's flirting with you," Frances told him. He looked more relaxed than I'd ever seen him.

Evan tossed bits of lettuce up in the air while the other two chickens ignored him. Frances went back to her easel, taking the time to rinse the brush she'd been working with and unwrap a new one. I glanced at her canvas and was amazed. She'd finished painting the chicken coop and had one chicken nearly complete, somehow managing to capture its inquisitiveness with the tilt of the head and the sharp little eyes. She had certainly found a nice way to spend her time.

We must have sat there for close to an hour. It was getting hotter and the hay under my butt was starting to get itchy. Lander had moved off the bale a while ago and had stretched out on a thick patch of grass with his head resting on his bag. He appeared to be sleeping. Evan was watching the chickens, but periodically I could see his head jerk as if he were on the verge of conking out as well.

I decided it was time to roust them. Lander awoke with a jolt, sitting upright so fast that he scared Helen, who had been softly clucking beside him. She flapped and lifted off for a couple wobbly feet before landing with an irritated *ba-gawwk*. Lander looked around groggily.

"Oh man," he said. "I was out cold." He staggered to his feet and brushed himself off. I watched the play of emotions on his face as he remembered his current circumstances.

"Don't forget your notebook." I pointed to the grass. "One of the chickens was working on it earlier. I think she thought the strap was a worm." I'd watched her pull the leather strap in fits and starts as she tried to drag her treasure away from the others. He collected his notebook, inventoried his bag and tried to shake himself awake. Evan didn't look much better than Lander.

We thanked Frances for letting us sit in on her flock and headed for the car. She raced on ahead of us and detoured into the house, returning seconds later with the remaining cupcakes.

"I think you young people could use these more than me." She handed the box to Evan, then gave me a quick hug. "Take care. We'll plan some time together soon."

I had expected more discussion on the way home about our encounter with Annalise and Dick. Or maybe some talk about what Lander planned to do now. But Lander was quiet, a cloud of depression appearing to descend. They didn't say much when we got to my house. After a brief debate, they decided they would probably be safe at Evan's tonight. I wasn't really sure why they'd thought they wouldn't be safe last night, but I was more than eager to help them reload their belongings and the old mattress into Evan's car and see them off.

CHAPTER TWENTY-ONE

Addie and I had a great evening. My new car was safely tucked away in the garage. I'd cleaned away the clutter from my overnight guests and treated myself to a giant salad in an effort to offset the sugar spike from the afternoon. Addie had worked on her Kong without interference from Henry, and by eight o'clock, we were curled up on the couch streaming a rom-com and forgetting all about the drama of the past week. To top it off, I slept straight through the night, unperturbed by noises or dreams.

I woke Sunday morning feeling good, clouded only by vaguely dismal thoughts of Seth. He'd obviously had a lot of problems, but he hadn't seemed like a bad person when I'd met him, more like one of those people who was genetically inclined to make bad decisions. He had been Lander's best friend for years, though, and I could only imagine how hard this was for him. I wished there was something I could do to make him feel better, but how did you cheer up someone whose best friend had just died, particularly when that best friend had likely been trying to kill him? Flowers didn't seem right. Alcohol was a depressant. You couldn't just give someone a dog, even if that was the ultimate comfort. I kicked around the kitchen. Nell had mentioned he loved macaroni and cheese, and since I couldn't think of anything better, I'd try that. I knew it wouldn't really help, but it's not called comfort food for nothing.

I was just draining the noodles when my doorbell rang, followed by a series of thumps as if someone was banging on the frame. Oh, no. It had to be Larry. I glanced at the clock. It wasn't even eight yet. Addie was at the door growling, fur rising in a narrow strip along her spine. Ugh, definitely Larry.

There was no point in pretending I wasn't home. I cracked open the door, pushing Addie back with my knee. "Hey, Larry." Larry was dressed in a rumpled dress shirt and slacks, and he leaned one arm up against the door frame, the sweat stain under his armpit exactly eye level. I stepped back and pushed my foot against the door to brace it. A noxious mix of garlic and alcohol emanated from his pores and Addie turned to make her way back to the couch, still growling in intermittent rumbles.

"Good morning to you," said Larry. "Looks like you spent another sad Saturday night with your dog." I pushed the door closed, but he caught it and pressed it open until it caught on my foot.

"Do you need something?"

He put his arm down and hitched at the waist of his pants. "I had a great night. Want to hear about it? Larry is back!"

"That's great, and no, I don't want to hear about it."

He sighed. "Well, if you're going to be unfriendly like that, I do need something. Didn't I give you one of my keys?"

"Keys to what?"

"My house. You know, for emergencies."

"Nope. No key."

"I was sure I had." He rubbed his nose. His face was puffy and pale. "Okay, then. I need to go over your fence. I think I can get in through the back."

"You locked yourself out?"

"My date could hardly keep her hands off me, and I guess in the excitement, I left my keys at the bar."

"So, go get your keys from the bar."

"They're not open yet." He yawned, stretching both arms up to reveal matching sweat stains.

"Where's your car? Still at the bar too?"

"Yeah. She lived pretty close, so we walked to her house. She couldn't wait, if you know what I mean." He did a little hip swivel.

I closed my eyes and tried not to think about it. "You're home awfully early. You could have taken her to brunch or something until the bar opened and then picked up your keys."

He resumed leaning. "She was in a mood when she woke up. Maybe her time of the month or something. But she was not as friendly this morning as she was last night." He yawned again. "She said she could drive me home or I could wait outside the bar for my car." He scratched his belly. I could only imagine her buyer's remorse when she'd woken up this morning. "I could hang out here until it opens. You could drive me over?"

"Let me get my stepladder," I said. "I'm sure you can get over the fence." Larry looked longingly at the couch. Addie narrowed her eyes at him and raised her lip, exposing beautiful white teeth that looked impressive against the darkness of her face. I dragged my stepladder from the coat closet and out to the patio.

"Here you go," I said. "Don't break anything."

Larry looked at the ladder, then pushed his lower lip out. "Don't you think it would be easier if I just waited with you?"

"No. I'm busy. You could always call a locksmith."

He grunted and pulled himself up. "That'd be a hundred bucks for the guy to just show up. I don't think so." Standing on the top step, he angled one way, then another. Finally he put one foot on the top board and launched himself over. I winced as I heard him crash to the ground.

"Okay, see you later," I said, collapsing the ladder and heading inside. I paused and listened for movement to make sure he hadn't hurt himself too badly. After some muttered cursing, he dragged himself across the patio and began beating on his own back door. I went inside. The cheese sauce was just beginning to simmer when I heard glass break. I cracked the door open and listened.

"Great," Larry muttered. "Gah, that'll probably cost more than a locksmith."

I closed the door as quietly as I could and returned to my cheese sauce. There was something about this episode with Larry that was tickling a thought in the far reaches of my brain. I mixed the sauce and the noodles, sprinkled a little extra cheese on top and popped it in the oven to bake. I considered making some dog biscuits while I had the oven on, but I wasn't in the mood. Instead, I plunked myself down beside Addie. She rolled against me and shifted to expose her belly, hoping for a rub. I leaned my head back, closed my eyes and complied.

I thought of William. He'd been in the hospital more than a week now. I thought of Frances and the joy she was finding with her chickens. What if someone attacked her? She was around the same age as William. What kind of monster could attack an older person? Why hadn't I gone in to help William? Maybe he wouldn't have been hurt. I rubbed my temples until Addie pawed at me, irritated that I'd stopped her massage. I resumed the soft stroking.

Could Seth really have attacked William? And if it wasn't Seth, who could have done that? I tried to imagine CiCi or Nell, Annalise or even Dick whacking William in the head hard enough to nearly kill him. I couldn't picture any of them doing this. Could William and I have just interrupted a garden-variety break-in? That actually seemed more likely. I had no problem imagining a hardened criminal attacking William that way. But what about everything else? The attack on us at the bayou? Seth's death?

The smell of baking cheese interrupted my thoughts, and I got up to check on my casserole. The top had oozed into a crispy brown and I fought the impulse to siphon a bowl for myself. I set it on the counter to cool and ran to get dressed. There was still something about Larry breaking into his own house that bothered me. Somehow we were missing something. Had Lander ever figured out if something was taken from his break-in? Or had William and I interrupted the burglar before they were able to pilfer what they came for? Nell's diary floated into my consciousness and the picture flipped. What if someone hadn't broken into Lander's to take something? What if they had broken in to return something? I felt a surge of energy, sure I was on to something. Maybe we should take a trip to Lander's house and figure out if anything was missing or added.

I raced down the stairs and called Evan. His phone went to voice mail. Maybe they were still sleeping. I'd call back in a bit. The mac and cheese had cooled to a touchable temperature, still too warm to put in the refrigerator. I grabbed a noodle from the side, cheese stretching as I pulled. I was going to have to get this to Lander before I lost all control. I covered it with foil and called Evan again, this time leaving a message.

"Hey, I know this is kind of weird, but I made some macaroni and cheese and I thought I could bring it over for breakfast. I'm gonna come over, and I have some ideas we need to talk about. Anyway, call me when you get this."

Addie hadn't moved from the couch and showed no interest in going for a ride, so I left her a biscuit, grabbed my purse and put the casserole in a cardboard box. Stowing it on the floor, I headed for Evan's. This would also save me the aggravation of having to drive Larry to whatever bar he'd left his keys and his car at later. I felt a zing of excitement, sensing that I was on to something.

I was only about a mile from Evan's when my phone rang.

"Hey," I said, glancing and seeing Evan's name.

"Hey," he said. "You can definitely bring the macaroni over, only Lander's not here. We could have it later, though."

"Oh," I said, feeling slightly deflated. "Where is he?"

"He left early this morning. He said he needed to get some work done. I guess he's really behind and his agent called last night. Or maybe it was his editor. I don't know. But he said he wasn't getting anything done at my house and he decided to go home."

"Should I go to his house, then? I could just drop this off if he's busy, but I had an idea. We need to figure out if anything was taken that night of the break-in. Because I had a thought— what if someone left something instead of taking something?"

"What? That doesn't even make sense," he said. "Look, let me call him and see if he's okay with the interruption before you go over there. I'll call you right back."

I was at an intersection, debating whether I should continue on to Evan's or just go straight to Lander's. My phone rang again.

"Hey. He's not answering." Evan sounded slightly anxious.

"Oh. Well, maybe he turned his phone off while he's working," I said. A flutter of apprehension tickled in my chest. "I could go by his house. If he's busy and doesn't want to be bothered, I could just bring this over to your house?"

"Do you think he's okay?" Evan asked.

"Probably," I said. I thought of William. "I don't know. Look, I'll just check. He's probably fine, just working."

"I'm coming over," Evan said. "I just have to change. We had a clog... anyway. Wait for me. I'll be there in a few minutes."

The flutter of apprehension was ballooning and I tried to tell myself that this was just a little PTSD from the night William had been attacked. If Lander needed to work, he probably didn't want any interruptions. Traffic was almost nonexistent, and it took me less than eight minutes to get there. I pulled to a stop on the grassy strip across the street and cut the engine. My heart hammered in my chest now, although everything seemed peaceful. Lander's car was in his driveway and the repetitive four-note song of a dove cooing in a nearby tree was the only sound I heard. Evan had told me to wait for him, but I wasn't sure how long he'd be. There weren't any other cars on this tiny, secluded street and there wasn't anything that looked amiss. I would just go knock on the kitchen door and make sure he was okay. If he was ready for a break, we could have some macaroni.

I pulled the casserole dish from the floor, put my purse strap over my shoulder and stepped quietly into the street. I bumped my door closed, holding the handle to muffle the sound. I don't know why I was being so paranoid. If I truly thought Lander was in trouble, I should go charging in, making as much noise as I could. But I didn't. I crept as quietly as I could through the grass along the side of the driveway so my shoes wouldn't make any scuffing sounds.

Tiptoeing up the porch steps, I took a deep breath and had a little conversation with myself. I was being stupid. Lander was fine. Maybe he wouldn't be thrilled with the interruption, but I wouldn't stay long. I approached the door, shifted the box to my hip and peered through the window. I hoped to see him taking a coffee break, but instead the room was empty, yellow beams of morning light streaming onto the massive quartz island. I wished I had an island like that for my biscuit-making.

I raised a hand to knock then reached for the door handle instead. It was unlocked. There was no way Lander wouldn't have locked his door. None. I hesitated, the urge to run nearly overpowering. But I thought of William and how I'd left him there, bleeding alone on the floor. I put the box down softly on the porch and pushed through the door. Everything was quiet.

"Lander?" I called softly. I took a breath, looking quickly around the pristine kitchen for a handy weapon. A rustle from the direction of his study nearly made me flee, but my feet refused to move. I was rooted, uncertain of what to do when Annalise poked her head around the door of Lander's study.

"Oh, hi," she said, looking as surprised to see me as I was to see her. "I thought I heard something." Her face changed as she recognized me, a scowl suddenly marring her perfectly put-together look. "Are you *following* me?" she asked, incredulous.

"Where's Lander?" I asked, staying close to the door.

"He's in the bathroom," she said. She stepped from his office into the living room, holding a paper in her hand. We stared at each other, my apprehension clouded with confusion. This seemed so mundane.

"Lander?" I called. He wouldn't have let her in if he thought she was dangerous. Right?

"He's in the *bathroom*," she repeated, looking at me like I was some sort of weirdo. I noted her pale pink capris and white linen top, strands of deep pink stones draped in casual loops around her neck with matching dangling earrings. She did know how to pull an outfit together.

"I didn't realize you knew Lander," she said. She was in the middle of the living room now, and I walked a few feet into the kitchen, listening for any sign of Lander in the bathroom. Maybe I *was* a weirdo.

"Yeah, I sort of know him. I didn't know he was going to have company," I said, trying to sift through what was going on here.

"I guess you didn't."

"I didn't realize *you* knew Lander," I said, suddenly remembering I wasn't supposed to know she was his ex-wife. "Is he one of your clients? Did he hire you to dress him up for his book signings?" I tried to smile, but my lips felt stiff. I heard a noise from the other side of the island. A slight scuffing noise. And then a small moan.

We both froze, neither of us blinking. I was transfixed, suddenly understanding how squirrels felt as they planted themselves in the street and stared down oncoming cars. I was close enough to the door that maybe I could race through it and get to my car.

"That old air conditioner," she said with a chuckle. "It's always made the oddest sounds." She took a small step towards me. "I'm his wife. We're talking about a reconciliation and we needed to make sure we have some paperwork in order." She waggled the paper back and forth and I wondered what that was. Suddenly I knew whatever had been going on with Lander could be explained by the sheet she held.

"That's nice," I said. "I'm glad you're working things out." I didn't know what to do. Let her talk? Run?

"Look at this house," she said, almost in disbelief. "It's beautiful. Did you know I lived here once? Back when we were married. Only it didn't look this way. It was a big ole mess." She took another step. "I have a nice house now, don't get me wrong, but I feel like Lander and I were always meant to be together." She smiled and it sent a cold chill up my neck.

"Okay, well, you two obviously have some things to talk about," I said. "I should go."

I heard another moan.

"Lander?" I called. She was still staring at me, running a sharp fingernail along the fold of her paper. I glanced towards the sound but couldn't see past the island. I wanted to run. Every instinct in me screamed to sprint out the door and go get help. But I'd followed that instinct before, and I'd left an elderly man to suffer. I had the feeling this outcome would be even worse.

"It's nice that you're getting back together," I said, my voice shaking. This was surreal. I needed to act. Maybe she was insane. Maybe Evan had been right with his *Misery* comparison —he'd just cast Nell as the crazy one instead of Annalise. "I didn't realize he was married. I'm sorry."

She was about ten feet away, not moving now. Just staring at me.

"Yeah, well, I mean we *were* divorced, but lately we've realized that was probably a mistake."

"That's great," I said. "So. I guess I should go. I just wanted to check something with him." Maybe if I went around the island the other way, then I could get to Lander before she could reach me. But then what? I inched my way to the island, cursing Lander's neat kitchen. There was nothing nearby that I could use as a weapon.

Annalise took a few steps towards me. She didn't actually look insane. She looked conflicted, as if trying to work out what she was going to do next. I guessed that put us in the same boat. I'm not sure how long we would have stood staring at each other, but suddenly Lander hauled himself up on the far side of the island, listing unsteadily. A small amount of blood dripped down the side of his forehead, and a knot the size of a robin's egg rose from under his hair.

"Lander!" I rushed towards him. Annalise surprised me by turning away and flouncing towards a chair in the living room, where a bright pink purse rested on the cushion. Whatever she wanted to get from that purse was going to make this a whole lot worse. I left Lander's side and raced the length of the room towards her. I'd never tackled anyone before, but I'd seen enough football games to know how it was supposed to go. At the last minute, I chickened out of a diving tackle, opting instead for an awkward sideways body block that sent her tumbling. Those cute sandals she was wearing didn't have the solid grip of my sneakers.

Annalise cried out as she fell, her knees cracking against the hardwood floor. I grabbed her purse, slipped the strap across my body and turned to face her, knees bent, fists up. There was no time to check her purse for weapons, even if I could have used one about now. Adrenaline flowed through my cells and I maintained my stance, hoping that she wasn't going to get up and come at me. I'd never actually been in a fight before, and I was scared of getting punched. Then again, I was scared of getting killed too.

She rose slowly, her hair falling loose and covering half her face. The scream she let out as she suddenly charged at me made my blood run cold. At the last second before impact, I darted sideways. She'd been expecting to strike me full-on, and the momentum carried her sailing past me into a wooden coffee table. Her shin cracked into the solid wood edge and she crumpled to the floor, yowling in pain.

She'd dropped her paper and I scooped it from the floor before fleeing towards Lander. He'd managed to prop himself against the counter and was holding one hand to his head while he squinted at his cell phone, trying to dial with the other. A wooden cutting board was on the floor, a smudge of blood marring the edge. This must be what she'd clocked Lander with. I picked it up, thinking I could use it as a weapon, but it was lighter than I expected. Probably lucky for Lander that it was. I set it down on the counter and looked for another weapon. Seeing none, I unzipped Annalise's purse and pulled out the small revolver that rested on top.

Lander had gotten through to the 911 operator and was giving his address. Annalise looked up, tears streaking her mascara, her breath coming in coughing hiccups. She watched us through streaming, half-closed eyes and I braced myself for another attack, but she seemed to be recalculating her next action. The wobbling gun in my hand probably had something to do with it.

"Lander," she sniffed. "Baby, I love you." She wiped at her face and looked sideways at him. He calmly repeated his address and said he needed the police because he'd been attacked in his house and could they please hurry.

As he disconnected, she scrambled to her feet, looking on the floor behind her. Frantically turning in circles, she brushed her hair behind her ear and bent to look under the nearest chair.

I unfolded the paper in my hand and looked at the top. It was the last will and testament of Lander and Annalise Jones, dated nine years ago. It was only one page, a simple form leaving everything to the surviving spouse. This must have been drawn up when they were first married, when Lander Jones didn't have a dime to his name and the two of them were living with his best friend because they couldn't afford their own apartment. And all these years later, here he was, a multimillionaire, churning out best sellers year after year. And there she was, about to be the third ex-wife of Dick DeLuca. I handed him the paper.

"What's this?" he asked. He scanned it. Then looked at it again. "You're kidding me. Where was this?" He shook the paper at Annalise and she stilled as she saw what he was holding.

"It was where we put it, baby. Remember?" She waved towards his study. "In the pirate chest—in that secret drawer." Of course there would be a secret drawer in a pirate chest. I knew it had to be cooler than a blanket chest. She rubbed a finger under her eye, trying to rid herself of the mascara pool. "Baby, remember when we first got married? It was one of the things on our list. Remember? How to be adults." She gave him a watery smile.

"You didn't think this was still valid, did you?" Lander's voice rose, a mix of astonishment and anger. "Tell me you did not do all of this"—he brandished the paper—"all of this because you thought you would get my assets if I died?" He'd straightened up, no longer aware of his head injury. "You were willing to *kill* me? Attack my neighbor—my *elderly* neighbor, my friend! And Seth? What'd you do to him? Did you kill him?" He advanced towards Annalise. She stiffened with alarm, an ingratiating smile flickering on and off.

"Baby, it wasn't like that."

"Did you run us off the road? Was that you too?"

Annalise's shoulders hunched forward and she held her hands balled against her heart as if deflecting his words. "Lander—"

He was close enough now that he grabbed her upper arm. She pushed away and ran for the door, pulling it open and flying through. I saw a shadow just outside the door immediately before I heard a collision of bodies and the oomph as someone's breath was knocked out of their lungs. Evan had arrived.

CHAPTER TWENTY-TWO

The kitchen was hot, but William still wore a heavy sweater over his plaid button-down shirt and corduroy pants. Evan, Lander and I sat at William's table, using our napkins to blot ineffectively at the sweat dotting our faces while we sipped tall glasses of lemonade that dripped lines of condensation down the sides. William had been home from the rehab hospital for almost a week and I was happy to see how much better he looked. The gaunt, wobbly confusion that had persisted while he'd remained in the hospital was being replaced by the confident contentment of being in his own home.

A sunny caregiver in pale pink scrubs set a plate of cookies in front of us and excused herself to the other room. Lander had sprung William sooner than the doctors had wanted, with assurances that he would be back for all his physical therapy and he would have care at home for as long as required. The arrangement seemed to be working well.

Evan took a cookie and broke it in half. "I knew it was your wife," he said to Lander. "I told you from the beginning."

"You did not. You thought it was Nell or Lander's mother," I pointed out. "Remember how you thought CiCi poisoned your tea?"

"What was this?" asked William, his twinkle making a real comeback. I told the story of Evan thinking his tea was poisoned and pouring the contents down behind the couch cushion. William laughed till he coughed, patting his chest with a thin hand. Evan hmphed and popped the second half of the cookie in his mouth.

"So, did your mom get her task force?" I asked Lander.

"She did," Lander said. "And when I did my FBI interview, they didn't care at all about my books. Well, except one agent did ask for an autograph."

"Did she ever notice the couch?"

"I'm not sure. She never mentioned it."

"What about Annalise? Where is she now? Hopefully in prison awaiting trial?" The thought of running into her had been leaving me with low-level anxiety.

"Dick's got enough money he probably got her out," said Evan.

"I don't think he has," said Lander. "And her parents don't have that much money. The police said they'd let me know if she bonds out."

"She'll probably start accessorizing the inmates," I said. "I mean, she really had a talent for pulling outfits together." Too bad she couldn't see me now. I'd actually taken some care with my outfit for our little reunion, and I looked pretty good if I could say so myself. Not that anyone noticed.

"I saw a snippet somewhere," said William, frowning with concentration. He still had some small memory glitches, but they seemed to be smoothing out. "Anyway, I do believe wherever I saw it, it said that Dick is starting divorce proceedings."

"Well, she did say you guys were reconciling. So here's your chance," I said, giving Lander a poke. He shuddered. "I still can't believe she did all this thinking that she would inherit your money," I said.

"Annalise has always been obsessed with money," Lander said. Shades of sadness still colored his tone. We'd talked in the weeks since Annalise had been arrested, and I knew he was still dealing with feelings of guilt that he was somehow responsible for Seth's death and William's attack. I'd tried to make him realize he wasn't, but truth be told, I still had swells of self-reproach over what I had done, or rather hadn't done, myself. It was easy to tell Lander he wasn't responsible for Annalise, but I knew where he was coming from. At least he was doing everything he could to make it up to William, but the confusing mix of emotions over the loss of his best friend, who'd actually tried to kill him, was a whole other quagmire.

"Was she behind all those things you told us about that first night? The food poisoning, the tire blowout? All that?" I asked.

"I think some of it was coincidental," said Lander. "It's just that there were so many bad things happening at once that I couldn't tell if I was jinxed or if someone was really out to get me."

"I still don't fully understand this whole thing," said William, pulling at a frayed cuff of his sweater. "You've been divorced for years. Why now? Why this extreme?"

Lander sighed. "I'm not entirely sure. The police haven't told me everything she's said, but from what I can gather, she knew that her marriage was close to being over. Dick's not known for long-term relationships."

"I'll bet he's dating that woman we saw him with outside his office," Evan said. He pulled his phone out and began scrolling to locate the picture. "Or maybe he's seeing a dancer. Didn't I hear something about that?" I didn't want to point out that he was the one who'd overheard that tidbit in his inebriated state at the men's club.

"Well, everything I've seen sounds like Dick DeLuca knows how to work a divorce," said William. "I had Julie, she's my Tuesday caretaker, help me look up some stories on my iPad. It's remarkable what you can find on the internet. Have you seen some of these news websites? Their stories are quite salacious. At any rate, there was a lot of information on his first two divorces that they've dug up, and let me tell you, if Annalise knew even half of it, she had to know she'd be lucky if she ended up with two nickels to rub together."

"So she decided to look up Lander," said Evan.

"It seemed kind of confusing, whether she was trying to get back together with you or kill you," I said.

"I think she was okay with either," said Lander. "Whatever was easier."

"One of the papers—well, it was a tabloid really—wrote that she had hypnotized Seth into being her hit man," said William. He reached over and patted Lander's hand. "I know how hard this has been for you."

"Is that how it happened?" Evan asked. "Did she really hypnotize him?" He looked semi-freaked out, as if he could be hypnotized against his will and turned into an assassin at any time.

"I think it's more like she took advantage of his financial issues," said Lander. "He was desperate. Desperate people do crazy things."

"Did she poison him when it didn't work out? Did she know you were going over there to talk to him? Did your mom give her the poison to do it?" It was going to take a long time for Evan to get over this poisoning apprehension. I gave him a gentle kick under the table. Lander didn't look like he wanted to go into this kind of detail.

He looked at Evan with the patient look you'd give a bothersome child. "I think she used a bunch of pills. They said Dick had knee surgery last year and had some leftover pain pills. And she got sleeping pills, and I don't know what else. And then she mixed it in with some high-proof vodka. That alone could have killed him, but all mixed up like that, he didn't stand a chance."

"How'd she get him to drink it?"

"Who knows. Maybe he knew. Maybe he was already drinking when she got there."

"But why did she have to kill him?" William asked softly.

"I'm guessing at the end, Seth was going to come clean. Annalise could read people. She knew she was losing him. He did what he did..." Lander paused. "But it wasn't who he was. I like to think he regretted it."

Everyone murmured soft words of accord.

"Which one of them was the one that..." William faltered on his question and absently touched his head where he'd been hit. "Was here the night Jessie and I..." He trailed off. "I still don't remember that night." Lander had already filled Evan and me in on the timeline, but he'd wanted to spare William any more than he was ready for.

"It was Annalise who hit you," said Lander. "Remember when I thought someone had been in my house?"

"And you had the locks changed?"

"Yeah. She had used her old key and taken the will out of the trunk in my study. I had completely forgotten all about that. I guess later she realized that it would look weird if she came forward with this old will after I was dead. She didn't want to draw attention to herself, so she tried to put it back in a more conspicuous place. Only she couldn't get in because I'd changed the locks. So she broke in and was in my study hiding it in some of my papers when you walked in."

We all looked at William, assessing how he would take this news. He shrank into his sweater for a moment, then straightened his spine.

"I never did care for her, you know," he finally said. "I always knew you were too good a man for her."

"And, Jessie"—Lander turned to me—"I've been meaning to mention this. I think the reason she acted so weird when she saw your rental car at Limitless Learning was that she had seen it that night you were here with William. But she didn't know who you were."

The caretaker poked her head through the door. "Mr. William, you doin' okay?"

"Never been better," he said, smiling. He finished his lemonade, licked a finger and collected his cookie crumbs from his plate. "I've been thinking it's time for me to get back to work to finish up that birdhouse I started, seems like years ago."

"Now?"

"What better time than now?" The caregiver looked like she was going to argue with him, but Lander said he would go out to the workshop with him and keep him company. He said he had a dedication to write for his latest book. Judging by the look he gave William as he stood to help the older man, I had a feeling I knew who this latest effort would be dedicated to.

Evan looked at me. "I know you're not really into video games, but do you want to come over? My new system is amazing! I think you'll like it." Excitement lit up his whole face. I certainly didn't want to be the one to deflate his exuberance.

"Sure. It sounds like fun." It's the little things you do with your friends that cement the bond and keep you connected. And hopefully keep them from ever thinking they might need to kill you. "Let's go."